PRAISE FOR

Four and Twenty Blackbirds

"Southern Gothic at its best. An absorbing mystery told with humor and bite."

—Kelley Armstrong, author of *Industrial Magic* and the Otherworld series

"Cherie Priest has created a chilling page-turner in her debut novel. Her voice is rich, earthy, soulful, and deliciously Southern as she weaves a disturbing yarn like a master! Awesome—gives you goose bumps!"

—L. A. Banks, author of *Minion* and The Vampire Huntress Legend series

"Breathlessly readable, palpably atmospheric, and compellingly suspenseful, *Four and Twenty Blackbirds* is a considerable debut. It's written with great control and fluency, and it looks like the start of quite a career."

—Ramsey Campbell, World Horror Grand Master

"*Four and Twenty Blackbirds* is a rare bird, the novel you wish you'd written yourself—excellent!"

—C. J. Henderson, author of *The Things That Are Not There*

"Wonderful. Enchanting. Amazing and original fiction that will satisfy that buttery Southern taste, as well as that biting aftertaste of the dark side. I loved it."

—Joe R. Lansdale, Stoker- and Edgar-winning author of *The Bottoms*

"Cherie Priest has mastered the art of braiding atmosphere, suspense, and metaphysics into a resonant ghost story that offers even more than what you hope for."

"*Four and Twenty Blackbirds* is an extraordinary first novel—heck, it's an extraordinary novel, period. It's a ghost story and a voodoo mystery—and like any good Southern Gothic, it has a healthy obsession with race and inbreeding. But *Blackbirds* is more than the sum of its traditional parts. Cherie Priest's writing, while decidedly capable of giving you the creeps, is infused with a refreshing spunkiness and interesting, believable characters. . . . Fans of supernatural horror should keep an eye on Cherie Priest!"

Four and Twenty Blackbirds

CHERIE PRIEST

A Tom Doherty Associates Book
New York

FOUR AND TWENTY BLACKBIRDS

Copyright © 2003, 2005 by Cherie Priest

Unrevised, shorter version published in 2003 by Marietta Publishing

Edited by Liz Gorinsky

Book design by Nicole de las Heras

A Tor Book
Published by Tom Doherty Associates, LLC
175 Fifth Avenue
New York, NY 10010

www.tor.com

Tor® is a registered trademark of Tom Doherty Associates, LLC.

Library of Congress Cataloging-in-Publication Data

Priest, Cherie.
    Four and twenty blackbirds / Cherie Priest.—1st Tor ed.
        p. cm.
    "A Tom Doherty Associates Book."
    ISBN 0-765-31308-1 (pbk.)
    EAN 978-0-765-31308-9
    1. Orphans—Fiction. 2. Young women—Fiction. 3. Blessing and cursing—Fiction. 4. Racially mixed people—Fiction. 5. Signal Mountain (Tenn.)—Fiction. 6. Birthfathers—Fiction. 7. Georgia—Fiction. I. Title.

PS3616.R537F685 2005
813'.6—dc22

                                                                            2005040584

First Tor Edition: October 2005

Printed in the United States of America

0 9 8 7 6 5 4 3 2 1

This book is dedicated to the kids in my life—
my little mortality markers,
Alex and Chelsea.
Now you two are getting old enough to hear
my really *good* spooky stories.

Special thanks to Adrien for the insight and determined patience, and to Jym for the constant motivation. Thanks also to Dad, Donna, Mom, Aunt Wanda, Jan Haluska, Wilma McClarty, and Eileen Meagher—who knew it all along.

Yet another round of public appreciation goes to some new friends and colleagues, without whom this edition would have never seen the light of day. Unending thanks to my agent, Lantz Powell, for defending me against the mad pirate; to my editor, the indefatigable Liz Gorinsky, for always being on my side; and to Warren Ellis, for giving me a remarkable chance.

Four and Twenty Blackbirds

I

Eden

I

"Draw me a picture of someplace you've been that you liked very
much," Mrs. Patterson suggested, pronouncing each word with the
firm, specific articulation peculiar to those who work with children.
"It can be anyplace at all—an amusement park, a playground, a tree
house, or your bedroom. Maybe you went on vacation once and vis-
ited the beach. You could draw the ocean with seagulls and shells.
Or maybe you went camping on the mountain. You might have
gone down to the waterfall for a picnic, or up to Sunset Rock. Pick
a place special to you, and when you're finished, we'll put your pictures up on the bulletin board in the hallway."

I cringed, staring down at the blank sheet of coarse cream paper.
Before me was a plastic tub filled with fat, fruit-scented markers,
ripe for the choosing. While the other kids at my table dove into a
frenzy of scribbles I stalled for time, popping the lid off each color
and sniffing for inspiration.

Red is for cherries. Purple is for grape. Green is for . . . I didn't
recognize the scent.

But green is for . . . yes, green is for water.

I jammed the lid onto the back of the marker and began to scrawl a wide pool across the bottom half of the sheet. Green is for water. And for alligators. I picked up the yellow marker (supposed to be lemons, but smelled like detergent) and drew two periscope eyeballs poking up through the swirls. Then I outlined them with black (licorice) and drew a long snout with two bumps for nostrils.

Brown. Brown was chocolate.

I sketched tall, thin trees that reached up past the top of the page. And snakes. Brown is for snakes. Wrapped around one trunk I placed a spiraled serpent with a wide open mouth. I gave him a strawberry pink tongue shaped like a Y.

But I was missing something. I chewed on my thumbnail and tapped the brown pen. A house. A brown house set on blocks for when the water rose too high, with a cherry red canoe tied to the front porch just in case. A brown chocolate house, made of flat boards with a sloping gray roof that let the fresh rainwater run into a barrel. Gray is for . . . A gray roof.

And gray is for . . .

Gray is for . . .

Mrs. Patterson's hands fluttered into my vision. "My goodness, Eden. What a vivid picture you've made! Now, where is this?"

"Gray is for ghosts!" I blurted out.

For a moment the other kids were quiet, but then a few began to giggle. The giggle traveled halfway around the room, then died of shame under our teacher's withering frown.

"Class," she addressed it as a warning. "Eden has drawn us a very good green swamp with alligators and snakes, and a house."

I sank down into my chair and repeated myself more softly. "And gray is for ghosts, Mrs. Patterson. I haven't put the ghosts in yet."

Mrs. Patterson understood. Small and frail, she was a shriveled and sweet black woman who'd emerged from retirement to figure-head my kindergarten class. She made cookies every night before she went to bed because she knew some of her kids didn't get any breakfast before school. She crocheted all twenty of us little sweaters during the winter and took us to the city pool for free all summer. She was simply kind, but all the same, she terrified me.

Not on purpose, of course. She wouldn't have scared me deliberately, but whenever I saw her tiny, wrinkled hands I thought of dead birds; and every time she breezed by my desk they were flapping their bony, naked wings.

I think my fear hurt her feelings, or perhaps she thought something terrible was going on at home for me to be so silent and frightened all the time; but all was normal in our household so far as normal goes. I was raised by my aunt Louise and uncle David. They had no children of their own, so it was just me and that was just fine.

Everything was fairly ordinary until I started school. Until then I'd never had much interest in doodling, finger painting, or any of the other sloppy activities of early childhood, but once I entered the hallowed halls of elementary school, people handed me crayons and watercolors at every turn. Suddenly there was construction paper, glitter glue, Popsicle sticks, yarn, and paste. We used ink to make thumbprint caterpillars and paper bags to make cartoon hand puppets. We had sidewalk chalk to make Van Gogh-esque night scenes on black paper or hopscotch squares on the four-square courts outside. Our educators wanted us to expand our brains, to think outside the box—to look inside our gray-matter nooks and bring forth *art*. Most of the time, it was fun.

So although I was deathly afraid of Mrs. Patterson and her skinny, swift-moving hands, I sought her approval, and I wanted to fit in. I crafted the standard benign animals out of modeling clay and rainbow scenery from felts, and I usually got gold foil star stickers or smiley faces on these uniform endeavors. But anytime we had free-thought art projects things got iffy. Any time I had to delve too deeply into my imagination I found myself confused and unnerved. The "someplace special" project was no exception.

When I was finally done, Mrs. Patterson dutifully tacked it up on our bulletin board with the rest, though she discreetly sent it to the lower left corner.

When the classroom emptied for gym or for recess, I don't remember which, I lingered behind and stared at my creation with a morbid intrigue. My elderly teacher sent the class ahead with one of her colleagues and she stayed behind, letting the door quietly close us into privacy.

"Who are they?" she asked. "Who are the three gray ghosts looking through the trees? You didn't give them any faces."

I concentrated—tried hard to focus. I could hear their voices, singsong and sad, but sometimes fierce. Sometimes demanding. Always close.

"Do you know who they are?" she asked again, the same non-threatening tone she always used on me, like I was a stray cat on the verge of fleeing before she could slip me some cream.

"They're . . ." The memory flitted fast, and was gone. "They're sisters who died. He killed them."

"That's very sad."

"No, it's very angry—they're angry he did that to them. They loved him and he killed them." The words fell across my lips, dropping down into a pile at my feet and accumulating there before I could make sense of them. "Now they stay in the swamp, because he cut them up and threw them into the water for the gators and the birds to pick apart. And their blood turned the green water black, but I didn't do that part because I don't like licorice."

"You don't like . . . oh. I see. The markers."

"Yes. The markers." My whisper trailed away to something less audible, and I realized how foolish I sounded. With a flash of paranoia I turned to her and almost took one of her scary bird hands, then changed my mind at the last moment and folded mine together, praying to her instead. "But you can't say anything to anyone.

If you do, they'll send me to the pine trees, like they sent my mother, and you won't let them do that to me, will you, Mrs. Patterson?"

"No, Eden," she assured me after a perplexed pause. A quick light brightened her face for a moment, but then her forehead wrinkled again. "No one's going to send you to the pine trees. No one's going to send you away."

Mrs. Patterson tried hard to understand, but how could she have known? I didn't know either, back then, that you're not supposed to remember those things at all, those traces of the lives you've had before; but I've carried them with me as long as I can recall. Sometimes they rise out to meet me in subtle ways—in the gentle fears and convictions that old ghosts bring when they haunt you from the inside out. But sometimes they manifest in visions, in nightmares, or in kindergarten art projects.

I went back to drawing bubblegum butterflies and marshmallow puppies. Mrs. Patterson invited the social services people to come and observe me, but I put on a good show. I could give them what they wanted. Eventually she gave up trying to corner me and seemed to accept the undercurrent of madness that ran beneath my crayon creations.

But once in a while the three ghost women would cry, and I'd find myself inserting their six searching eyes into plastic-wrap windows, or cotton-ball clouds, or watercolor trees.

I wanted to make sure they could see me.

II

Here's another one.

Later that same year. I'd not yet turned six.

I lived on Signal Mountain, one of a chain that surrounds Chattanooga like the rim of a bowl, split down the middle by the river. Signal is populated by rich white people on one side and poor white trash on the other, which made my family's ethnic ambiguity something of an oddity. But I was a social creature, and the mountain was a safe playground for everyone. My cronies and I had free run of the tree-covered ridges, and we spent more time carousing through the woods than we did in our bedrooms.

Sometimes it was hide-and-seek, or tag, or—before I knew any better—blue versus gray. We wandered briskly in cutoff shorts and sneakers that let our legs get shredded by the brambles, and in long-sleeved shirts that caught on low branches and trapped pinecone seeds and needles. We stomped through streams and climbed up rocks. We chased one another senseless every day after the big yellow bus dropped us off at our neighborhood's entrance. And most of the time, it was good.

Most of the time I ran with my friends until my lungs burst, alternately stalking them and being stalked, hiding behind wide round trunks and under piles of mulching leaves in shallow ravines. Most of the time I didn't have to worry about anything more profound than spiders or ticks.

But then the women, no longer content to lie quiet and filtered, became dissatisfied.

One day, they began to speak.

I was behind a tree, squatting in a pile of leaves lest I be discovered—so I guess it was autumn. Yes, because come to think of it, I was wearing a chunky blue sweater over my shirt. When I saw the first woman she was standing still. A few dead leaves dropped from overhead, wafting back and forth until they settled at her feet. The mountain was dying its yearly death, and rot was in the air. Even the dirt between my sneaker treads smelled of compost. But until I saw them there that afternoon, what did I know of decay?

With the corner of my eye I caught a long flash of palest gray, almost white. I thought of an old dress, dangling on a wire hanger from a tree branch. I stood and turned to see better, not yet aware enough to be afraid, and even when I saw her more clearly I was only surprised. It took me a minute to remember I was not asleep.

She held there motionless, tugged only by the faint gusts that rustled the trees. The wind made her dress barely billow around her legs, so she must have been there, real in one way or another. Her face was as pallid and indeterminately hued as her dress, and her eyes were more of the same.

"Hey," I said, not to greet her but to get her attention. "Hey."

Her eyes rolled to meet mine.

She opened her mouth but did not yet speak. Instead it seemed every sound in the forest was pulled inside her gasping lungs and I was standing in the vacuum. I knew my friends were only yards away but I did not hear their small, fast feet shuffling through the undergrowth. No birds sang and no squirrels knocked winter nuts down into empty trees. Even the shadows stopped crawling across the rocks as the sky held the clouds above in place.

My breath snagged in my throat and refused to leave my chest.

Tears came to the woman's eyes and dripped to the forest floor unchecked. Her head swiveled slowly, looking past her left shoulder and then her right. Her choked, thin voice cried out to the others.

Willa, Luanna—she's over here.

Two other women appeared, one on either side of her. They had the same vaguely African features as the first, with hair bound into submission by scarves tied in loose knots. Their faces might have been round once, but their skin was drawn back and their wide cheekbones made shelves that shadowed their hollow jaws. Their teeth were exaggerated by fleshy lips robbed of their firmness, and when they spoke to one another it was a terrible sight.

There she is, his darling one.

His pretty one.

Oh, Mae, she's returned to you. She's returned to us.

Mae crouched low to examine me with her enormous, brimming eyes. *My baby,* she said, reaching one scrawny arm to my face. *My baby. Miabella.*

But when the back of her hand brushed my cheek, the horror of her dusty, dead breath broke the spell and my screams split the supernatural quiet that had descended over the mountainside. I howled until my cries went hoarse, and the women withdrew. Mae left me last, turning with a slow, miserable sob and vanishing into the crowded trees. The last thing I saw before I shrieked myself unconscious was her retreating back, slashed and stained with long, dark streaks that could have been nothing but blood.

III

It should come as no surprise that I ended up a regular patron of the school counselor's office. Mr. Schumann was short and wide, with red hair that grew shorter every year. His ears protruded north past the narrowing fringe, straining to listen even when his round blue eyes appeared impassive. He always watched me with squinty concentration, like the face a cat makes while trying to figure out a bathroom faucet.

"Why don't you tell me about some of these pictures you've made?" he began our last session together. "Mrs. Patterson thinks they're very good, but she wants to know what they're about."

I stared at my shoes. "I already told her. They're about the sisters."

"Yes, the women who died. You said someone killed them."

"Uh-huh."

His brown office chair squealed as he shifted his weight. He leaned forward and pressed his palms together. "That's a scary story to tell someone, don't you think?"

"It's for real. It's a for-real story. I didn't make it up."

"Where did you hear it? Did you see it on TV or in a movie?"

I shook my head, aggravated because I couldn't make him understand. "I didn't hear it anywhere. I just know it. It's in my head."

"But stories like that have to get into your head from somewhere. Where did you pick them up?"

"Nowhere. I came that way. I was born with the story. It happened to me before I was born."

He tapped the tips of his index fingers against each other, then reached for a pad of paper and a pen. "I've got an idea. Why don't you tell me the whole thing, then—from start to finish."

"I don't know the whole thing," I sulked. He still didn't believe me.

"Then tell me the parts you do know. I'd like to hear them."

I closed my eyes and saw flashes, frames of action disconnected and surreal. A house like the one I'd sketched for Mrs. Patterson, surrounded by swirling green-black water. The slick jerking motion of an alligator sliding off a bank into a fetid pool of stagnant backwater.

One.

Two.

Three women. Me in their arms, passed from one to another.

"My mother and her two sisters," I said, eyes still shut.

Mr. Schumann rifled through a folder before pausing to read something. I heard his asthmatic breath aimed down at the desk, blowing against his loose papers. He scratched his head with his pen. "Eden, it's my understanding that your mother died when she had you. I know you live with an aunt and uncle; is there another sister too?"

"Yes, but that's not who I mean."

"But you said—"

I balled my hands into tight little fists, squeezing the story out like toothpaste from a tube. "Not my mother *now*. My mother *then*. When I was his prettiest one. It was a long time ago. Whole lives ago since he killed them."

Mr. Schumann held still for a minute. He thumped his wrist down on the desk and used his scritchy little pen to jot notes across his pad of lined paper. "Who is this 'he' you mentioned?" he finally asked.

I always saw the women so clearly, it seemed strange that I couldn't conjure his face. I felt his arms, broad and muscular when they picked me up to sit on his shoulders. I recalled the sweat and musk and tobacco smoke I smelled when I pressed my cheek against the crook of his neck. But these were only photographs.

I needed a scene. I cracked my eyes open enough to peek over at Mr. Schumann's fidgeting hands. They fumbled, disassembling the pen into pieces and placing them in precise east-west alignment with a granite paperweight and a letter opener shaped like a sword. Such anxious hands. Not like my father's at all. Not like the long, dark fingers so lean and strong and always sure.

My father's fingers held glass vials filled with funny liquids and powders, and he poured them one into another, another into a greater one, and another onto a small burner. One more bottle. Three drops of brown, smelly stuff on top of it all. When all was done simmering, he removed it from the heat with a padded glove and poured it into a Mason jar that might have otherwise held peach preserves.

His sleek back stretched a damp undershirt to its breaking point. He was at a rough desk, reading something from a book beside the vials. He leaned his head backwards over the chair and gripped his hair with both hands. Tight black wool.

He was frustrated, angry. Something was missing.

"Papa?"

"What are you doing in here? Get yourself away now."

"But Papa, I wanted to know where—"

"I said, get yourself away now."

"Papa?"

"Now!" He shouted it, rising out of the chair with enough force to throw it towards me. His elbow struck the book and knocked it fluttering to the floor. The pages flipped from beginning to end with a shuffling flap. Another flash: the shuffling of cards in my mother's hands before she laid them out in a cross-shaped pattern on a purple silk scarf. No. My father. His book.

I was fascinated by the yellowed, dirty pages as they waved back and forth. Back and forth. Back and forth until the thick cover clattered still. And before my father could whisk the book closed and throw it back up on the table, I saw what was mounted inside.

Dry and nasty, shrunken and crooked, a black, mummified hand with a gold ring on each finger was fixed against the inside back cover of my father's book. Not a picture but a real one, with stick-fingers splayed open and lacquered shiny.

I screeched and popped out of my chair in Mr. Schumann's office, forgetting for a moment where I was. I only wanted to step on the hand, to squash it, to kill it, to destroy it somehow. But my father was gone, and his book was gone, and the only hands I saw were the counselor's confused ones that were putting his pen together again.

And his letter opener, conveniently shaped like a sword, was lying close to me. So close that I barely had to reach out to grab it, and it took less than a second to slam it down through his pasty white palm.

It took him almost a full second more to realize what had happened enough to join me in my screaming. Not until the blood spurted through both sides of the wound and sprayed his notepad and the pen fragments with sticky crimson did he find his voice enough to call out, and by then I was well on my way to running the mile and a half home.

Lulu was waiting for me at the door.

2

Lulu

Aunt Louise is a goddess. She's nearly six feet tall, with huge, melon-firm breasts and a tiny waist. From my very earliest inklings of sexual aesthetics, I wanted to look like Lulu. I wanted her black, spiral curls, her olive skin, and her deep brown eyes. I wanted men to fall over themselves for me the way they did for her. She was my mother's older sister, but only nineteen when she came to care for me. As Mr. Schumann said, my mother died when I was born and I was passed down along the maternal family members.

Back when I was a baby, we all lived with my grandmother and my mother's younger sister, Michelle. Lulu assumed most of the responsibility for my upbringing, and she took me almost everywhere. By the time I was two I'd been to concerts, coffeehouses, and poetry readings enough to scar me for life. But if Lulu had been a homebody, she would have never met Dave, and then where would we be?

Dave, shortly to become my uncle David, found me wandering away from Lulu while she investigated the meager Dashiell Hammett selection at a used bookstore. I'd found a display offering free fudge samples, and although I could not yet read, I understood enough to help myself. Dave worked at the store part-time, and when he finally peeled me away from the fudge plate, I was smeared with enough chocolate to frost a cake. But he didn't scold me, or demand to speak to my guardian. Instead, he propped me up on a pile of discarded books and left to get his camera.

Eventually Lulu noticed I was missing. She found me atop the pile, opening random volumes and pretending to read while Dave took pictures. What can I say? I was a doll. I *did* have Lulu's curls and her skin, and I was probably the cutest thing the bored clerk had seen all day.

Of course, then he saw Lulu. And both of them promptly forgot about me.

So now a word on Dave.

Dave is roughly the color of the fudge I bathed in that day at the store. Back then his head sprouted long, erratic dreadlocks knotted with beads and hemp thread, and he wore clothes spattered with political slogans like "Free Tibet" and "Stop Animal Testing." He asked Lulu if he could borrow me sometime to take pictures. He was working on his portfolio, and the folks at the Urban Art Institute were going to apprentice him out as soon as it was complete. For that matter, perhaps Lulu wouldn't mind posing for him sometime.

We three have been a unit ever since.

Four weeks after meeting Dave in the bookstore, Lulu took me and moved in to Dave's apartment, which he had turned into a makeshift studio. We went through countless rolls of film in those first months. The shutter flicked incessantly, like Lulu's cigarette lighter when she sat on the balcony in her underwear after photos or sex.

Lulu started telling people what everyone already assumed, that I was their daughter, and Dave adjusted our bodies into exquisite, astounding compositions of intimacy and danger. He laid us out in silks, in drapes, in only skin.

Once he sat me on a shelf draped with black velvet and placed two giant wings behind me. He said they were turkey wings; I can't imagine where he got them. Although they were mottled shades of autumn leaves, when photographed in black and white they were dark enough to be the limbs of giant ravens. I leaned back and raised my head, cocking it against one wing as though I were utterly exhausted, worn out from carrying all those dead souls back and forth from the underworld.

He pressed a button.

Click. I was in a contest. Then on the cover of a magazine. Then a calendar of my more endearing toddler poses, the less morbid ones that the unwashed masses might purchase as Christmas gifts for teenage girls or middle-aged housewives with nail polish that matched their kitchen curtains.

But the pictures of Lulu were the ones that made us both stars. Lulu is a goddess to more than just me, you see, and Dave's pictures brought the world to attention. Suddenly, we were rich. We moved up to the mountain with the rest of the rich people, and I started school.

And I started seeing the dead women.

And I stabbed my counselor with his own dull knife.

And I ran away from his office, all the way home, where Lulu was waiting for me.

She was holding the door open with one hand and the telephone with her other. The phone's pigtail-curled cord barely stretched from the kitchen, where the machine was mounted on the wall. She'd already gotten the call from the principal.

She stepped aside and let me run past her. I was panting and gasping for air, unable to dash another yard but unwilling to quit trying. In the living room, I did laps around the coffee table while she closed the door and placed the phone back on the receiver. She joined me by standing in the way of my loop, forcing me to stop or run into her.

She did not raise her voice.

"What'd you do that for?" she asked. "Why'd you hurt Mr. Schumann's hand?"

I shivered and shook, though it was warm where I stood, in the patch of sun cast through the huge picture windows. "It was moving. And he wasn't—it wasn't him. It wasn't his hand. It wasn't his hand I wanted to stick!" I hollered. "It wasn't his hand I saw! It was a different one. A little wrinkly one. The one in the book."

Her eyebrows perked. "What book?"

"The book I saw. It was old, with old pages all yellow and dusty. And when it fell open, there was the hand stuck to the back cover. It was moving."

"Moving, huh?"

"Yeah. And then when I opened my eyes Mr. Schumann was there, with his fat wiggly hands all moving in front of me—and I don't know. I don't know why I did it. I'm really really sorry. I didn't mean to hurt him. He's a big dumb dork, but I didn't mean to hurt him."

"Come here." She picked me up and sat on the couch, wrapping her strong arms around me, letting my head sink against her breasts like one of the most popular pictures of us together. She leaned her mouth close to my ear and whispered the rest.

"You see so much you shouldn't, poor baby. Just know this: know that the sisters would not hurt you, and they would help you if they could. They're looking for something they lost, years and years ago, they're not looking to harm you at all. They would never harm you, even if they could—and I figure that they probably can't."

"But there's this book, Lu. Are they looking for the book?"

"Good Lord, no, or at least I don't think so. Don't you think any more about that book. Maybe one day you'll outgrow the sight, and you won't see them anymore, but this is our blood, baby. Someday

I'll tell you who the women are, and why they follow you with their pleading eyes and reaching hands. You should think of them as your guardian angels, and don't be so afraid. They love you, and so do I. But don't you ever expect anyone else to understand it.

"Tomorrow the police will come and a social worker will want to see you, but that's all right. You tell them you're sorry about Mr. Schumann's hand, and that it was an accident. You tell them that you closed your eyes, you fell asleep, and you had a nightmare. That's close enough to true for now."

Something awful occurred to me—something more awful than the thought of any school suspension. I sniffled and wiped my nose on her blouse, not even sure how I should broach my fear. "And they won't send me to the pine trees?"

"To the what?"

"To the pine trees?"

She continued to stroke my hair, but didn't respond right away. "What do you mean about the pine trees, darling? Where'd you hear that?" she asked quietly.

"I dunno." I'd picked it up in some conversation held above my head when I was too young to recall the specifics. It was one of those things I'd heard in passing, not really understanding either the meaning or the context. I had only a dim impression that you got sent to the pine trees if you did bad, crazy things. And if you were *especially* bad and crazy, you never came back from the pine trees. They swallowed you whole.

Lu snuggled her chin down against the top of my head and kissed me there, where the hair parts. "Okay," she said. "So you've heard just enough to be afraid. I'm sorry for that, and that's just one more thing that I'll have to tell you more about someday. But don't worry about that for now, either. There's no such place anymore. Not the pine trees you're thinking of. No one will ever send you there, or anyplace like it. And any time you find yourself frightened of the pine trees, you remember what I said about those three sisters and you can stop being afraid. They won't let anyone take you off to the pine trees, and neither will I."

"Never?"

"Not so long as I live."

3
Branches

I

I took Lulu's words to heart. I envisioned the ghosts as visitors, not malicious boogies, and I began to look for them, though I'd not seen them outside my dreams since that time in the woods. I even started to wander the mountainside seeking them.

Occasionally I'd feel the eyes on me and I'd stop my play to look around. I might have invited them to come out to me if I'd known how. But no, the women kept their distance. I could have forgotten them altogether except for their passing smell of old clothes, drifting sometimes by. Mothballs and cedar. I felt nothing of them except ephemeral words of curiosity, and once of caution. Only one other time in my childhood did they raise their voices, and then they saved my life.

I was alone under the trees that day. It was the year I turned ten, or maybe eleven. The bottom and fringes of my jeans were wet. It had been raining for several days on the mountain, as it often does in early summer.

Bored to death with cabin fever, I'd watched eagerly as the

clouds began to crack and steamy beams of light fell through. Then I grabbed my rubber shoes and dashed out of the house before Lulu or Dave could stop me. I took my bicycle and rode over to the neighborhood playground, which was old but in a good state of repair. If any of my friends had managed to escape their own houses, they'd surely join me soon.

I was disappointed but not surprised to find it deserted. The merry-go-round creaked forlornly when I shoved it, spraying water in a big, lazy circle that soaked my pant legs even more. The puddle at the bottom of the slide would have only done worse if I'd splashed through it, and the monkey bars were slick with dangling drops of dew. Sighing, I wiped the water off a swing and sat down to wait.

The scent of musty fabric wafted by. I raised my head. The odor returned, stronger in my nostrils. Scarves and sweaters too long in a drawer. Lingerie washed and neatly folded, put up in a chest.

"Hello? Are you there?"

Get away from here. You get yourself gone.

She was standing beside the spring-mounted animals that had handles on either sides of their cartoonish heads. She wrung her hands together as she spoke.

"Mmm . . . Mae?" I asked. I tightened my grip on the rusty chains that held the swing, but I did not jump or run.

Get away from here. He's coming for you.

"What are you talking about?"

He's coming for you!

"Who?"

She vanished. And behind the spot where she'd stood I saw a man. He wasn't much older than a boy—he might have been a teenager still. He was tall but hunkered over, and terrifically thin. He held his arms close to his torso, as if they were plastered there by his soaking wet shirt. He must have been outside a long time to be so wet. He must have been waiting for me.

His hands were tucked under his armpits and his feet were bound in soggy black boots with laces that trailed off into the grass. At first he held so immobile I thought he might have been another apparition, but when he spoke his voice was mortal enough.

"There you are."

I didn't move. We faced each other across the playground like it was the O.K. Corral. His eyes were partially obscured by his sloppy wet hair, but even at that twenty-yard distance I could see blue and madness in them. I did not know how or if I should reply.

I let him speak again.

"This will be hard. You're not what I expected." His hands began a slow release, creeping down the sides of his rib cage. "You're just a pretty little girl now. That old devil, though. He'll package anything up all pretty."

I tried to match his stare, moment for moment. All around me I could hear the women whispering their warnings, but this man kept me in something like a thrall. I didn't want to flee yet. I wanted to hear him talk some more, in his slow, strong drawl—southern twanged, but not so clipped as the way people in the valley spoke.

He took a small step forward.

"Oh yes, anything at all. Even that ugly ol' soul you've got behind those tiny little-girl ribs. That old devil, he's something else. He thinks if he hides Avery someplace sweet and pretty, that I might think I've made a mistake. He wants me to think you're just a precious innocent. But I know better. I know who you are. I know they brought you back, Avery. I know you'll keep coming back until I find that book, but I'm sworn to do what I can."

He took another muddy step and I found my voice when he said that bit about the book. "What are you talking about?"

He laughed. "Your baby-doll voice won't fool me. You've heard the three sisters too—I know you have. I've heard about it. You can't escape them, Avery. They're God's own furies, chasing you down. They've led me to you."

"Nuh-uh," I argued. "They warned me about you. They said you were coming to get me."

"Then . . . then it's because they're a portent of your death. They wish to witness your destruction."

"You're crazy." I said it deadpan, with a creeping hint of ice. "You're some crazy stranger, and I'm not supposed to talk to strangers. You go away before my friends get here."

No, my baby. I heard her, but I couldn't see her.

No, my baby. Don't you bother talking. He's as mad as the moon, and you'll only make him angry. You've got to run. You've got to start now. You have to outrun him.

One of his hands slid free of his side and in it I saw the black glint of metal. He'd been hiding a handgun, shiny and damp and heavy enough to make his wrist droop. Before he could lift it enough to aim, I finally followed the ghost's advice. I turned and dashed, parting the slender trees with my flailing arms.

Bang.

The first bullet blasted out of the barrel and split a tree trunk to my right.

Water dumped down from the shaken leaves to drench me, but it did not slow me. He was on my heels, but he was not so quick as I was. I knew my way through the ravines that crisscrossed the woods and scarred the hills. This was my world, and I was the wisest scout of all. Even my own friends—kids who knew the wooded gullies as well as I did—couldn't keep up when I started running.

Bang.

Another shot, even farther off base than the first.

Even in my breathless, choking fear I found myself calculating, aiming my flight through the densest clots of trees and down the sharpest, rockiest cuts of earth. I leaped across rain-flushed streams in one fast skip.

He tumbled behind me, gradually losing seconds from his clumsy pursuit. He didn't know which rocks were steady enough to jump from and which would tumble into the water at the slightest touch. He didn't know which piles of leaves masked solid ground and which concealed slime and sharp sticks. Not like I did.

Bang.

I was moving roughly in the direction of home. Going about it the long way, of course—no sense in bolting for the main road where he'd have an open shot at a straight-moving target. Home. It wasn't far. I could make it. I could make it with room to spare.

But what if I wasn't enough ahead of him? My lead was growing, but behind me he was still staggering doggedly through the forest. What if he caught up before Lulu had time to get a gun? What if he came inside? What if he hurt my Lulu? The thought nearly paralyzed me. I stumbled, but recovered. A new plan, then. One that wouldn't bring him so close to my aunt. I shifted my course.

My legs were tiring, but my resolve was fresh. I would draw him away from my beloved goddess. I would shake him on my own. I believed in Lulu, she was unstoppable and unbreakable, but if he caught her by surprise—and if he got off a bullet or two before she had time to know what was happening . . . I couldn't stand the thought of it. So I kept running farther from her, away and up the mountain, farther from help.

I did this even though I didn't know the area farther up the mountain behind the house.

The rule of thumb in my neighborhood was always, "go down, not up." The playground was down; the safest woods were down. The convenience stores and gas stations were down. The roads that went up headed to either the government parks or to undeveloped real estate.

Naturally, childhood apocrypha had turned the hinterlands into a realm pocked with monsters and malevolent Civil War ghosts; but regardless of what the uncharted lands held in store, I was less afraid of those possibilities than of the skinny man with the gun who would certainly kill me if he caught me. And he might even kill Lulu if he caught her, too, so I had to keep my two-pronged goal in sight: I had to keep him away from home, and keep him away from *me*.

Bang.

Up and over. Into new territory. I was comforted to see that it didn't look much different from what I usually played in. Nothing but dripping wet trees too thick to let me see far ahead. I dived and weaved, wondering how much longer I could keep it up. Adults marvel at the energy of children, but though it is vast, it is not infinite. I didn't dare glance over my shoulder, lest I run into one of the innumerable trunks. I heard him thrashing and charging, but he was falling behind. I kept my eyes open for a good hiding place, but saw nothing except trees and big rocks in every direction. Maybe on the other side of that precipice . . .

Not that way!

Mae's warning was too late.

I reached for a handhold to throw myself across a rock about as big as I was. I grabbed it, and launched myself half over, half around it. I landed on a pile of leaves and sticks that gave way beneath my weight.

I fell, sliding heels over head down a sloping hole.

At the bottom I lay still, my wind knocked thoroughly out, and I stared up at the vaguely circular patch of sky maybe fifteen feet above. Damp dirt rained down after me. My shoulder hurt. When I lifted it up and looked crooked-necked at the back of my shirt, it was only to notice with encroaching panic that I was bleeding. I'd landed on something hard, sticking up out of the ground. I poked my fingers into the dirt around it and unearthed the head of a shovel. I had brief hopes that I might be able to dig it out and use it for a weapon, but the handle rotted away when I pulled it loose from the ground.

Somewhere above, the crashing feet of my pursuer slowed near the spot where I'd disappeared. I tried not to move, not even to breathe.

An inch at a time his wet head peered over the edge of the hole. "You cannot," he puffed the words laboriously, "outrun justice. You can't. God has promised it." His hand reached over and pointed the gun down at my head. I desperately rolled myself towards what I thought was the edge of the hole.

Bang.

I didn't stop against a wall of dirt. I kept on rolling, down a little farther. My turn took me beyond the friendly skylight and all was dark. I felt wildly around for anything substantial, grasping at dangling tree roots and squeezing handfuls of mud. I dragged my knees up off the spongy ground and forced them to ratchet me into an upright position.

I was more than a little surprised to learn that I could stand without impediment, and finally I wandered a couple of steps farther to lean on a thick square timber. I pressed my wounded back against it and tried not to wonder how much blood I might be leaking.

Overhead I heard the scrambling scuffle that signaled I was still being pursued. The boy yelped when his legs surrendered their balance and he tumbled down after me, landing exactly where I had.

He was wheezing. "There's nowhere for you to go now. You can't stay in this . . . well, or cistern, or whatever, forever . . . it won't hide you long."

It's a mine shaft. Hold your ground. He's blind. Let him pass you.

I dug my back hard into the tunnel wall. Small, squirming things wriggled wetly against me. I jammed my eyes shut, which made almost no difference in the underground dark. Something with many slight legs worked its way up my neck. I pressed my lips together and willed my ears shut too. The bug worked its way up my cheek and across my scrunched eyelid before heading on past my forehead and over my hair.

The boy tread into the blackness with halting legs. "Give yourself up. I'll do it quick."

He stopped no more than a foot in front of me. I could smell his breath, stinky with corn chips, ranch dip, and cola. I felt the swish of air parting for his waving arms, groping ahead. I unsealed my lips and exhaled as quietly as I could, then slowly sucked in more moldy air through my wide open mouth.

Breathe in. Mustn't make a sound. Breathe out.

He kept moving, another step. Than another. Deeper back, farther from me.

Push the beam, child.

I didn't understand. She said it again.

Push on that beam. Shove your good shoulder against it.

Still afraid to move too much, I leaned a little weight on it and heard a creak.

He heard it too. His footsteps stopped.

No, do it hard. All at once. Then get out of the way. Go back the way you came.

No time to argue. He was turning, his shoes squishing an about-face in the muck.

I lunged, heaving with all my might. The timber groaned and cracked, then collapsed. I darted past it and back towards the patch of sunlight just in time to hear the walls falling in. My pursuer called out but his cries were stifled by the falling wood and mud. Hand over aching hand, knee over scraped knee, I crawled up out of the hole and left him there.

Back topside the rain was falling again, or maybe it was only the wind bothering the trees. It was lovely.

I tumbled back down the side of the mountain until I reached the road to my house, gripping my stinging shoulder as hard as I could, almost crying with relief.

Lulu, keeper of the hearth, was waiting at the door.

They made me go to court.

Lulu was wearing a fitted blue dress that stopped at her knees, and a pair of high heels that made her calves discreetly convex. Dave wore a black T-shirt and jeans. I was trussed up in a green skirt and blouse with cuffs that clenched at my wrists. Since we weren't regular churchgoing folks, it wasn't every day I was forced to present myself in such a manner. The clothes made me uncomfortable even more than the dozens of appraising eyes, all of which were pointed at me.

"And then he what?" the lawyer pressed.

My eyes lurched around the room and caught Dave, who flashed me a wink and a lopsided grin of sympathy. I sat up straighter. "Then he lifted up the gun and he started shooting at me."

"What did you do?"

"Well, mister—I ran like the devil knew my name."

The defense attorney also asked me a round of questions about my early "episodes" in school, trying to convince the jury that I might have provoked the assault, or even imagined it. But *my* family's lawyer had bullets dug out of trees and rocks waiting in a sealed plastic bag, and the other guy couldn't much argue with *those*.

I indignantly related the rest of my testimony while the defendant, Malachi Dufresne, sat dourly silent with his hands twisted into a pair of knobby fists. He never looked at me once. He never raised his eyes, not even when his great-aunt took the stand to tell the courtroom what a nice boy he was.

She said it in a mellow accent that sounded like his.

"He's *such* a good boy. Always has been. Ever since he was a small thing and his parents used to leave him at my home for the summers. He was always so kind to the horses. He's nothing but gentle. I'm sure there's some good reason he came after that child, or at least he thought he had a good reason. My poor nephew needs a doctor, not a prison. If y'all would just let me have him I could get him the best money can buy."

Dave leaned over and whispered in Lulu's ear, mimicking the old woman's scratchy southern voice. "I'm filthy rich. Don't you *dare* send him to jail."

Lulu nudged him in the ribs and whispered angrily, or maybe fearfully, back. "You stop that. She's got money enough to see it done." And she was right. When the end finally came a few weeks later, the man in charge of jurors' row announced that Malachi should go to a hospital to be evaluated.

Dave shot to his feet, nearly jerking my arm off as he rose. "That's not enough!"

The judge clapped his gavel down and pointed it at Dave's head. "Contain yourself, sir. It is my ruling that Malachi Dufresne be remanded to the Moccasin Bend mental health facility for psychological evaluation, and then he will be returned to court for sentencing in sixty days' time." He dropped the gavel again and stood.

The rest of us rose too, and people began to mill about the courtroom, draining gradually through the exits like a congregation slipping out of church after services. A bailiff came to escort my assailant back into state custody. Lulu put an arm around my shoulder and guided me towards the aisle. "They'll keep him," she told me, squeezing me quickly. "They won't let him go for a long time. Don't worry."

Just then the white-topped aunt came thrusting her elbows forward through the crowd. She knocked aside a middle-aged man talking to a boy about my age and did not even turn to acknowledge them. Instead she turned sideways to pass us by, glowering over her shoulder with chilly blue eyes. She opened her mouth as if to speak, but Lulu cut her off.

"Keep on walking, Tatie."

"I was just going to say—"

"I *said*, keep on walking, Tatie Eliza. You will leave this child alone."

The crone could not disregard the giantess Lulu, but she was not afraid of her. "Blood will tell," she said, her voice reeking with contempt. "That's all I was going to say."

"And now you've said it, so you keep on moving."

But the little old lady blocked our escape. She dropped her gaze from Lulu to me. Lulu tried to push me back behind her, but I wouldn't go. I wanted to look at this ancient matriarch who refused to stand aside.

She wanted to look at me too. "They haven't told you, have they girl? Not half the truth, I bet they haven't."

I shifted to dislodge myself from Lulu's sheltering grasp, but she wouldn't have it, so I stayed put whether I liked it or not. I craned my neck around her waist and inquired across the aisle. "What . . . what are you—stop it, Lulu, I want to—"

A small head was in the way. It was the boy she'd pushed apart from the man I supposed was his father. The boy stared at me, or through me, as if he could see something inside that I wanted to keep hidden. I tried to lean around him, but his sharp nose demanded my attention. I reached for him to push him away, but his father grabbed him first—like he didn't want me to touch his kid. He drew the child away from me as if I was contaminated.

I glared at them both and he continued to stare blankly over his shoulder, his eyes not leaving mine and his expression not changing. They left through the main doors and I was glad to see them gone.

"Hey, old lady," I said once they were out of the way. I think I was almost loud enough to embarrass Lulu.

"Go on, now, Tatie," she said over my head. "You and I can talk later if you want, but you leave her be." I couldn't believe it. Lulu was actually pleading with the dwarfish, crooked woman in expensive makeup.

Tatie fired her question at me again. "Do you know who I am, girl?"

"You're the crazy guy's aunt."

"And you know who else?" she prompted, shimmying closer.

"Some screwy old lady?"

All the wrinkles in her face sank down to the brim of her nose. She looked positively wicked. She was Snow White's stepmother in a designer dress. "You come here, you mixed-breed brat."

"You leave her alone!" Lulu almost shouted it, forcing me towards Dave.

One of the bailiffs raised an eyebrow and exchanged a glance with the judge, who hesitated at his bench but made no move to intervene. Lulu rotated me a full one hundred and eighty degrees, trying to force me out the other way. But I turned my head and shook it, answering Eliza well enough.

"I," she raised a gnarled finger and repeated the pronoun, "*I* am your aunt! Hers too—that hussy who'd close your ears if she could. How you like that, girl? An' how do you like that, hussy?"

Lulu was behind me then, pushing me with her knees along the pewlike bench and shoving me towards the door. "Devil take you, Eliza. You and your maniac boy both."

"Maybe he will," she called back. "But I said it already—*blood will tell*. And that girl will follow him soon enough. You hear me, girl? You'll join him soon, like your mother before you. They'll take you off to Pine Breeze too!"

And we were clear.

Lulu dragged me down the steps and out into the parking lot before I could hear more. My dress shoes clacked and scraped on the asphalt as I hurried to match her long strides towards the car.

"Is that right?" I demanded, squirming my arm free and nearly sprinting by her side. "Is she our aunt?"

When we got to the car, Dave unlocked the door and hustled us into the front seat. "Yeah, is she?" he asked. Together we ganged up to stare down a sullen Lulu. I was surprised by the alliance, and by the fact that there was something about me and Lulu that he didn't know.

My aunt drew her shoulders back, pretending that the seat belt chafed. Without looking over at either of us, she grumbled her unhappy response. "Yes. She's distant kin. Don't make more of it than needs to be said."

"Wow," Dave said.

"Wow," I echoed. Out the back window I saw two policemen guiding my cousin, Malachi Dufresne, into a van with iron mesh bars on the windows. He paused and scanned the crowd, one foot poised midair.

One of the cops pushed him forward, and he disappeared into the vehicle.

Later that night I cornered Lulu in the kitchen. You corner Lulu and you're taking your chances, but I was feeling brave after what I saw as my victory in the courtroom. I sidled up alongside her at the sink and broached the subject I knew she least wanted to see brought up. "So what is that place, what Aunt Eliza said?"

"Don't call her that."

"What was it you called her? Tatie? What's that mean? It's not like 'Katie,' is it? It's not like a name or something?"

"Just call her Eliza. She never needs to hear more than that from you."

I hopped up on the counter and picked at a foil bag of potato chips. "All right." I stuffed a crispy potato shingle into my mouth and talked around my chewing, so I could pretend that Lulu had misheard something in case I needed an excuse to backtrack.

"So it's Pine Breeze, huh—not the Pine Trees like I used to think. And it's for real; I didn't make it up. I really heard it someplace. Are you going to tell me what it is, or not?"

"No, I'm not going to tell you, not yet. And don't ask again. I'll bring it up when I think you're old enough to hear about it."

That wasn't what I wanted to hear, but it wasn't as harsh a reaction as I'd nearly expected.

I grunted, still gnawing on that salty chip. "Maybe I'll ask again, and maybe I won't."

"Well," she said, taking the bag away from me, "you'd better not."

III

I missed two weeks of school during the trial, and when I returned I was something of a celebrity. Chattanooga isn't a big city, and anyone's business is everyone's business, especially if that business makes the news. Lu mostly kept me clear of the television during those weeks, though I don't think she did me any favors. Not surprisingly, the media had gotten wind that my case was related to an older, equally perplexing one. Soon everyone in town knew more about Leslie than I did.

Leslie. She was my mother.

Her picture had been plastered across the screens almost as often as mine. I don't know which one they used for either of us. My fourth-grade portrait was a likely candidate for me . . . but for my mother? I couldn't even swear I would recognize a photo if I saw one. The only one I knew of was grainy and distant, of the three sisters linked by a tangle of arms thrown over shoulders. Lu couldn't have seriously thought she could keep me from hearing something the entire valley considered old news. She must have known that someone, somewhere would bring it up.

Within a few hours of my return to the classroom, someone did.

There was a new girl in my class. Her name was April, and she was from *up North*. Not *up North* like over the river, or *up North* like Nashville or Louisville, but farther away—Chicago, she said, and you knew it was true. You could hear it in her vowels, and in her almost audible sneer. She believed that the more snow you got for winter the smarter you were; and consequently, the hotter your summers the more likely it was you'd marry a cousin. By the time I met her, she was the most hated member of my class. This is not to say she had no friends; on the contrary, she was quite popular with the richer kids, for they envied her cosmopolitan air and her bizarre clothes, which she insisted were the veritable height of fashion. But make no mistake, they hated her too. They hated her for the reason we all did: she thought she was better than us, and we were afraid she was right.

On my second day back we took a field trip to the train station, the Chattanooga Choo Choo. My apathy knew no bounds. Everyone knew it hadn't been a real station for years, and it had since been converted to a Holiday Inn. After all the excitement of my last month, a mere hotel was not going to engage me. I might have complained aloud, but at least I wasn't stuck in a classroom pretending to pay attention to the goings-on at a chalkboard. Any field trip—even a field trip down the mountain and into the ghetto— was better than a day of diagramming sentences.

I sat sourly in the bus on the ride down the mountain, taking an entire seat to myself so I could spread out, lean my back against the window, and let my head knock against it during rough patches of road. We parked, unloaded, and then all us fourth and fifth graders milled about together while our teachers made arrangements with guides. I stood in the parking lot with my peers and stared up. And up. And up. At what was really quite a grand building.

Yes, it was grand—even despite the nasty urban rot surrounding it. Across the street was a series of restaurants and lesser hotels that hadn't seen a customer in fifty years, boarded and blackened with pollution and mildew. Down the road both ways I saw only more of the same, and except for the large parking garage next to the station, it seemed that everything for blocks around was decrepit and deserted.

But the *station*. I was grudgingly impressed.

Our teachers ushered us into the lobby. By then my neck was aching, but I couldn't stop myself. An enormous domed ceiling in gold-and-red glass loomed above us, and even the most cynical of students gaped at the glittering glass-and-iron chandeliers. I finally dropped my head and saw my own reflection in the polished marble floor.

The guide started talking in a squeaky old-man voice that matched his appearance in every way. "In 1840," he began, and my mind was already wandering. God, to have stood so long, to have seen and survived so much, only to be turned into a cheesy hotel. It was positively criminal.

With increasing irritation, I sensed someone pressing close to me in the crowd. For once I was actually listening to the lesson and enjoying it, and I didn't want anyone interrupting. I shuffled forward a foot or two towards the front, but April followed me. I knew it was her. I could smell her expensive cherry lip balm even before I saw her, and everyone else knew enough to leave me alone.

I tried to ignore her, but when she whispered into my ear there was little I could do to pretend she wasn't there.

"So it's you, huh? You're the one everyone was talking about."

I nodded, acknowledging that I'd heard her without admitting guilt. I kept my eyes forward, still dutifully watching our guide. "Maybe."

"It *is* you. I knew it was."

"Then why'd you ask?" I muttered over my shoulder, still refusing to face her.

"Why didn't you just say *yes?*"

I didn't answer, hoping without real hope that she might go away.

"Why did your cousin try to kill you?" she asked bluntly.

41

The question startled me so much I evaded an answer without even meaning to. "How did you know he was my cousin?" I hadn't even known it until the trial was over, and I'd found out in the privacy of my kitchen. What did this girl know, anyway?

"*Everybody* knows. They said it on the news. And they said your mother was in a crazy hospital when she had you. They said she was only a teenager and she died and you don't even know who your father is. They said your cousin thought you were a wicked witch and that's why he did it."

Warm color crept up my neck, but thankfully my shirt collar hid it for the most part. "You can't believe everything you hear on TV," I admonished, but I couldn't help but wonder. Suddenly I wished I watched more television, and it began to dawn on me that there might be a reason Lu had gotten our cable turned off. "Why do you keep asking questions if you already think you know the answers?"

"Because I keep hearing these really stupid things about what happened to you and I can't believe they're true—even down *here*."

I gritted my teeth. "Which things?" I almost growled.

She lifted her nose in the air and sniffed like a small, greedy animal. "*All* of them."

"What do you know, anyway? You weren't there." My voice was rising, but I couldn't really stop it. I wanted to smack her, and it was only out of respect for my surroundings that I did not do so.

"I didn't *have* to be there. Everyone heard about it. Everyone knows." She folded her arms, challenging me as surely as if she'd offered me pistols at sunrise. I wasn't sure what to do. I didn't even know if the allegations were false—and if they were true, whether or not I should be upset or ashamed. I stood there confused, wanting to either retreat in disdain or defend myself, but not knowing which course of action was appropriate.

From pure desperation, I opted to misdirect. "Shut up, I'm trying to listen. You're going to get us in trouble. We're not supposed to be talking."

She went on anyway, her voice just low enough to keep our teacher's head from turning. "I mean, it's not like it matters. You don't have to say anything. I know it's true, and I'm going to go home and tell my dad and stepmom that I got to meet you. I'll tell them it's *all* true, just like they heard on the TV, and that I'm stuck having class with that witch. They'll love that. Maybe they'll love it so much they'll take me out of this stupid *redneck* school."

I closed my eyes, concentrating on the old man, who went on speaking in his dreary drone about things I would have found fascinating under different circumstances. He gestured at the ceiling and said something pithy and rehearsed about the glass, and then he pointed back out at the restaurant and revealed another historical nugget.

It all sailed past me.

My rage was positively palpable. I wasn't too offended by the *R* word; heaven knows I threw it around plenty myself. Even so, I wanted to slug April more surely than I wanted to wake up the next morning. My fingers wrung themselves into a white-knuckled frenzy, but I clutched them at my sides, paralyzed by indecision.

"What's the matter, witch? Can't think of a good spell? Are you going to turn me into a frog?"

One after another I measured my breaths, deep and slow. "I wish I could. We *eat* frogs around here." Well, I'd never eaten any personally and I didn't know anyone who *had,* but I'd heard that it was something that rednecks did.

She laughed out loud. "Jesus," she blasphemed happily. "Nothing you people do would surprise me. Shit, I want out of here so bad."

"Then go home. Or one of these days I'm gonna send you home *airmail,*" I threatened, fists beginning to shake.

"I believe it, too. My dad says you guys are the worst kind of southerners."

I couldn't stop myself. I had to ask, even though it meant asking a question when I already knew the answer. I just wanted to hear her say it. I probably should have kept my mouth shut, but that's the story of my life.

"What do you mean, *you guys?*"

"I mean," and she drew her mouth up to my ear once more. I hadn't yet faced her and she wanted to make sure she still commanded my attention. I believe she would've crawled inside my head if she could have, to make sure I heard her. "You guys who aren't all white and aren't all black. You're not *anything* except the worst mix of a bad lot, and it don't surprise my dad at all that a family like yours would have something crazy like this going on."

"Thank you," I said quietly.

"For what?"

"For making this *really* easy."

Later she called it a sucker punch, but she knew it was coming. She practically begged me for it. Right beneath the ribs. My knotty little knuckles slammed into her stomach and then, as she fell, my other hand came up and caught her square in the face. Blood spurted from her nose, surprising me but not stopping me. She reached out and tried to grab my hair but I knocked her hand away and shoved her backwards. Back she went, onto a couch in the lobby and then over it.

Her head must have hit something somewhere along the way, for she did not get up again. Instead she lay there moaning, wiping at her face until scarlet streaked her cheeks and the sleeve of her shirt, even smearing the lovely marble floor.

It was only then, when I stood there panting, fists balled and feet parted, that I realized the old man had quit talking. Silence filled the lobby, despite the crowd gathering in a cautious circle around the scene. Our teacher ran to April's side and lifted her to a sitting position, where she cried and snuffled.

Our other chaperon, Mr. Wicks, found his way to me. He grabbed me by the shoulders and shook me harder than he needed to. "What did you do?" he asked, his runny gray eyes mere inches from my face. "What did you do to her?"

"She—she was, she said—"

"You don't just hit people like that!" He squeezed and I grunted.

I was frightened by his grip, and by the nearness of his breath. I couldn't stand him being so close. I lashed out, mirroring his self-righteous tone and hoping to push him back with my words. "Then why did you ask? Why does everyone keep asking me questions when they already know the answers, or else they don't care?"

He clapped my face in his beefy hand and held my chin so high I had to stand on tiptoe to keep from hurting. "If there was a problem, you should have taken it to me or to your teacher. Now quiet down right now, and unless you want to get kicked out of school the second we get back, you *stay* quiet!"

We stood that way for several seconds, me with lifted neck and him with menacing veins bulging at his temples. Our nostrils flared a complementary tempo until he released my jaw and we each stepped back.

Inch by inch, the muffled veil that had dropped over the place lifted and small daily noises once again echoed off the glass, brass, and stone. With it came hushed, feverish discussion amongst my schoolmates. I caught quick phrases, nothing I wanted to hear or repeat, as I slumped down on the lobby sofa over which April had stumbled. There I stayed while the tour continued without me, and without April, who was taken back to the school nurse by a chaperon who'd brought her own car. Mr. Wicks sat on the couch opposite me and glared, not speaking.

In order to avoid his laser gaze, I stared at the walls, and into the bar, and out through the glass at the gardens where the train tracks had once run. I strained to hear the rest of the tour guide's speech, but no matter how hard I listened it was lost to me. I gave up, closed my eyes and tried to pretend like I didn't feel like crying.

But I *did* feel like crying. I was desperately angry and hurt. I wanted my aunt but I didn't want to look like a baby asking for her. Besides, the odds were better than fair she'd get a call as soon as we returned, and I didn't want to face her wrath after yet another principal's message. Probably she wouldn't be angry. Probably she would understand . . . but she might not. Sometimes it was hard to judge.

And my hand ached. I'd never hit anyone before, and it seemed I'd bruised a knuckle or two. Did anyone care? No, of course not. I absently rubbed my wounded hand with my unharmed fingers.

A second teacher appeared to join Mr. Wicks. "Is everyone behaving here?" she asked, eyes boring hatefully into me. Again, I was hurt. She was the advanced reading group teacher and I liked her. I'd thought she liked me too, but she must not have, or she wouldn't have looked at me like that.

"Yes, and it had better stay that way. She'd *better* be sitting there thinking about what she did."

"Oh, I *am*," I mumbled with meaning.

"What was that?" they asked in perfect unison.

As if to assert himself, Mr. Wicks leaned forward. His forehead crumpled with disgust and his upper lip lifted at the edge to flash one of his nicotine-stained teeth. "What did you just say?"

"Nothing."

"What?"

"Nothing. I didn't say anything."

The reading teacher folded her arms and lurked behind Mr. Wicks. "You're in plenty enough trouble here, Eden. Don't get smart on us. I just don't understand this sort of behavior from you. I mean, I know you've had . . . some *family* trouble recently . . ."

I could have sworn I saw one corner of her mouth twitch, as if she'd made a little joke. Mr. Wicks's similar dull grin confirmed my suspicions. With sudden, glaring clarity it became perfectly apparent that they were making fun of me. I clenched both hands again, even the sore one, and dug them into the tops of my legs.

The reading teacher shook her head, trying to cast the smile away. It half worked. She went on. "But if you were having problems with another student you should have called it to our attention. You never take matters into your own hands like that."

I rummaged around in the steaming pile of anger in my chest and found my voice. I lifted it up and offered it out. "And what would you have done?" It came as a whisper, not a very steady one.

The teachers looked at each other, and Mr. Wicks answered for them both. "That depends on the circumstances. We could have sat down and talked things through, and if she was being rude or unkind—then we would have taken action."

"Like what?"

"That depends. But you have to leave that up to us. We're the ones who make the decisions around here."

I sat silent for another moment, growing calmer before looking at either of them. A lesson was coming together, and I sensed it was important. Behind me a pair of high heels clattered on the shiny floor, and phones rang at the check-in desk. Oh yes, it was a hotel now. I looked over my shoulder and out the front windows beside the doors. Across the road the sad, sagging ruins of other hotels and restaurants forlornly decayed to uniform shades of gray.

I raised my eyes. "Can I ask you something?"

They nodded, once again in full accord aligned against me.

"Why is this still here? I mean, people take care of it and keep it pretty. It's not like the rest of everything out here that looks like it's going to fall down any second. Didn't you guys see when we were driving here? The Choo Choo isn't like everything around it. It's different, but people protect it and love it, they don't abandon it or tear it down. This whole part of town looks like it got sick and died. Why does this place still look alive?"

After a few seconds of blank stares from them both, the reading teacher shrugged and softened a little. "I guess because, well, just because it was able to evolve. When it couldn't be one thing any-more, it became something else and kept on living that way . . . and it did it with style."

"But it's not the same."

47

"But it's still here," she restated my point without contributing anything new. "In the end it outlasted everything else."

So that was it—the lesson unintended.

Yes, it was important indeed. I learned more on that field trip than my school had ever expected, though it wasn't from the teachers. I learned volumes more than I might have gleaned from a blackboard, and I learned it from a big brick hotel that patiently wore a tacky neon sign like a plastic crown—not because it looked good but because it had become a necessity.

I closed my eyes again, wanting to remember the beauty of the place instead of my violence there. I listened for the churning engines of long-rusted trains, straining to hear them dragging themselves along the tracks and puffing to a laborious stop. I did not see them on that visit, but in the rear of the hotel, dozens of retired passenger cars were permanently parked on the remaining tracks. Gradually they were being renovated and restored, eventually to become luxury hotel rooms. All the ghosts in the old Pullman and Cincinnati cars cried out the rueful truth in voices like whistles, steam, and crackling lumps of burning coal.

Now you know, now you know. It is not enough to simply survive and to be victorious . . . it must be done with grace.

4

Interregnum

I

The summer I turned thirteen, Lu and Dave sent me to Camp Lookout, on the next mountain over. I was none too pleased with the prospect, initially, but once I got there it was all right. It wasn't a full-fledged summer camp, anyway—it only ran for two weeks out of the year, and I was near enough to home that a phone call would probably have summoned my aunt and uncle faster than a pizza.

I tried not to feel too betrayed as they drove off and left me, and I tried to remember that it was only a couple of weeks. This was supposed to be fun. Dave said that I was there to taste some independence, and when he put it that way, it didn't sound so bad.

The camp itself was civilized enough, which is to say, at least there weren't any tents. I didn't like the thought of tents. I like having more between me and the elements than a thin sheet of canvas, and I've never seen the point of going out of your way to pretend you haven't got any plumbing. Therefore, I was greatly reassured by the sight of cabins and a couple of communal bathroom buildings. As long as I could flush, I'd be okay.

I twisted my hands up in the duffel bag straps and shifted the weight of my backpack on my shoulder. Some other kid a few feet away was crying and clinging to her mom. She was about my age, and I found myself uncomfortable on her behalf. I wasn't entirely thrilled about the situation either, but it wasn't something to make a scene over.

"Good grief," I muttered, just in time for a counselor to tap me on the shoulder and offer to show me to my bunk.

The counselor's name was Maggie, and she had a bone-deep tan that promised she'd look like a saddle in twenty years time. She had enormous teeth, as unnaturally white as her skin was unnaturally brown, and she was near enough to my age that I anticipated a difficult time taking her seriously. But she was wearing the official camp staff T-shirt and a name tag that identified her as a "Senior Assistant," so I let her tell me where to go.

She led me to a big A-frame structure that was supposed to look rough-hewn, and it succeeded enough to worry me about its potential bug population. But inside, the place was clean, and the four narrow beds appeared free of any obvious infestation.

Two of the beds had stacks of personal belongings staking them out as claimed, so I went to the far corner and dropped my stuff down on an empty mattress.

"Your bunkmates are already lined up for roll call and introduction. Let's get you out there with them, okay?"

"Okay."

"How about we get you introduced around, and then we can get you all unpacked and settled in?"

"That sounds fine," I agreed, happy to follow instructions since I wasn't sure what was expected of me.

"After Mr. Joe and Miss Candy finish with their opening welcome, we can get ready for lunch, okay?" I would come to learn that Maggie always talked that way, in questions. I don't think she was stupid, but she seemed as uncertain in her authority as I was—it was like she was asking my permission to tell me what to do. I found her discomfort almost endearing, but not exactly confidence inspiring.

The campers were all gathered outside in a small amphitheater, shuffling bottoms on the split-log seats. Some were chatting with cronies of previous years, and others were new, like me. The latter group played laser-tag games of eye contact, wondering who would be worth chatting up and whom to avoid.

I took a seat on the outer edge of the seating's crescent, making a point of keeping plenty of personal space between me and the next kid in line, a boy a couple of years my junior. I crossed my arms over my knees and leaned forward, waiting for the action to start.

Mr. Joe kicked things off with a knobby-kneed bang, doing a little hop as he came forward to begin the official greetings. "Hello, boys and girls, and welcome to Camp Lookout!" he announced, speaking with inflections that expect a cheer to follow.

He was rewarded with a discordant buzz of leg-slaps and whistled hoots, and Miss Candy stepped down front to join him. Miss Candy had bangs that had been teased with a curling iron and sprayed into place before the rest of her hair was pushed under a Camp Lookout baseball cap, and I figured that was pretty much all I needed to know about *her*.

Neither one of them impressed me much as people I should get to know, and I don't remember much of what they said. Mostly they gushed excited promises of games, swimming, and crafts—none of which spelled "summer fun" to me, exactly, but at least I was surrounded by new people. Everyone at school knew who I was, knew all about the court case and—almost as notoriously—the time I broke April's nose in the Choo Choo; but there at the camp, so far as anyone knew I was just one more awkward kid. The more I thought about it, the more I found the prospect of anonymity intensely appealing.

I met my roommates back at the bunks after opening remarks. We introduced ourselves and made idle chitchat while we unpacked, and then Maggie came bounding in behind us to perform a redundant round of roll call for our benefit.

"This is Anne," Maggie began, making a sweeping gesture at the crybaby I'd seen earlier in the parking lot. Anne was no longer sobbing, but the waterworks hadn't cleared up completely. She nodded to acknowledge her name and lifted her hand in a little wave.

"And Lisa." Lisa didn't look up from her methodical unpacking, but she also lifted her hand in a small wave to the room in general.

"And Eden." I followed suit, unwilling to break the routine.

"And this is Cora," she finished. Cora mumbled a syllable that might have been "Hi," but spared us the beauty queen hand twist. Maggie decided that her work with us was done, at least for the time being, so she left us all to "get acquainted, okay?"

Within five minutes I realized with a passive displeasure that I had been stashed in the oddball cabin. I never did decide if they put me there because my cover was blown and they thought I was one of the oddballs, or if I was just lucky.

Cora was the easiest to get to know, since she didn't tear up at the drop of a hat or freak out if you bumped the side of her bed and caused her socks to fall out of alignment, so I chose her as my first potential camp buddy. We had a number of things in common, and it was easy to talk. She was also tall for her age, and like me, she was the sort of girl who got asked a lot where her parents were from, since that's more polite than wondering aloud about somebody's racial makeup. Cora had never been to camp before, and she didn't know anyone else either.

"I've got a grandfather who's dying," she informed me over supper.

"I'm sorry," I said, just being polite, and she called me on it.

"No, you're not, but that's okay. It's kind of sad, but I don't know him real well. I'm just telling you so in case I go home in the middle of things, you'll know why. Mom didn't want me to come at all, since Grandpa's sick and we might have to leave for his funeral, but my stepdad said they could always bring me home if it came to that. Are your grandparents still alive?"

I had to think about it a minute. "My grandmother is, I think. I don't know. For some reason, we don't have much to do with her. I'm not even sure what she looks like."

"Why don't you have much to do with her?" Cora asked between a couple bites of cornbread.

"Not sure, exactly. Had something to do with my mom, maybe. It's a long story though, I bet." I tried to summon some memory of Lu's mother. I knew we'd lived with her until Lu met Dave, and I was a couple of years old then. I thought I might remember some half-heard voice that may have been hers, but then again, it might have been somebody else. I couldn't remember seeing her at Malachi's trial, and even my rarely seen aunt Michelle had come out for that one. "I think my grandmother's still alive, but I'm not sure we'd go to her funeral if she had one. I don't think she takes much interest in us, anyway, and I guess it's mutual."

"Oh."

Anne, who was sitting beside Cora on the other side of the table, began to sniffle. "I miss my grandma. I go to her place after school twice a week while my mom's at work."

We didn't pretend not to stare as she started crying again, but at least we didn't laugh, and Cora handed her a napkin. "That's sweet that you're so close," she said while Anne blew her nose. "But I bet she hopes you're having a good time. You're only going to be here two weeks, and then you can go home."

"Two whole weeks," Anne echoed mournfully, and then it was my turn to hand her a napkin.

"Geez, honey. Suck it up."

"That's not very nice," Lisa said without looking at me. She was too busy making sure her peas were lined up in tidy rows to raise her eyes and scold me in earnest, which was fine. It had been four hours, and I'd already figured out that it didn't matter how rude or gentle you were with Anne, she was going to cry anyway and there wasn't much you could do to improve or worsen the situation.

"It's okay," Anne said behind her improvised tissue.

"What about you?" Cora asked Lisa, who was deeply engrossed in her vegetable arrangement. "Why do you always do that thing where you have to make everything look just right?"

"Yeah, that's way weirder than Anne's crying," I agreed, and I peered over Lisa's shoulder, as if getting a closer look at her edible artwork would cause it to make more sense.

She elbowed me away without any real malice. "I like it this way."

I accepted the explanation, but I couldn't withhold judgment. "Bizarre," I concluded, and even Anne managed to nod through the snot to agree.

"I don't care," Lisa replied. Something about the way she said it made me believe her. That only made it stranger, so far as I was concerned, but at the same time it made it more tolerable too. At least I didn't have to feel sorry for her.

Across the table, Cora shrugged at me and I shrugged back.

Cora was easily the most normal of the bunch, and she probably thought the same thing about me, which only begged the question of what was really wrong with her. Before the week was out, I'd have my answer.

Thursday night we had a bonfire. There were marshmallows to be turned to dripping torches and dropped into the dirt; and two of the male counselors broke out guitars to compel a sing-along. I'm a fairly good singer so I joined in on the songs I knew even though I felt a little silly and didn't understand who Michael was, or why he needed to row the boat ashore.

Later, they wanted to tell ghost stories. Mr. Joe told the first two or three, but they sounded more like jokes than real events. Cora thought so too. She leaned over on the splintery log and said as much in my ear, but she wasn't any good at whispering and Mr. Joe overheard just enough to feign offense. "Cora." He found her on the far side of the fire and made sure everyone else saw her, too. "What do you mean they're not *real* ghost stories?"

She shifted on the log and tried to make herself look smaller. It didn't work, and all eyes were on her, so she had to answer. "I mean they're not, that's all. Real ghost stories don't have punch lines, Mr. Joe."

"They don't? Well, how should they go, then? Why don't you tell us, since you're the expert."

I was thankful for the dimly bright fire, because it camouflaged the flush that was creeping up my neck. I knew everyone was looking at Cora, but she was sitting next to me, and there was a chance someone would later remember me when presented with the mental prompt of "ghosts." I held my breath and waited for my new friend's answer.

"Real ghost stories . . . they're not whole stories," she said slowly. "You can't tell them like a joke, because you never know the whole thing. There's too much left out, and if you know the whole thing, it would take you longer than a couple of minutes to tell."

I found myself nodding along to her words, then I stopped myself, lest I be singled out as a fellow "expert" and asked to testify. But she was right, and I knew that better than anybody. It made me wonder how she knew it so well.

"Would you like to tell us a *real* ghost story, then?" Mr. Joe went on, and all at once I deeply hated him for forcing the subject. He didn't understand at all; if you had a real ghost story, you probably didn't want to tell it to a whole bunch of people who were only going to laugh at you if you believed it.

Cora opened her mouth and then closed it. She looked over at me, then, for general support or maybe something more specific. I didn't know how to help her, though, so she glared back into the fire. "I don't have any real ghost stories to tell, Mr. Joe. Yours are fine. You should tell us some more of them."

Her flat tone was utterly lost on our counselor, who needed only the barest hint of permission to make a further spectacle of himself. He happily began a new tale, and as he talked he stuffed another unfortunate marshmallow onto the end of his unbent coat hanger.

Cora let out a sigh of relief and uncrossed her legs.

"He's stupid," I whispered—and I'm good at whispering, so he didn't hear me. "Don't worry about it." Then, because I wanted to establish to her that I 'got it,' and that she could tell me if she wanted to, I added, "If you've got a real ghost story and you want to tell it later on, I promise I wouldn't laugh at it."

Cora rubbed her toes into the dirt and stared into the flames. "Yeah," she said, but I wasn't sure what she meant by it, so I just said, "Okay" in response, and we didn't talk about it anymore for a while.

That same night, I heard her humming to herself. I want to say that she was doing it in her sleep, but I don't think that was the case. I think she was afraid, and she was singing to herself all quiet, the way people do sometimes. Some people pray, and I imagine it has about the same effect. It gives you something else to think about, something else to dwell on besides what you're afraid of— but not something so complicated that you can't spit it out by heart if you get too scared to think on it. Having a strand of words to string together helps.

I rolled over on my mattress and faced her bunk, straining to listen. There was a beat to her breathy muttering, but no melody that I could discern. Must be a rhyme, I thought. Maybe it was a child's prayer, or a verse repeated so the familiar sound is a comfort.

I went ahead and asked her about it over breakfast, but in case it had something to do with any real ghost stories, I asked it on the sly—in private as much as I could. I waited until the other girls had

56

taken their trays to the drop-off line, and then I leaned over to Cora.

"Last night I thought I heard something. I thought I heard you talking in your sleep." It was a lie, but it was a polite one. It gave her an out, and let her pretend she didn't know what I meant if she didn't intend to fill me in.

"I don't talk in my sleep," she argued. "You might've heard me, but I was awake."

"Were you saying your prayers?"

"No." She said it matter-of-factly, not like it was the most outlandish suggestion in the world, but like it wasn't the correct one.

Cora didn't volunteer any more information, but she hadn't acted like it was something that embarrassed her, either, so I picked at the question a little more. "Were you talking to yourself? 'Cause I do that sometimes, too."

She thought about it for a second, then nodded. "Something like that. It's this thing I do when I can't sleep."

"Oh." That made sense, but it wasn't very interesting. I hoped that wasn't the end of it, and I might have asked more questions but our roommates returned without their trays. It was time for camp games. I hoped they'd let red rover drop and move onto something else. My arms were sore, and if they tried to make me play that stupid game again, I was going to look Mr. Joe straight in the eye and tell him I had my period.

Thankfully, it didn't come to that. We played something else, or maybe we went swimming. I don't remember. The middle of that day was the least interesting part; and it wasn't until well after lights-out that things got interesting again.

I made a deal with myself that I'd stay awake long enough to see if Cora did it again, but I was worn out and I broke that deal.

I didn't stay asleep long, though. I woke up to a gentle shake, and it was Cora. She looked like she'd seen a ghost, and believe me, that's a look I know all too well. "What's going on?" I meant to ask, but she shushed me and widened her eyes into two wet, worried orbs.

"It doesn't always work," she said in that loud whisper that meant someone would wake up if she kept talking for long. "It isn't like a proper prayer, maybe that's why. I don't know any real prayers, do you?"

I nodded my answer and sat up, wiggling out from under the blanket and fishing around with my feet. "Let's go outside or something," I proposed, finding my sneakers and pulling them on despite my lack of socks.

"That's why I woke you up. I've got to go *use it*, and I don't want to go by myself. Will you come to the bathroom with me? Please?"

"Yeah," I said. "I'll come with you. Hang on." The room was chillier than you might expect for a southern summer, but we were on top of the mountain so it wasn't such a surprise. Everyone packed a sweater to be on the safe side, and I pulled mine out to wrap it around my chest. When I stood, my feet felt small and damp inside my shoes.

Cora was talking to herself again, and I was almost sure it was a rhyme—something straightforward and Mother Goosey. She was repeating it to herself a little louder now, as if volume had something to do with the chant's potency. By the time we got outside, I could catch about every third word.

"What is it, that thing you keep saying?" I broke down and asked. "And why do you keep doing it?"

My companion had brought a red plastic flashlight. She aimed a big yellow circle at the ground and we did our best to keep our feet inside it as we walked across the grassy, gravelly ground between our cabin and the bathroom building. When we were about halfway there, she answered.

"It's a thing I say when I'm scared. If I say it over and over again, and I think about it as hard as I can, they don't bother me."

"They who?"

"I'm not sure, exactly. But they hang around and I see them sometimes when it's dark. They especially like to hang around mirrors—at least I think they do. Maybe that's just when I see them best. I don't know."

I stopped, and she aimed the light at the spot between our shoes. The puddle of illumination seemed awfully small against the wooded night. I shifted back and forth between my sweaty feet and rubbed one heel up against an itch on my leg. "Does this have something to do with your real ghost story?"

"Yeah, but don't stop here. Let's keep moving. Let's get it over with. I've really got to go, you know?"

I could stand to take a pee myself, but I held my ground. "And you didn't just ask me to come along because you're scared. If you were scared, you would've gotten Maggie up and made her come with you, since that's her job and all."

"Yeah," Cora said again. She grabbed a handful of unruly black hair and tried unsuccessfully to stuff it behind her ear. "I kind of figured you might—I mean, I wanted to know if, um . . . Well, last night when everyone was laughing at me you weren't, and I wondered if maybe you would understand better than the rest of them."

"And?"

"And . . . I wanted to know if you could see them too."

That was the root of it, and it was what I'd suspected. On the one hand, I couldn't hold it against her—and I'd wanted her to confide in me, hadn't I? But on the other hand, the bathroom building was only a few yards away, and it was filled with mirrors. I glanced back at the cabin and considered my bladder capacity.

"Please? Don't make me go by myself. For real, I don't think I can do it. I'd rather stay in the cabin and wet the bed or else go pee in the bushes than go in there by myself. Please?"

I didn't mean to make her beg, but that dimly glowing bathroom building was looking less and less like a direct necessity. "If you're serious, about the bushes I mean, I could run in there and get you some toilet paper. And I could keep a lookout."

She fidgeted, doing the universal hopping jig of a needy kid. My offer made sense, but it wasn't exactly what she wanted. "We could do that, yeah. But I really want to know if it's just me. If you can see them too, and it's not just me, then . . ." Her voice sputtered out. She wasn't sure how to finish.

I understood better than she knew. If you're the only one who sees them, then maybe they aren't there. Maybe it's you and you're crazy, which isn't ideal; but maybe it's *not* you, and there really is someone or something closing in around you. Damned if you do, damned if you don't. I didn't know what the better option was any more than she did.

"All right," I caved. "We'll go. Come on."

We cleared the last stretch in a few seconds. Cora stopped before crossing the threshold, flipping the switch to turn off her light. Everything inside was already brightly lit with an ugly fluorescent glare, and she needed an excuse to hesitate another moment.

"Do you hear anything?" she asked.

I did the auditory equivalent of squinting, even closing my eyes so nothing would distract me. I heard things, yes; I heard crickets, and, nearby, an owl was interrogating the mountain. I heard a restless sleeper turn over on a squeaky mattress, and a row of creaking boards beneath an insomniac counselor's feet. But I knew what she really meant. She wanted to know if I felt anything, but she didn't know how to ask that question.

I wouldn't have known exactly how to answer it, anyway. Maybe there was something, but I couldn't have told her what. It might have been nothing more than trees and wind on the edge of the sounds I could sift from the near-silence.

"No," I answered, because that was the easiest thing to say. "I don't hear anything. Let's go, if we're going. Don't look at the mirrors, if you're scared to. You can run right into a stall. You don't have to look over to the right at all. I promise I won't tell if you don't wash your hands."

"Yeah." She dipped her chin and dropped her eyes, crooking her head over to the left. "But you stay here. You look, and you tell me if you see something."

"All right."

She took off, slipping slightly on the dingy tile, and she flung herself into the nearest available stall. Her bottom connected hard with the seat and I wondered how she'd had time to bypass her underwear.

I took up a position in the next stall over, doing my business and listening to the sound of my friend's rushing torrent. I finished up faster than she did, and I went to wait for her by the sinks. By the mirrors.

I held still, trying to feel out the room. Whenever I'd seen the three women, there had always been a change in the way the air felt—everything went empty and dry. The bathroom building was anything but dry, and it couldn't possibly feel empty with every stray, slight sound echoing from tile to tile and from door to bent metal door.

From within the stall, Cora was talking to herself again, or maybe to me. It was hard to tell. "It's like talking to babies. It doesn't matter what you say, it's how you say it. You can change the words around however you want, as long as they sound nice, and as long as they make you feel better."

Although I deliberately hadn't done so yet, now I turned to face the crusty old mirrors. To call them mirrors at all was to give them more credit than they deserved; they more closely resembled polished strips of sheet metal. You could see yourself in a vague sort of way, but your reflection was an impressionist representation composed of fuzzy colors. I stood facing the nearest square full on. I couldn't for the life of me figure out what Cora was so afraid of. I barely recognized my own familiar shape, and I couldn't imagine she'd see anything distinct enough to be threatening.

"Sing a song of breath mints," she continued, now singsong, through the door. "Banana cream pie. Four and twenty blackbirds take to the sky."

"I know that one. That's not how it goes," I mumbled. I was watching her stall over my reflection's shoulder. I didn't see anything, I didn't think. The whole thing was so blurred as to be hopeless, anyway. The longer I looked, the less worried I became.

"I told you, it doesn't matter. I like banana cream pie. So that's how I say it goes."

"Fine." But even as I said it, there was motion in the clouded glass. At first I figured she'd kicked the door from within, but I didn't hear any kick and she was still steadily peeing, so I had a good idea of where her body was. I wondered how long her legs were.

"Sing a song of breath mints, banana cream pie. Four and twenty blackbirds take to the sky. When the sky is filled up . . ."

More motion. Definitely, this time. It was white, and fast, at the mirror's upper left corner. It could have been anything. An owl, even, drawn by the light. Anything.

"With all the feathered wings . . ."

"Cora?"

"The birds will come protect me . . ."

"Cora," I said again, but I could hear everything I needed to know in the tremor of her voice. She knew she wasn't alone, and she knew it more surely than I did.

"From all those other things."

"That's a good rhyme," I whispered. "Maybe you should say it again." As soon as she'd quit talking the white thing had come in closer.

"I'm almost done," she whispered back. I heard her stand and shuffle her pajama bottoms up around her waist. "Okay."

"Okay."

"I'm going to come out now, and I'm going to run for the door. Will you be behind me?"

"Oh yeah. Maybe in front of you."

"Don't leave me—"

"Okay, okay, okay. I won't. You first." The white thing was taking form, growing solid in the battered, filmy surface I couldn't take my eyes away from. I didn't dare turn around; I didn't want to know what it looked like any better than my foggy view already allowed. It wasn't one of the sisters three, I knew that much, and that meant it could be friend or foe; I didn't feel like sticking around to find out which.

This was not like anything I'd felt before. This was not dry and quiet and distant. This was something damp and invasive. I tried to pick out a shape more specific than "personlike" but I wasn't having much luck.

"Hey, Cora, do you see anything?"

"No, my eyes are closed."

"If you opened them, would you see anything?"

"I'm not going to open them."

"Okay, but if you *did* open them—what would you see?"

"Forget it," she said. She knocked the door open with her knee and came out blind, one hand over her face. In the moment I turned to see her, flailing toward the door and past me, I saw the white thing better. I saw it well enough to know that it was there, and it was different. It was not like the women who had hovered so gently near my side. This thing reached, and it moved like it could grab. When it followed Cora past the stall's door, it pushed against the metal slab and the rusty hinges creaked.

It saw me, then, and for a moment it forgot about its pursuit of my friend.

The empty place where eyes ought to be gazed me up and down. It lifted one arm like a tentacle of smoke and it nudged the door again, deliberately opening it farther. Back and forth it rocked the door, and the sound the metal made was a beat like the one Cora spoke to comfort herself.

It had made its point without a word: it knew I could see it too, and I knew it could touch me if it wanted.

Cora was long gone, outside now, calling to me in her too-loud quiet voice. We were pretty close to Miss Candy's cabin; it was only a matter of time before someone woke up and knew we were out of bed. "Shut up," I called out of the side of my mouth, but I don't think she heard me. I took a step back and my tailbone met the hard porcelain of the sink. I reached back, gripped the edge, and squeezed.

The very white thing stopped playing with the door and began to come towards me. It might have been only following the sound of Cora's voice, but it was going to have to go past me or through me to get to her. Either way, it was getting closer.

I was glued to the spot by sweat and fear. I wasn't sure how to move out of its way if I tried, and I didn't think for a moment that a mangled nursery rhyme was going to help me any.

"Eden," she called, sharpening the letters on her fright. "Eden, run!"

That was as good a plan as any, but my feet wouldn't hear it. I couldn't lift them, not with all my strength, and my arms weren't moving either. Maybe it did something to me or maybe I was only petrified by my own terror, but I froze up when it pressed against me. I turned my head and closed my eyes, and the side of my face the thing pushed against went numb. It went prickly and painful, like when you accidentally sleep on your arm—you wake up, and you can't feel it for a second, but then the blood flows back and it hurts all over like someone's jabbing at it with pushpins. The awful sensation spread down my neck, and shoulder, and clipped one of my knees before it faded.

"Sing a song of breath mints," I heard, and it was an insistent line, said with all the force of the Latinate chants of an exorcism. Cora's hand wrapped around my wrist and pried it loose from the sink.

64

"Banana cream pie. Four and twenty blackbirds take to the sky."

I opened my eyes and she was looking back at me, teeth locked together. "When the sky is filled up, with all the feathered wings . . ." She drew me forward, dragging me out of my horrified haze.

"The birds will come protect us, from all those other things. Come on, Eden."

I wrenched my other hand from the sink and let her lead me stumbling away, back into the darkness, away from the fluorescent buzz and the white thing in the bathroom. I looked over my shoulder and saw nothing but the big pale rectangle of light where we'd left the main door ajar.

"You can't stop for it," Cora breathed as we tripped and hopped back to our cabin. "You can't ever stop for it. You can chase it away with words, if you mean them when you say them, but you can't ever stop for it."

We reached the cabin breathless and awake, with twigs caught in our shoes and scuffs on our knees from all the falling. But we were alone, except for the snores and unconscious shufflings of our roommates.

Cora and I climbed into the same bunk and yanked the covers over our heads, turning the flashlight on to illuminate our private little space beneath the blanket. For a few seconds, we panted back and forth, catching our breath and listening for the worst.

"What was that?" I asked, suspecting she didn't have a much better idea than I did.

She shook her head to confirm it. "Dunno. But at least I can make it go away. And at least I know it's really there, now. At least you saw it too."

"Yeah, I saw it too. And you did—you did make it go away."

"I told you. You've just got to say the rhyme."

It was my turn to shake my head. "That's the dumbest spell I've ever heard," I said. "I can't imagine why it worked, but I'm glad it did."

Cora smiled wide and all the way, for the first time in the few days I'd known her.

"If we knew why it worked, it wouldn't be magic, would it?"

The next day, when we returned from an hour's worth of swimming, there was a message waiting for Cora from her mother. Her grandfather had died of a stroke sometime while we were doing cannonball leaps from the diving board.

Her parents came to pick her up that afternoon, and she did not return.

The next year when I came to Camp Lookout, I looked everywhere for her. I wanted to know what had happened with the mean white thing and if she'd ever learned how to make it go away completely.

But I never got to ask her. She wasn't there.

II

That summer at Camp Lookout set the pattern for most of the rest of my youth: even the good parts were often overshadowed by omnipresent specters and knowledge of the insanity in my family woodpile. In time, curiosity and adolescent confidence outweighed my fear of Lulu's wrath, and I came to watch her constantly for a moment of weakness, a time when I could pounce on her with my unwelcome questions. But I had to wait for that moment, long and patiently, and with faith. I waited until high school, miles and years removed from lonely train stations and tangible interactions with other girls' ghosts.

My time came one night when I came home from school and found Lulu in her room, lying face up on her bed. A bottle of coconut rum lay on the floor beneath her hand, and her eyes were red-rimmed and swollen. The phone on the nightstand was off the hook and shrieking a dull, whining busy signal.

She opened her eyes when I came in, then closed them again.

"Damn," she said. "I thought you were Dave."

"Sorry," I responded, pinned to the spot where I stood. "You okay?" I asked.

Her eyes stayed shut so she could lie to me without looking at me. "I'm fine."

I'd have been a fool to let it go at that. "What's the matter?" I asked.

"Your grandmother's dead. Last night. A stroke, they're thinking."

Lulu and her mother hadn't spoken since Lulu had moved out of the house almost twelve years before. I couldn't recall having ever met the woman, though I guessed she must still live in town. That's why it was so confounding to be presented with the sight of my beloved aunt in shambles, sprawled across her bed, pushed to this point by the death of a woman we'd not seen in so long.

"You know what the kicker is?" Lulu slurred. "You know what really makes me . . ."

She stalled. I sensed she was hunting for a word, but when she realized what the right word was, she decided not to use it. She began the thought again. "You know what really makes me mad?"

"What?"

"She's dead now, and that means me and Shelly's all that's left," she said, meaning her younger sister who now lived in Nashville. It had probably been Michelle who had called with the news.

I had an idea. I had a *question*.

It leaped out of my mouth with a little more glee than it should have.

"Just you two and old Tatie, eh?"

Lulu sat up fast, eyes blazing as though she were looking for something to hurl my way. I stepped back and braced myself

67

against the doorframe with both hands, ready to run if I had to. Lulu settled on a bottle of cough syrup on the nightstand and chucked it drunkenly towards my head. It stumbled against the wall by my elbow, then clattered harmlessly to the floor at my feet. I held my ground.

"I didn't mean anything by it—just to say that I guess there's another whole branch of the family there someplace. It's not just us, not really." Of course I meant something by it. I meant I wanted to know more, but I wasn't dumb enough to anger her over it if I could help myself.

She laughed without a trace of mirth and let her body fall back onto the bed. "That's true, I guess. Lord, but wouldn't we be better off if it wasn't so."

"It doesn't matter now anyway," I broached, still clinging to the doorframe. "'Cause they sent Malachi away to Pine Breeze."

Lulu snorted, and something told me I'd screwed up. "Who told you that?" she asked.

"But they did, didn't they? They sent him off to Pine Breeze for the next twenty years and he's gotta stay fifty yards away from me for the rest of forever."

"Yeah, well. You're part right. But he's at the state facilities. You heard the judge say that part about the Bend, or did you forget? He's not over there at Pine Breeze."

Pine Breeze. It was all I could do to contain my excitement. For all of her promises to fill me in one day, she'd never done so. And if she wasn't willing to volunteer any information, now might be the best time to quiz her. I sighed my next question, desperate to make it come out casually. "How come?"

"It's been shut down for fifteen, sixteen years. Since you were born, anyway. You do the math." One long arm reached over the side of the bed, feeling for the rum and fumbling around.

On the other side of the house, the front door opened and Dave dropped his keys onto the end table by the couch, like he always did.

I ran the tip of my tongue over my upper lip and took another deep, measured breath. Lulu found the rum and took another swallow.

This was as close to vulnerable as I might ever expect to see Lulu. Now or never. I was too curious to pay any attention to the twinge of guilt that warned I was taking advantage of her. I asked my next question anyway.

"Where is Pine Breeze, anyway?"

Lulu's eyes squinted low and close together. Uh-oh. "What do you want to know for?"

"I just do." I slid one foot back and forth and shifted my weight. She didn't answer me for a few long seconds, so I spoke again to fill the pause. "Just wondering."

"I told you, it's been shut down."

Dave appeared beside me. "She all right?" he asked quietly, but Lulu heard him.

"Would she have called you back from Atlanta if she was all right?" she spat, not budging from her prone position except to stuff a pillow up under her head. "And now this little thing thinks she can, she thinks, she wants to know about Pine Breeze, if you can believe that. . . ."

My uncle pulled me outside the doorway and leaned close. He peeked around the corner back at Lulu, and he lowered his voice. "You got plans with friends or anything? I mean, are you going off someplace tonight?"

"Not sure. Maybe I will, and maybe I won't."

He ignored my attitude and moved to his next query. "How bad do you want to know about Pine Breeze?"

No sense in lying. I dropped the nonchalance. "Pretty bad."

"Okay. Stick around. But give me a minute here. Let me get her to sleep." He nudged me farther down the hall and stepped into their bedroom, closing the door behind himself.

I stood there, baffled. It had occurred to me before that I might pump Dave for clues, but he always allied himself with Lulu, pleading ignorance or parental alliance. I wandered into the living room and flipped the television on, wondering if he was actually going to make good or if he'd only been trying to get rid of me.

Dave was a great guy, but it was a rare, rare day that he'd go against Lulu's wishes.

After an hour or two I heard the bedroom door open and close softly. Then boxes were shifting across the hall in the studio. Papers were shuffled. Boxes were replaced and the studio door swung shut.

Dave tiptoed past the bedroom door and joined me on the couch. He was holding an album I'd never seen before. He opened it across his left knee and my right one. Despite the expanse of the living room, the length of the hallway, and a shut door separating us from Lulu, my uncle's voice barely crested a conspiring whisper.

"Pine Breeze," he began, "has been closed since you were about six weeks old. That's why you've never heard anything about it. Your mother was sent there before anyone knew she was pregnant with you. The facilities weren't any good—it was a home for messed-up teenagers, it wasn't a hospital—and she bled to death before they had time to spank you into breathing on your own. That's why they're closed. They were supported by private donations and government funding, but when your mother's story got out it all got pulled. No one wanted to be talked about.

"Lulu and I got thinking about it once and I decided to go poking around. It's out towards Red Bank, on the north side of the river, and I swear they just abandoned it. I don't think they packed up a single thing except maybe some of the furniture. They just left it."

Dave flipped the first page of the album, to a photograph of an enormous brick building covered with ivy. The windows were cracked and dirty, and random bricks had fallen out of the masonry down to the untrimmed shrubbery. At the bottom left corner of the photo Lulu was staring into a window with her nose pressed flat against it, her hands against the pane to shield away the glare.

I ran my fingers lightly across the picture's edges. "Is this it, then? Is this Pine Breeze?"

"Part of it. The complex was scattered all over that whole hill. There's about eight or nine buildings altogether, I guess. We thought this one was the main administrative office."

"They needed eight or nine buildings to house crazy teenagers?"

"It wasn't always an adolescent ward. The first parts were built around the turn of the century, for a health spa or something. I'm not sure what. But after that closed, it was bought out by someone else, who turned it into something else and added a new section or two . . . and so forth. By the time your mother was there they only used a couple of the buildings anymore. The rest of them were shut up, I guess, but I've always been under the impression that there weren't more than fifteen or twenty kids left there when it closed."

He turned the page to reveal another Georgian brick building— two or three stories with wood-slat shutters and a tiny square porch, all overgrown with weeds and vines. A skinny tree sprouted around a rain gutter and worked its roots through the mortar between the dirty red walls. "It's a beautiful place, even now. I mean, even the last time I saw it, a while back. It's completely desolate; unless you go inside the buildings it looks like no one's touched it since 1978."

"Why? What's inside the buildings?"

"Graffiti. Homeless people and teenagers have trashed it, but I never saw another soul while I was out there. At least not until the cops showed up and kicked me out. My jeep was parked down at the foot of the hill, that's what gave me away. There's nowhere to park if you want to get out and walk around. The cop was pretty cool, though. He just told me that there was no trespassing allowed and that I needed to get on my way instead of being an asshole about it."

"Is it still there? Could I go running around up there?"

Dave flipped through the remaining few pages before he answered, and then he talked slowly. "I'm not sure. I heard the city was going to tear it down, but whether they have or not, I couldn't tell you." Ah. Being careful about what he said. I couldn't blame him.

His voice picked up to its usual pace once more as he finished, "And I am officially forbidding you to go there, even if it is still standing. Didn't you hear the part about homeless people and vandals? Besides, it's falling apart. The place isn't safe."

He may as well have quit when he implied it hadn't fallen down yet. I hadn't heard anything past the part about the city only *maybe* tearing it down. "Where is it? Red Bank, you said?"

"No dice, kid. I just said, it isn't safe. If you want, I'll run you out to the library tomorrow afternoon. They've probably got some stuff on it under local history if you feel like looking. You can explore the place via your friendly neighborhood librarian, but you are *not* going to check the place out in person. Not with my permission, and not on my watch, missy."

"Okay, the library, then. We could do that."

Dave clapped the book together and stood. "Of course, this is all under the strictest condition that you don't say a word to the goddess."

"Fear not, dear uncle." I smiled.

"Don't call me that. It makes me sound old."

"You *are* old," I said.

He smacked me gently on the head and went to go hide the album back in the studio closet before our goddess arose.

Dave was as good as his word. We went to the library and he left me to roam while he crossed the street and soaked himself with coffee at a hole-in-the-wall establishment. He promised me an hour at least before he came after me, and I set my watch to make sure he didn't cheat.

I went to the third floor of the ugly concrete building and chatted up the reference librarians, who pointed me towards a jungle of gray filing cabinets. Fine white spiderweb dust lifted into the air when I opened the proper drawer and shuffled for the correct file. Maybe one day they'd get around to putting all this on microfilm, or microfiche, or whatever medium a twenty-first-century library is expected to use. But sometimes I think it's true what they say about this part of the country—you may as well set your clocks back twenty years.

And there it was: "Pine Breeze."

The file was thicker than I'd expected, and the old sticker label was peeling its slow way free of the folder. I pulled the whole thing out with both hands and closed the cabinet with a shove of my hip.

The first page was a mounted newspaper clipping dated March of 1930. "Tuberculosis Hospital to Close, Reopen," the headline read. I scanned it hastily, picking out the phrases that looked important and ignoring everything else. Established 1913. Staffed by Red Cross, Salvation Army nurses. Bought by private investors—a local family. To be converted to a health spa. Interesting, but well before the time period relevant to me. I lifted the sheet out and prepared to put it aside, but not before a passage had time to leap off the page—"where some two thousand people perished during the TB epidemic . . ."

Two thousand people? That sounded like an awful lot.

I reached for the next item in the folder.

1946. A neat diagram of the campus compound, laid out on yellowing paper. I counted nine buildings, including a nurse's station set away from the main grouping. I concentrated hard, trying to decipher the tiny writing on the key at the right of the page.

Building 1: Administration headquarters. Former infirmary.
Building 2: Auditorium/gymnasium.
Building 3: Furnace house (for disposal of contaminated corpses).

Contaminated corpses? Then they burned the bodies of the tuberculosis victims, and they needed an entire building to do so. Maybe that two thousand estimate wasn't so high after all.

Building 4: Doctors' offices.
Building 5: Outpatient services.
Building 6: Cafeteria / food service facilities.
Building 7: Inpatient therapy.
Building 8: Rehabilitation dormitories.
Building 9: Nurse's station.

This was helpful. I made a mental note to hit the copy machine before leaving.

Next was a series of yellowed articles bearing headlines like, "Health Facility Seeks Federal Aid," and "Pine Breeze Sanatorium Investigated for Racial Inequality." The rest of the loose papers seemed to be articles about money problems, so I flipped past them in search of something more recent.

1968: Ah. There it was. "Federal Grant to Fund Hospital for Adolescents in North Chattanooga." Operated by Marion Finley. Would serve up to eighty patients, primarily substance-addicted and behaviorally problematic teenagers. Hmm. If Dave was right and the school was only serving fifteen or twenty kids back when it closed, then it really *had* fallen shy of projections.

Next page: A poor-quality black-and-white photocopy of another clipping. The words were hard to make out, but the photograph had transferred well enough. Eight girls, perhaps my own age, were sitting around a long table with sewing cards strung with yarn. All their round, pale faces were turned towards the camera, cards poised over the table. Each girl wore the same stoned, automaton stare, as if she knew her picture was being taken but wasn't sure what it should mean to her. "New drugs to modify behavior . . . activities provided . . . once-troubled girls into ladylike young

74

women . . . Finley claims high success rate, but says more funding still badly needed."

I put the picture away and began to flip down through another series of headlines, these too suggesting ongoing money problems. I idly wondered if the place had ever been solvent at all.

One wealthy family had withdrawn its support, though its members had previously contributed enough to have the dormitories named after them. Despite Ms. Finley's constant begging, the government couldn't be bothered to lend a hand. Enrollment was down. Pine Breeze was operating at cost.

1978: My mother.

I stopped. A giant picture of my mother stared out at me from the manila folder, buttressed by the caption: "Pine Breeze Patient Dead." I knew it was her, even though I only had the one old picture to guess by—and even before I caught her name beneath the photo. That spooky family likeness stared me in the face, and it chilled me a tiny bit.

I picked up the article. It crackled between my fingers as I read.

"Leslie Eve Moore, sixteen-year-old patient at the Pine Breeze adolescent facility, died sometime yesterday morning, apparently as a result of a difficult childbirth. Officials at Pine Breeze are withholding comment at this time except to say that the girl received the best medical care they could offer, and that they are deeply sorrowful. A spokesperson for the girl's family insists that they were unaware she was pregnant when she was committed to the institution. A lawyer from the NAACP has demanded an investigation, claiming that the family was never told of the pregnancy and that Leslie was not given proper medical attention, possibly because she was of mixed race. No details are available regarding the infant at this time."

My mother.

And me, now the same age as she'd been then. The picture was an old studio portrait in 1970s sepia tone, one she hadn't been happy to have taken. She wasn't frowning, but her smile was forced, and her hands were clenched in her lap, smashed hard across her thighs rather than folded there. The yellow dress she wore had a butterfly collar that made her neck seem too long and thin. She looked awfully fragile for a juvenile delinquent, but there was a certain stubbornness around the set of her eyes and the full line of her mouth. I'd have been lying if I said I didn't recognize it.

I looked quickly over each of my shoulders and, seeing no one, I folded the paper with my mother's face and stuck it in my pocket. Perhaps I should have made a photocopy, but I wasn't thinking. I'd only ever seen that one other picture of her, the one of the three sisters taken before their mother had sent my mother away. Lulu kept that picture to herself, stuck in the top corner of her dresser mirror.

Now I had one of my own.

I skimmed the rest of the folder's brittle fillings but I didn't expect to find anything more enlightening than what I'd already gotten. I was unsurprised by what it contained. Yet more accusatory headlines screamed out, complaining about the government funding going away and the place closing down over my scandal. I was strangely proud. It was all about *me*. There wasn't much extra information on my mother to be found, but at least I could say I knew a little bit more about her case. I'd never quite felt up to speed; ever since Malachi's trial in the courtroom and my own tribulations in elementary school I'd assumed the rest of the world knew something I didn't.

After I replaced the file, I ran down the stairs and out across the street to find my uncle. He was sitting at a small square table at the end of a narrow corridor where I knew he'd be waiting. He lifted his head when I entered, disturbing the bell at the top of the coffee-house door.

"Did you find what you wanted?"

I nodded and grabbed a rickety, skinny-legged seat across from him. "You've got to take me there."

His chin swung back and forth. "The goddess will not permit it."

"Then you only meant to tease me."

"No. I only disagreed with Lulu that you were old enough. Now you know. Now you've seen. The rest is up to you. I'll be in enough trouble when she finds out I told you this much. I'll be lucky to get laid for the rest of my life."

He was settled on the matter. It wouldn't do me any good to push. I'd have to find another way. I'd have to ask another question.

"Dave, do you know who my father was?"

"Uh-uh. Lulu thinks he was a white guy, his name might have been Allen, or Andrew, or something like that. I don't think anybody really knows. I'm sorry, baby. I've given you all I know."

With that, my uncle, Promethean traitor, finished his coffee and closed his book.

III

In a week or two, Lulu returned to her old self and life resumed in its rut of normalcy. I don't know if Dave ever told Lulu what he'd told me or how he helped, but we never spoke of it again, except for the odd occasion when I'd ask him to show me, and he'd shoot me down.

I finished high school; I spent a couple of years at the University of Tennessee at Chattanooga pursuing some of nothing and some of everything. I spent long enough in college that I had no excuse to leave without a degree, but that's what happened. After a while, I just got tired of going.

For the most part, the university gave me an excuse to fall in with a snobby crowd of disaffected poets who thought I was a psychic diva because of the poetry I wrote—mostly about the three sisters and about my cousin Malachi, who rotted away in a state institution as far as I knew and cared. Oh yes, people still knew of the case. People still talked about me at least as much as they discussed the widow of the man who killed Medgar Evers. She lives near here on one of the mountains and everyone knows it. South of the Ohio River there is no such thing as old news or ancient history. Drive around downtown and look for pickup trucks with rebel flag stickers, if you don't believe me.

Eventually I quit taking even the loosely enforced poetry workshops and sank further still down the academic totem pole by joining a small clique of slam poets. They worked out of a scuzzy bar on the south side of town, assembling their vicious rounds of bad tournament poetry to amuse or bore the meager audiences. Occasionally a local band would play before the spoken word performers took the stage, and then there would be more of a crowd for the poets to scream at.

Once upon a time, I lived for those nights when the joint would be packed and the beers would flow freely. I never did drink beer, not even the good stuff, but I could be conned into a glass or two of wine if the mood was right. It loosened me up for the show; it made me more gloriously slick and tragic.

Don't you know it, everyone loves a lost little girl in a black corset top and leather pants. Everyone wants to save her or fuck her, not understanding that neither is necessary. But so long as she is at least a small measure beautiful, and so long as she is young, they will come to hear her. So long as she can sell the illusion that she is innocence and pain in search of defilement and rescue, she'll have them at her feet—their eyes and teeth parted in mock blessing, their idle lust a lascivious parody of worship.

Never mind her poetry. It doesn't have to be good.

My poetry was good, or at least it was predictably shocking, peppered with obscenities and sexual slang. Oh, all right. It might not have been that good, really, but it served my purposes. I got free booze all night anywhere I chose; and by the time I was old enough to use my real driver's license instead of the phony one, I was plenty beautiful. I had grown into a mini-Lulu, smaller and thinner, with breasts not quite so ponderous but full enough anyway, and the same long-lashed eyes and fat lips on a fair face. In a bigger city I might not have been so special, but the valley is a small pond and the fish are easily impressed.

I was especially interesting to the valley boys because of my peculiar heritage.

Ordinarily I checked "Other" on any form requesting racial information, for what was I to say? I was probably more white than black, but given the roulette wheel of genetics there wasn't any good way to guess. If I straightened my hair I could possibly pass for Caucasian, but most folks recognized on sight that I wasn't of any Nordic strain. In fact, much to my irritation, men had a tendency to think of my appearance as a conversation starter, or more often than not, as a precursor to a lame pickup line.

Almost any given night I could expect to climb off the stage and have some good ol' boy waiting for me, offering me a beverage I wouldn't accept, because even simple politeness is more encouragement than they need.

"That was real good," the evening's Romeo always began. "So what *are* you, anyway?"

Ah, Dixie. Where even if they don't care anymore, they can't help but notice.

I might choose to play stupid and toy with him, to force him to ask the question the way he meant it. "I'm a student." "I'm a poet." 'I'm a girl." And I'd bat my eyelashes slowly and stupidly.

"No, I mean, like, what *race* are you?"

What was the point? Once on a day trip to Knoxville I bought a baby-doll T-shirt that said, "Not black, not white, HUMAN." I wore it mostly on days that I didn't feel like answering questions.

Another mixed-race girl worked the circuit with us, and she got the same crap as often as I did. Terry was some unlikely combination of disparate backgrounds—German and Indian, or African and Eskimo, or Mexican and Arabian, something along those lines. Something that left her not a shade darker than me but a touch more exotic.

As far as I was concerned, she was still a teary-eyed poser. Although I couldn't stand her, Lu says I shouldn't be so hard on her, and she's probably right. In a roundabout way, it *was* my fault that she died.

It happened the night of my last slam. Terry took the stage and held it hostage with her typical set of four-minute diatribes on (1) the fascist Republican regime, (2) her confusing cultural heritage, and (3) her whiny, ongoing battle with an eating disorder that wasn't working for her half so well as a balanced diet might have.

Despite Lulu's warning that it's cruel to speak ill of the dead, I wasn't a fan of Terry's work or her personality—and on that final night Terry was at her worst. She tromped up to the stage in a leather outfit that would have looked great on someone else, but was a most unflattering contraption on her bulky shape. When she turned around and faced the audience I could see she was sporting glitter eye shadow again, so the spotlights flashed and sparkled on her shiny form as she clutched the microphone and raised her eyes to the ceiling.

"Sex is like . . . a triple-layered . . . frosted cake . . . of danger."

She punctuated it with the heavy-handed pauses of Captain Kirk, but without the smiling self-deprecation that keeps William Shatner from being truly awful. To give credit where credit is due, she *did* have a good voice. She spoke mellow and low, and if she hadn't been trying so hard her poetry might have achieved some kind of comic sensuality.

"I want you . . . as badly as a diabetic child . . . at a birthday party . . . with no clowns."

A friend of mine grabbed my elbow and squeezed it in affected agony. "This is just *surreal*."

Surreal. It was his word of the week. "This must be one of the circles of hell Dante accidentally left off the list." He gestured at the bar with one languid white hand that poked out of a ruffled shirt straight off Robert Smith's back. "Want another drink? I'll buy, since you were darling enough to come and join us. *Redeem* us, even, from this steaming puddle of cat piss." *Redeem* was last week's word.

"Jamie, you're a master of understatement. Of course I'll get up there and make you look good. It *is* your show tonight, isn't it? You're the one who put it together this time?"

"Uh-huh," he mumbled, scrutinizing a leggy brunette new to the group. He caught me catching him, and he returned his eyes to the stage, pretending his attention had never left it. *Christ*, I thought. *He must be a Pisces.*

Terry hadn't even finished her first piece. "I think . . . I might have to take a bite out of you . . . before your attraction to me . . . grows stale."

Pause. A couple of people clapped tentatively. She cut them off.

"Love is . . . a stale piece of leftover party cake . . . at the bottom of a black garbage bag on the floor . . . of the kitchen. . . . My father will take you to the curb . . . in the morning."

She bowed and nearly toppled forward, but recovered before we had time to laugh. "Thank you. My next piece is dedicated to my lover, Trent, to whom I have given my entire body and soul. Ahem . . ."

Jamie dragged a hand down my shoulder and wrapped an arm around my waist, pulling me closer so we could speak without being overheard. "Poor Trent," he purred. I'd had three glasses of wine, one over my usual limit, and I didn't care enough to push him away even though I should have. He wasn't repulsive, he was merely delusional, which could be forgiven. "We should get out of here after your set," he went on. "Let's go get something to eat, or something else to drink. What do you say?"

"Why do we let her get up there and do that week after week?" My voice was loud enough to shove him back a few inches. "Why don't we just tell her she can only do four minutes and then she has to sit down and let someone else have a turn? Dammit," I swore, knocking Jamie all the way outside my personal space, "I've got half a mind to shoot her off the stage myself, before she does any more harm."

The gunshot that followed surprised no one more than me.

Bang!

A beer bottle, a pitcher, and a window shattered, all in one neat line.

Terry flopped backwards, still clinging to the microphone stand. The cords and plugs ripped loose from their mounts in the floor and splayed about. Everyone dove for cover, screaming and hiding under tables, behind chairs. Behind the bar and down the hall. Out the back, for those who could make it.

I was too tipsy to wrap my head around what was going on; or maybe I was drunkenly solipsistic enough to think I'd caused it. "Aw hell, I was only joking!" I shouted above the screams. "I was only joking!" But people were shrieking and Terry was shuddering, one black shoe jerking about at the edge of the stage.

Another shot reverberated but this one hit the roof above me, sending plaster raining down on my head. I wrestled with a sneeze and half dropped, half fell to the floor, officially losing my cool. I wondered where Jamie had scuttled off to, and I took brief, apathetic note of how swiftly he'd abandoned me at the first sign of trouble. I rolled over to an overturned table and scooted behind it, smacking headfirst into another bystander who had also sought shelter there. He lifted his face to mine and I saw shock and fear there that matched my own.

"Hey, Eden, are you okay?" he asked, lightly freckled upper lip trembling.

"I never get any complaints." Ha-ha. I'm not any funnier under pressure than I am onstage, really. But *someone* had to keep a level head and something about the chunks of vomit on his shirt told me it wasn't going to be this guy.

I didn't know him, but there were more than a few people who knew me without my knowing them. I didn't recall seeing him at a slam before and I didn't think I knew him from school. I started to ask who he was, but then I heard the scuffle created by two large men in the process of tackling the gunman to the ground.

"Now the wrath of God has been satisfied!" the shooter was shouting, even as strong hands forced him into submission. "Vengeance is mine—vengeance is God's!"

No. Oh, no *way*. No, it couldn't be.

"I'll kill him as many times as I have to!"

Seeing that the danger had passed, Jamie had crawled out from under his rock of choice and up to Terry; he pressed his ear to her ample chest. "Terry?" he called, manipulating her head with his hand. "Terry?"

I climbed to my feet and walked in a furious, fearless daze towards the writhing mass of limbs that made up the three men— two holding fast and one resisting. It could not be. Surely someone would have told me if he'd been released. Surely.

No. There he was, fighting feebly against the brawny arms that pinned him. His hair was much the same, no longer, no cleaner, no drier than the last time I'd seen him, and he hadn't gained a pound. Blond stubble burst from erratic patches on his chin and cheeks, and his eyes had new, blue circles drooping below the bloodshot globes. He looked old and tired and weak, except for the total madness he exuded with such rapacious enthusiasm.

"Bars cannot stop the wrath of God. God finds a way. They tried to stop this, the agents of Satan, but that old devil cannot prevail. He cannot prevail against the Lord my God, and now His purpose is served. I don't care if they put me away again. I've done my work;

I've done the Lord's work. Blessed be the name of the Lord. Blessed be the name of the Lord. Blessed be . . . His name."

His conviction was horrifying.

I approached him with fascination diluted by the dawning astonishment that he thought he'd killed *me*.

Drunk or not, I managed to be insulted, though that was possibly unfair. He hadn't seen me in fifteen years, and Terry and I . . . well, to the passive, uninformed observer she and I had more in common than I liked to think. We were about the same age, and could have reasonably been of the same ethnic extraction. She was not ugly, and she carried herself with the same lazy air of a fat, spoiled Persian cat. As a card-carrying Leo, I like to consider myself feline in grace and appearance and, to tell the truth, if I were seven or eight sizes larger she and I could have passed for sisters.

Okay.

I can understand why Malachi mistook her for me after all the time that had passed since I'd last seen him. And *that* is as kind to the dead as I'm prepared to be.

Malachi watched me walk towards him, his babbling face revealing nothing beyond his blubbering triumph. I should have stayed back. I should have let him live with the illusion of his victory, but in all likelihood he would have learned of his error anyway. I don't believe it would have made any difference, and now that he was safely restrained, I was angry.

Astounded and angry. Genuinely, blindly seething.

"Vengeance is mine, sayeth the Lord," he mumbled, his vigor faltering as he studied me. "Vengeance is . . ." He stopped. He twisted his head around to see the crowd that had grown around the body up on stage. "Oh. Oh, I didn't. She's not." His forehead settled atop his eyes, narrowing them into a fierce glower that should have frightened me more than it did. "God will forgive me," he said firmly. "He will forgive me because He understood my intent. He judges us according to the light that we have. And His vengeance will be satisfied yet. He will forgive me, Avery."

I squatted before him, my leather pants creaking at the knees. "You'd better hope so, cousin." I smiled, showing all my teeth, and then I patted his cheek with the back of my hand. He recoiled as far as his captors would allow, which wasn't much.

I almost stood with surprise, but I stayed down close to him. How strange—and yet not. It should have occurred to me long before. He was as afraid of me (or at least of whoever he thought I was) as I had been of him. With one long, vindictive fingernail I scratched a fine white line down the side of his face. I leaned in close and put my mouth near his ear, like Jamie had done to me. "Strike two," I whispered.

Then I rose to my feet and stepped away, back into the crowd.

More than one person had commandeered a napkin and was already scrawling the next slam's badly eulogizing tribute poetry. I retreated from the rest of the poets as well. My wine buzz was blown and I couldn't stand their company for another moment. Jamie waved his arms like he wanted my attention, but I pretended not to see him as I made for the back exit.

Outside, sirens with red-and-blue lights flashed the arrival of police cars, or an ambulance, or both. The paramedics were too late for Terry, who had quit bleeding and would be quite stiff before long; and the police were too late for me, because whatever wrong I'd committed was at least a lifetime past. They could take Malachi back to jail for his bungled stabs at justice, but whatever provoked him would escape his wrath so long as I had anything to do with it.

I was actually starting to believe it.

I was parked out back, which I only remembered when I nearly tripped over my car. Good. I didn't want to talk to the police either. They'd probably come for me later, when they found out what Malachi had been up to, but I wasn't ready for them yet. I needed some time to pull myself together. My hands clenched the steering wheel to keep from shaking. I hate being scared. I hate it. And even worse, I hate feeling guilty . . . especially when I don't have any-thing to feel guilty about. Or so I told myself.

I took my time getting home. On my way back up the mountain I stopped in north Chattanooga, halfheartedly poking around to see if I could stumble across Pine Breeze. I didn't find it; I didn't even find the cemetery with a duck pond that was supposed to mark the turnoff. I was thinking harder than I was looking.

Avery.

Dave said he thought my father's name was Allen, or Andrew, or something like that. Was it Avery, instead? Once I'd gone through Lu's high school yearbooks seeking out a likely candi-date. My mother had been sent to Pine Breeze by the time school pictures were taken, so I didn't find anything of her—but in her class I thought perhaps I'd find the mysterious Allen or Andrew. Naturally, I found more than a couple Allens or Andrews. I painstakingly searched each black-and-white photograph for some hint of my own features, but I did this without reward. Not one of them was any more likely than another to have been my sire.

But had there been any Averys? I couldn't recall. Perhaps I should look again.

Finally feeling a little more centered—or at least less rattled—I gave up wandering the rabbit warren of roads that comprise the north-side neighborhoods and returned home.

Lulu was waiting for me at the door. Her body was haloed by the television light flickering in the living room. She was not happy.

"Jamie called to see if you made it home okay. He told me what happened at the slam."

"Oh." Well, at least I didn't have to tell her about it. I wasn't sure how I would have explained it anyway.

Lulu and I faced off on the porch. "You could have at least called to say you were all right," she said.

I shrugged. "I didn't know Jamie would call. I didn't know that dumbass would tell you about it. I didn't see any reason to worry you."

"Where you been? You left there an hour and a half ago. What've you been doing all this time?"

I shrugged again, like I always do when I don't know what to say. I do it when the truth isn't likely to be enough. "Driving around."

"Your dumbass friend said you talked to the gunman for a minute. He said he thought maybe you knew him somehow. Tell me, then, was it Malachi?"

"Yeah. It was him."

"What did you say to him?" she asked, closing the door behind her and shutting us both outside. "What did he say to you?"

So this was it—just me and her. I didn't get Dave for backup, and neither did she. All shields down. Unless I wanted to waste more of the night with the nervous shakes, I'd have to fire the first shot. "I don't see why I should tell you. You never tell me anything."

She held me in her gaze like a frogsticker with a flashlight. The challenge had been delivered. I couldn't tell if she was annoyed or impressed. She's hard to read. "What you want to know?"

Might as well start with the big one. "Who's my father?"

At least she wasn't surprised. She must have been expecting it for years. "Don't know. We didn't even know Leslie was pregnant when Momma sent her into that place."

"You must have known she was seeing somebody. She was your baby sister. You must have known there was someone up her skirt. Damn, Lulu, she must have been a couple of months along when you sent her in—the newspaper said she was only there for six. Come on, who was it?"

If she was surprised that I'd gotten hold of the old clippings, she didn't show it. "I told you. I don't know."

"Was it Avery?"

"No." The word flew out of her mouth without hesitation. "It wasn't him."

"Then who was he? Why does Malachi think I've got something to do with him?"

"Because he's crazy. He's crazy and he doesn't know shit."

"Now you're lying."

"Don't you call me a liar."

"Then you tell me the truth."

"Okay, the truth is it doesn't matter about Avery. He's been dead generations before you were born. And the rest of what I said *was* the truth. Malachi's a crazy little fuck stick to think you're Avery come back, and that's all there is to it."

"Then what harm would it be to tell me about Avery if it really don't matter? Maybe the police will let me talk to Malachi, and he'll fill me in," I bluffed.

"You won't really do that," she said, but I could tell she wasn't so sure. Her hand reached for the porch rail and her lips tightened. She was holding something back.

"Maybe I will, and maybe I won't. But I tell you what—I might."

Lulu was torn. She walked away from the door and sat down heavily in the wooden porch swing. The chains squealed reluctantly, rhythmically, as she rocked on her heels and the swing began to sway. She didn't look at me for a few seconds, maybe a minute or more. She was working something out, deciding how much to give up and how much to keep. Every sentence was a trade-off, and I wished to God I knew what she was playing to keep. But when she raised her eyes to me I knew she was giving up the round . . . at least as much as Lulu ever gives anything up. At least I'd gotten her into a mood where she was more willing to talk, and that was something new.

"Okay, then," she breathed. "You're right. Sit down beside me. You've not had a bedtime story in longer than I could say."

IV

"What year did they fight part of the Civil War here in the valley? What year was the Battle Above the Clouds, like old white people like to call it—you know, when they fought on Lookout Mountain? When was that?"

"I don't know," I admitted, joining her on the porch swing and kicking it into back-and-forth motion with the back of my heel.

Lulu dropped one of her toes and pressed it against the ground, slowing the sway but not stopping it altogether. "I don't know either," she said. "So I don't know exactly when this started, then. We'll say 1860-something. That's close enough. My great-great-grandmother was a house nigger named Lissie. She worked for the Porter family, who had a big house at the foot of Lookout—not too far from the thick of the fighting. The Porters had fled down into the valley when the shooting started, but they wanted some of their things from the house if they could save them, so they sent Lissie and her brother out after them.

"When they got there they found the place wasn't too bad off, so they started gathering up some of what had been left behind. Then Lissie heard someone calling for help out back. A shot-up Northern soldier had gotten separated from his fellows. He wasn't dying yet, but he wasn't in good shape either, and as regular as this city changed hands in those days, his position wasn't exactly secure. As the story goes, Lissie and her brother took him inside and hid him in the basement. Her brother took what he could carry and went back to the Porters, telling them his sister had been taken off by the Yankees—and let me tell you, they would have believed those Yankees were capable of almost anything, so they didn't try very hard to disbelieve him. Lissie stayed in the basement and nursed the soldier back to health enough to make it back to camp a few days later. When the war was over, his unit went back up North, and when the family got back home, Lissie was pregnant.

"She told the Porters she'd been raped by those damned dirty Yankee soldiers, and they felt sorry enough that they took pretty good care of her, by all accounts. She gave birth to a little boy, and she named him Avery.

"Maybe five or ten years later, the soldier came back looking for her, wanting to thank Lissie for saving his life. When he learned about Avery, he tried to be distantly helpful. He wasn't willing to have any contact with his half-breed son lest his wife find out, but he felt guilty enough to throw money at him. Some years later, the soldier—I guess I should mention his name was Harvey—maybe Lissie was trying to halfway name his son after him, the names do sound alike, don't they? Anyway, Harvey got divorced and then married again, to a much younger woman. She bore him two children. The younger one was a girl born around the turn of the century, and that's old Tatie Eliza, who you've met.

"Eliza never married and never had any children, but her brother did. His daughter was Malachi's grandmother, or great-grandmother I guess. Something like that . . . sort of a distant thing. So Eliza is my great-great-aunt, approximately. That's what *tatie* means—aunt. It's what all her family members call her, I think maybe because if they say it the French way, it's not such a public admission that they're blood to her."

"What happened to Avery?" I asked. "Why does Malachi hate him so much?"

"Well, Avery grew up. By the time Eliza was born he was probably thirty years old, and by the time he learned he had siblings he was married with a child of his own. At some point he took his child, his wife, and her two sisters down to Florida. I'm not sure why they all left—I think Lissie had other family down there or something. But they did, and no one ever heard from any of them again. One of the sisters, though, had a baby she left behind for her mother to raise. That baby was named James, and most everyone says that James was probably Avery's baby too. There seemed to be a lot of sharing going on. While no one really knows what happened to Avery and the girls, James and his wife, Susan, became my grandparents. They died in a car crash when I wasn't out of the cradle. I never knew them."

All very interesting, yes, but she was beating around the bush; or maybe it was all just a long story and I hadn't seen the point yet. "You still haven't answered my question: what was wrong with Avery that Malachi is still trying to kill him a hundred years later?"

Lulu held still, choosing her words and arranging them like Scrabble tiles before putting them down for me to know. "There's a word for it, for what they thought he was. There were rumors," she stalled, "that Avery was a *sorko*—a sorcerer. Lissie's parents were brought from Niger, and she was a witch in her own right. Lord Himself knows what she taught him, but he took to those African tribal and Indian religions like a duck to a pond. He felt powerless growing up; and sometimes people look for power in places they shouldn't go.

"And in case it's escaped your attention, your cousin Malachi is not so right in the head. Stir a healthy fear of God into the loony mix, and you get a kid who thinks his great-uncle was an immortal witch. I honestly don't know the specifics that make him tick, and I wish I did. Maybe he knows something from Eliza that I don't. It's never made sense to me that he chose to hunt you because you saw the ghosts. But then again, it's not such a far leap for a zealot to make—to say that a girl sees dead people so she must be a witch. That's how it works with some of those religious people, you know. Anything they don't understand—and sometimes, anything they don't like—it all must come from the devil. How he dragged Avery into it I couldn't say. I'll have to stand by my original story that the boy's a crazy fuck stick."

"What *did* happen to Avery and the women, Lulu? Someone must know."

"*I* don't. And you're the one who sees them, honey. If you really want to know, you could ask them. But there are some things that are better left alone. After all this time, it doesn't matter. I told you, Avery doesn't matter. It doesn't matter what he did, or what became of the sisters. You may not like the answer you get."

"Maybe I'll ask them anyway. I can handle the truth."

"I wouldn't recommend it."

"Why not?"

"Your mother couldn't."

5
Blood Tells

I

Newly fueled with information about long-gone family members, I decided to step up my hunt for information about closer relations. It took me half an afternoon of dedicated searching, but I finally found it. I located the cemetery right away, and you'd think finding an entire road right nearby wouldn't be so hard. Turns out the two-lane strip springs off the street at an angle that makes you think it's only a driveway. I must have passed the turnoff a dozen times before I saw the green sign, bent nearly to the ground.

Pine Breeze Dr., it said, plain as day—once I'd pulled up alongside it and craned my neck until my head was horizontal. I turned my small black car, affectionately dubbed the Death Nugget, up the steep road and downshifted.

Both sides of the drive were overgrown with hundreds of years' worth of vegetation that arched across the sky and made the day feel darker than it should have been. I rolled down my window and hung my head out, craning my neck to scan the sharp, tree-cluttered hills that loomed in close around me.

I drove slowly, but there were no other motorists to grow angry with me. No one came up behind, and no one approached from the other lane. This was the forest primeval, barely outside the city limits. Its dense thoroughness left me disquieted; this was not like the mountain, where the woods are patchy and easy to navigate. These trees were knitted together with infinite nets of kudzu that blocked out any friendly squares of light. This ravenous, parasitical weed spilled down over the grass and extended its needy tendrils to the road, where they were only barely stunted by the occasional traffic.

Yellow flashed sudden and brief, high up to my right.

I hit the brakes and slid to a stop, once again thankful for the solitude. I backed up and set the car's parking brake, then climbed out and peered up the hill. A bulldozer was parked in place where the green thickness cleared. Then, as I stood longer, a straight line implied itself. Then another. A wall, or a corner. Part of a building lost in the woods. I got back into the car and maneuvered it to the rock-strewn track.

My tires spun against the whitish dirt, spraying it out behind me in a telltale cloud. I wasn't approaching quietly, but there was nowhere to park down on the street, where the asphalt disintegrated into a deep ditch instead of a shoulder. About fifty yards up the hill, I pulled up next to the bulldozer and shut off my car's engine.

Another bulldozer and a couple of trucks shared the spot with me, and though I didn't see anyone manning them I could see they'd been busy. The foundations of two small buildings lay in rubble, and a third was half-demolished.

When I got out of the car I was greeted by silence, and again I had to remind myself that I was barely a stone's throw from civilization. "Hello?" I called out. "Is there anyone here?" Birds scattered from the treetops, but otherwise I received no reply. It was a Saturday, after all. I shouldn't expect to see any workmen.

"Hello?"

My scuffed old combat boots crunched in the gritty mess of weeds, pebbles, and crushed concrete. Beside one of the machines were scattered a few pieces of broken tile. I picked one up and turned it over in my hands. It was black and charred, as were the others. One smokestack held its ground, marked in construction-worker spray paint with a bright orange X that signaled its days were numbered. "The furnace house," I said to myself. They'd started their demolition with the charnel rooms.

I tossed the tile into the square pit beside the smokestack and turned my attention to what remained. A gymnasium squatted beside one of the buildings I recognized from Dave's pictures. I approached it first, but found it locked with a thick chain. I might have wandered around the fringes to see if I could gain entry, but the door on the other structure had fallen off its hinges, and the open doorway beckoned.

On, then, to easier conquests.

I paused at the tattered threshold, a pang of nervousness seizing my chest.

"Hello?"

No one responded and no human sounds approached or retreated, but my own breathing was loud in my ears and my heart knocked heavily against my rib cage. And just on the edge of my peripheral hearing . . . what was that? I could swear I heard an echoing heart, a repeating, lurching breath that mimicked mine.

"It's this place," I said, stronger than a mumble. "It's this creepy-assed place. There's nobody here."

A brownish lizard ran up the doorframe and darted inside, but everything else was still. Somewhere in the distance I thought I heard water dripping, but I could have been mistaken. I shook the half sounds out of my head and forced myself to proceed.

The small, rectangular concrete porch cracked beneath my weight where rain and time had weakened it. Inside I saw a set of stairs, and what was possibly an office, with a big wood desk. Also I saw soda cans and cigarette butts, and newspapers camouflaged by a dusting of dead leaves.

The lizard popped its head around the wood and licked its shiny eyes, then disappeared. I thought about the knife I had in my car's glove compartment, and about the flashlight in the trunk. It was broad daylight, and all the windows in this building were broken or open, so I didn't need the light. But I might want the knife, with its curved, serrated blade. It was a good knife, a solid, sharp knife—supposedly a climber's knife. I joked from time to time that I could filet a bear in under a minute with that knife.

I refused to remind myself of Dave's warnings about transients and vandals—but on the other hand, I might need to pry open a lock, or get into a drawer. With this handy, ego-preserving excuse, I ran back to my car and grabbed the weapon. I then returned to the dilapidated porch, feeling much safer.

After another moment's hesitation, I followed after the lizard.

Once inside I was slightly more at ease. The first floor was open and mostly empty, littered with a few overturned tables and chairs in addition to the inch or two of miscellaneous trash that covered the floor. There wasn't anyplace for a human-sized threat to hide.

This must have been the cafeteria. The dish room and kitchen at the far end confirmed my suspicions, but did not interest me much. The major fixtures—stoves, ovens, and appliances—had long since been stripped out, and the place was a boring shell. I returned to the front door, and to the stairs I'd seen there. The next floor was no more exciting. A pool table missing two legs leaned against the floor, and a faded cork dartboard hung on the wall next to a cracked chalkboard.

I went back outside.

Once in the sun, I realized I'd been holding my knife with pale-knuckled fingers. I coughed a laugh and folded it closed, putting it down into my boot and letting the belt clip cling to the edge of my sock. I rubbed my hands together to wipe the weapon's glaring red imprint out of my palm.

To my left, on the outside edge of the clearing where I stood, was a one-story, faux-marble Georgian lump with Latinate lettering announcing the Lapton Building. I recognized the name, and I was not remotely surprised. The valley has three or four local families with nothing better to do with their money than to build stuff they can carve their name on, and most of them have been doing it since the Civil War. Three of the original five superfluous columns that flanked the Lapton Building remained, though the overhang and the porch had fallen in years before. I stepped inside unhindered by the door, which was lying in the front yard.

It was like walking into a vacuum.

The air was utterly motionless, and hung around my head as if it were a sedating gas. Feeling faint, I reached one hand for the wall to steady myself. I watched dazedly as my hand went through the weak, old plaster, but I did not hear the sound of it falling in chunks to the floor. A ball of wadded newspaper tumbled by the entryway, accompanied by a platoon of leaves. A dark bird flew briskly by a window, but I did not even hear the startled flapping of feathers, or the rustle of wind-pushed papers.

I reclaimed my hand and clutched it to my collarbone. "It's just this place," I said again, though my voice was not so sure. "What *is* it about this place?" Seeing that I'd dusted myself with white plaster leavings, I slapped my hand against my thigh and left a pale handprint there on my jeans.

Two signs pointed down opposing wings—one read Boys' Residences, the other (predictably enough) said Girls' Residences. I waded through the debris like it was honey, struggling against the disorientation that crept up on me from all sides.

I followed the sign that pointed to the right and came to three doorless rooms.

Each white-painted, concrete-block cell held at least one rotting set of box springs and two chests of drawers, which could only in good conscience be called chests, for all the drawers were missing. Stray metal hangers tinkled together like wind chimes when I opened the closets, but nothing else remained inside them. Every room had a largish window covered on the inside by a metal grate that could have been sturdy chicken wire. Huge tiles hung down from the ceiling, damp and moldy, and dead wires straggled from the holes to mingle with the hanging weeds.

A discolored scrap of magazine thumbtacked to one wall turned out to be a heart-encircled picture of Donny Osmond. Graffiti beside the photo declared that Michelle, Tammy, and Sharon had shared this room in 1978. It also said that Michelle Wants Them All, Tammy Has Them All, and Sharon Does Them All. Nice.

In the next room I was rewarded with more teenage scribblings. Lisa and Penny lived there, also in '78. They too had an inordinate fondness for Donny, in addition to several other alleged heart-throbs whose faces I didn't recognize.

But where was Leslie?

Next room.

"Leslie Was Here."

I read the handwriting out loud, though to see the words had made my throat squeeze shut. I didn't see any other names, or anything at all to indicate she hadn't been alone. Her room was indistinguishable from the others as far as the contents went, but I snooped around it anyway, hoping to find . . . hoping to find heaven knew what.

I found nothing. I left the room wishing for a souvenir, but there was nothing to salvage.

I trudged back to the front, where a secretary, nurse, or receptionist's desk was lodged in a corner. Its top drawer was empty, but the next one down held a stack of mail. I rifled through the assorted scraps of stationery until I saw my mother's name. A paper clip held a note to the envelope.

"Another one from A. Have sent the letter to her file in Brach."

Brach. Another rich old family likely to have a building named after it, if I looked around hard enough. I took the empty envelope and folded it over, wedging it into my back pocket and wanting to leave. By that time, any destination would have sufficed. The atmosphere was overwhelming in the dormitory—if I didn't leave it soon, I was going to pass out.

The air lightened when I stepped outside, but the heaviness did not release me completely. The weight followed, or rather I carried it with me. My walking felt more labored, and my head seemed stuffed with cotton. Again at the edge of my conscious hearing came the heartbeat, just slow and distant enough not to be mine.

"I'll check that one more place, and that's all. Then I'm leaving." The knife casing in my boot rubbed reassuringly against my ankle. I thought about pulling it out, but then I thought about being stopped by a cop and I decided against it. Better to appear unarmed, if caught. Besides, if there were only hobos or other humans present, they would have made their presence known; and any other unknown watchers were unlikely to be intimidated by a four-inch blade.

"I'll leave it there for now. One more place, though, before I go. Just the one."

I couldn't be sure if I was talking to myself anymore. I knew there must be ghosts—surely there had to be ghosts in a place where two thousand people had died a hundred years before. Yes, there had to be ghosts, and therefore I should be unafraid if they wanted to watch. What harm had ghosts ever done to me?

Leslie.

My mother's name. No. I was focusing on it. I was only imagining it.

Leslie.

The second time I knew I'd caught it, each consonant sliding out from an ectoplasmic throat. I took a deep breath. No, I'd never come to harm from a ghost, but the only ghosts I knew were Mae and her sisters and Cora's easily dissuaded specter—and they were surely not the only dead people, so I could hardly consider them representative of the spirit world as a whole.

"Who's there?"

My question invited the presence closer. Something was different about this entity. Something about its voice, or its touch, suggested more strength than mere spirit had ever shown me. I clenched my fists and held them against my thighs, refusing to move. A faint, chuffing gust of air came and went close against my skin. It was sniffing me, smelling me—tickling the sticky inside crooks of skin at my elbows and under my chin.

It snorted a hard puff of stale air against the side of my face. *Not Leslie.* It didn't sound pleased.

"No," I admitted. "Not Leslie."

It drew close again, dusty breath rasping against my ear and ruffling my hair.

But I know you.

"No. I don't think so."

I know you, it insisted.

"You don't." My fright-induced patience was growing strained. "Go away. Let me alone. I'm not here for you and there's nothing you want from me."

Ah. It withdrew. *Now I do know you. And I will do as you command, for it was you that brought me here.* A hateful laugh, distinctly audible, bounded throughout the clearing and echoed itself into nothingness.

I felt alone again. Shaken, confused, and suspicious, but at least alone. I didn't care who the being thought I was, so long as it left me.

While I still had the nerve to do so, I sought out my last conquest.

Brach Hall was situated down the hill behind the gymnasium. It had the same run-down brick-and-white exterior as the other buildings, but it lacked the decorative columns and the sense of architectural frivolousness. The door to this one was attached, but unlocked.

I stood on the landing and half expected a cold burst of wind or will to shove me back, but nothing of the sort greeted me, so I let myself inside. I was pleasantly surprised by what I found. Inside waited a hallway with a dozen or more doors standing ajar and a big open room down at the end. Sunlight gushed and fractured through the jagged shards of glass that lingered in the windows, and even though this place was as filled with forest and human garbage as the rest, it seemed bright and almost friendly in comparison to the rest of the places I'd checked. Best of all, it held the four tall filing cabinets up against the wall. A fifth had toppled to the floor and splayed its contents across the room, so I knew they were full of files and folders.

All I had to do was find my mother's.

It took some time. The files were not so alphabetically arranged as they should have been, and they were organized according to some grouping system that I didn't understand—possibly by age or by classroom standings. By the time I pulled Leslie's up out of the others, the flood of natural light had dimmed into a late afternoon stream, or perhaps it had grown cloudy. It had certainly grown quiet, and in light of my earlier supernatural greeting, quiet couldn't possibly be good. I climbed to my feet and stretched my stiff legs, wondering after the comforting hum of bugs and birds that had been my background noise all day.

I wiped at my sweaty neck and listened.

Still in the distance water leaked and tapped, and down on the road below a car zipped by. I didn't hear the low, rhythmic pulse anymore, or the jagged breathing, but its absence wasn't enough to set my mind at ease. I could tell myself it was my imagination, but deep down I knew better than that. I wasn't welcome here. Whatever eyes were watching, they didn't belong to my late mother.

Without opening it, I lifted the lightly stuffed folder.

Another engine roared down the winding road at the foot of the hill. This one slowed as it approached the gravel turnoff, and

I thought I might have been discovered. But then the engine revved high again and left.

Back in the hallway I kicked aside the beer bottles and filthy, mildewed clothes and boxes that clogged the floor. Somewhere above I heard a muffled snap, and I froze, straining my ears. I heard it again, then again. It could have been a shutter flapping. It could have been a squirrel working on some nuts. I gripped the folder against my stomach and went back towards the front door.

Just before the last turn before the exit I stopped, my attention snagged by an open office. The nameplate on the door read M. Finley, and it was in surprisingly good order. On the wall to my immediate left was a classroom-sized chalkboard.

SHE KNOWS SHE WAS WRONG, it read.

The message made me uneasy. Surely it had been there for some time, drawn by teenage vandals. It meant nothing to me. Nothing at all.

Finley's chair was pushed back away from the desk, and it sagged and smelled wet but it was in one piece. I nudged it aside with my foot. One desk drawer was on the floor, its contents damp and unidentifiable; but in another I found files with billing statements. Fortunately, these were filed by last names. My mother's was easy to find. I pulled it out and set it inside the folder I already carried. I turned to leave.

Although I had heard no sound, and although I had looked away for only a few seconds, the chalkboard bore a new warning across its broad green slate.

SHES COMING BACK

I sucked in my breath so hard I almost gagged.

The heartbeat was coming close again, up from behind me, loud enough that I knew I was hearing it, and not imagining it. This time there would be no fooling myself. The exaggerated breathing had returned as well, panting as it approached. It was as if a chilled wind was rushing up against my back, and it grew colder and stronger every second I stood there. I read and reread the message and tried to figure how it must have gotten there.

One by one, without a noise, another series of letters offered me advice.

LEAVE!

I didn't have to be told twice. Sideways I slid towards the door, never for a second considering that I should look over my shoulder. The mysterious S H E did not welcome me there, and she was not a harmless shade. I had made her angry merely by not being my mother, and it seems I'd made her angrier still by unintentionally misleading her.

I fled shakily to my car, too baffled and afraid to give it much thought.

The Death Nugget was where I'd left it, its dark, roundish shape keeping the bulldozers company. I dug my keys out of my front left jeans pocket and fumbled with them, stupidly shaking as I unlocked the door and dropped myself inside. I tossed the folder on the passenger seat and threw the car into gear, backing down the gravel trail as though—and just in case—I was being pursued.

II

I didn't go home. Lulu and Dave would have asked questions, and I didn't have any answers yet. On Saturday night all the coffeehouses are crowded and loud, and the bars are worse because the patrons are not just bored but drunk as well. I wanted to be left alone, really alone, so I could shake the foggy residue of the poltergeists of

Pine Breeze and take time to analyze what I'd found there.

I opted for a small restaurant, an Italian joint whose name I always miss by at least one vowel. I like the place. It's quiet and low-lit, with small booths set in walled-off sections that lend the illusion of privacy. I ordered a glass of wine from a blond waitress who probably wasn't old enough to serve it and who definitely should have asked for my ID, but didn't. She obediently brought the drink without any questions. After she'd gone, I opened the grimy file across the table and picked through the contents with all the precision of an archeologist. Any scrap of paper might be a clue.

The first dirty envelope was addressed to Leslie Moore c/o Pine Breeze in solid, precise handwriting in black felt-tipped pen. This letter betrayed only a little about the writer, but it revealed an entire world about my mother.

Dear L—

I hate them for reading these, and I hate them for reading what you sent—but please tell me at least that you're all right. Why won't you write? When I called there the woman assured me that you were free to do so, but she said you hadn't written anything to anyone hardly since you got there. She said you've refused us all—but you must not refuse me. You must write—or I swear I will come down there myself and take you away! I'll tell her to stop sending the money and then they'll have to let you go, whether you like it or not.

You said when you went in there that it was only for a short time, and you promised me you'd write. There are other hospitals, you know. There are other places you could go, places that are made for girls with our problem. I don't see why you want to stay out in that god-awful place. I could be with you—I could support you in this decision. Just say the word and I will make a place for you here, no matter what she thinks. I swear, if I don't hear from you soon, I'll stop the money.

—A

I set the letter on the table and swigged at the wine like it was whiskey. At the table next to mine, the diners had left their signed credit card receipt on a small black tray. I snagged their abandoned pen and attacked A's letter with it.

"Why won't you write?"

I underlined it. The people at Pine Breeze (Marion Finley?) had told him she was free to communicate with him. I had no way of knowing if this was true or not. Therefore, I did not know whether or not Leslie had ever written A in return—or, for that matter, whether she'd ever received the letter I had spread out before me on the burgundy tablecloth.

"I'll tell her to stop sending the money."

I circled "her" and stared at it. Her who? The same "her" who would not approve of my mother joining A wherever he was? Maybe. I had an idea who "she" might be, but I did not set the letter aside yet.

"There are other places . . . for girls with our problem."

I circled "our" and sat back in my seat to stare at the three little letters. *Our problem.* He knew she was pregnant. I leaned forward again, and tapped the tip of my borrowed pen against the paper. Because I was not yet ready to move on, I recircled the word and stared at it some more, glaring as if it was hiding something from me. *Our.* His and hers. Their *problem.* A slight flush of indignation tugged at the edge of my attention, but the situation didn't warrant it, so I forced it back. No sense in growing a grudge now.

I reviewed the first two lines again.

Pine Breeze officials read the incoming and outgoing mail. It was pretty safe to assume they knew she was pregnant too. This realization raised more questions than it answered, since Lulu—and, come to think of it, that newspaper article—had all agreed that no one knew she was expecting when she was checked in. Either my family was lying, or someone at Pine Breeze was helping hide a secret or two.

My eyes returned to A's only threat—that he'd shut off the money. Not his money, *her* money. Another elusive *her*. Whoever she was, A was close enough to have some measure of say about where her cash went. I finally succumbed to my curiosity and reached for the next envelope in the folder, setting the damning letter aside.

This one was addressed on an old typewriter with its *E*'s set low. This one wasn't *to* Leslie, it was *regarding* Leslie. Inside I found a canceled check from a popular southern bank, signed with a tall, thin, slanty signature that took me a minute to decipher and confirm.

Eliza Dufresne.

"Old Tatie," I said under my breath. "The million-year-old matriarch. Where do you live, Tatie?" I flipped the envelope over and held it up to the small, primarily decorative lamp on the wall. There was no return address, but the postmark read "Macon, GA." Ah *ha*.

In the dusty stack I found half a dozen more canceled checks, all with Eliza's spidery signature. She'd paid Pine Breeze every month on the first or second day like clockwork. Why? What did she care? Who was A to her that she would pay to hide his lover?

I might have lingered over this question longer, except that another letter captured my attention—at least my shock, and then, though I wouldn't have cared to admit it, my horror. It was simple enough in appearance, in an ordinary white sleeve with a damp-obscured postmark.

Mrs. Finley, you must give up that girl's baby. That baby should never be born. He's going to cause a world of pain to many people—not just myself. You may go to hell too, for all I know, just for protecting her there and helping her give birth to that thing. I don't know. But the best thing you can do is send her home and let her mother deal with it. Her mother knows what to do. Her mother wouldn't pussyfoot around like you people are. This isn't a

matter for an institution, it's a matter for family and you know it.
You're interfering, you're not helping. Send that child home or else
there will be consequences.

There was no signature.

I wondered if Lulu knew anything, but I only wondered it briefly. I'd never get it out of her. She'd buried my mother deep—and her own mother beside her. She'd marked their graves with a secret sign that she'd never share with anyone, especially not me.

What to do, then? My grandmother was dead, and her daughters were silent. I didn't understand it, but I was determined to find a way around it.

I thought again of the nameplate on the office door. Could Marion Finley still be alive? If she was getting threats like the one I held before me, maybe she'd had a good reason to help keep my mother's indiscretion quiet; though that train of thought brought me right back around to my own family, and the question of whether or not anyone really knew.

Someone outside the Pine Breeze staff knew, this much was clear.

I flagged the waitress down and asked her for another glass of wine and a phone book, if she could scare one up. She came back with both, and I thanked her. Inside I found a dozen or more listings for Finley, none of which were preceded by Marion. There was one R. M. Finley, though, so I filed that away for future reference. I knew more than a few people who went around signing their middle name instead of their given first. It was worth a shot. And later, I might even call a few of the other Finleys to see if there were any relations. Perhaps she'd married, or died. I closed the heavy book and pushed it away.

There should have been more letters, but I didn't see any. I gathered my findings up in a pile and went to put them back the way I'd found them, when a stray bit of coarse paper fell loose. It was another envelope, made of cheap paper with nasty yellow gum to seal it. A grimy smudge of a thumbprint made a dark shadow across the place where the return address should have been written.

I opened it and found nothing except another canceled check from Eliza. But all the rest had come from her in heavy white stationery, mailed with fancy stamps boasting pictures of flowers and birds. The postmark on this one was strange as well.

"Highlands Hammock, Fla."

Surely it was an error. Someone else's envelope, Tatie's check. Bureaucracies make mistakes all the time. The handwriting on the front looked like hers, though; I lifted another envelope to compare, and yes, the script matched up. I supposed she must have taken a trip, or at least I hoped so. Macon's only a few hours away, but it's a good six hours to the Florida state line from Chattanooga. Heaven knew how far south I'd have to go to catch her. Highlands Hammock. I'd have to look it up on a map.

Before I rose to leave, I went back to the first, most revealing item in the folder.

A's letter to Pine Breeze loomed beige and brittle before me. I read it for the umpteenth time, still amazed—still bewildered by a fact the letter made abundantly clear.

Leslie had *wanted* to be there.

I paid for my wine and left a good tip, even though the waitress hadn't been terribly helpful. At least she hadn't gotten in the way, and lately I felt even that much deserved to be rewarded.

The digital clock on my car's dashboard read 11:14 when I pulled into the driveway of the Signal Mountain house I still called home.

The next morning, over coffee and some doughnuts Dave hadn't killed off, I dragged out a more recent phone book than the one at the restaurant and scanned through the Finleys again. No Marion magically manifested in the latest offering by Bellsouth, so I gazed at the R. M. and wondered if it would be worth my time to let my fingers do the walking. It might mean Roger Michael or Rebecca Marion, or anything else in between. It was a long shot, to say the least, but I could either see about calling or I could do something rash like pack my bags and strike out for Macon.

For a moment, I seriously considered going with the devil I knew instead of the one I didn't; but Eliza's specter loomed in my imagination, and I shook the thought away. No. Not yet.

Before I started pressing buttons, I went to the window and pushed the curtain out of my way. Mine was the only car in the drive; and when I peeked into the garage, it was empty. Good. They were both gone. I knew from experience that mere silence could not promise that I was alone, but if both cars were absent, the coast was probably clear.

I reached for the phone and checked the numbers on the newsprint-thin page. I punched the soft round buttons on the handset and listened to the seven-note chime. Then I held still, waiting while the connection went through and the other phone announced my call. Four, five, six . . . after seven or eight rings I was confident that I wasn't going to reach an answering machine, which was unfortunate. To hear a deep, manly voice declare that I'd reached Randall Finley would have made the process of elimination all the more simple.

I hit the button to cancel my call and looked at the entry again.

Beside R. M. Finley there was an address, one that implied a location on the other side of town by the East Ridge tunnel. I didn't know the area well, but it was midmorning, and even if I lucked upon the right home within thirty minutes, I wouldn't be surprising anyone awake.

I fished around in the oversized coffee mug at the end of the kitchen bar. From the bouquet of writing instruments contained therein, I selected a black felt-tip pen and used it to scrawl R. M.'s address onto my palm. Maybe R. M. was out getting breakfast or, as I realized the day of the week, still at church.

I took my time going down the mountain, which turned out to be a good thing. Otherwise, I might have hit a pair of gawkers who'd stopped in the middle of 27 to catch a good stare at the UFO house. As I grouchily swerved past, I wondered how many auto accidents the spaceship-shaped domicile had caused in the last twenty years. In my rearview mirror, I caught the tourists flashing their middle fingers and swearing—because God knows *I* was the idiot who parked on a busy highway's hairpin curve for a science-fiction photo op.

I survived the rest of the drive without incident, though, and I made my way over to the city's east tunnel around 11:00 A.M. As you might expect of a city surrounded by mountains and ridges, Chattanooga has several tunnels that run conveniently beneath these ridges to provide a fast outlet into the suburbs at the east, northeast, and north sides of town. All other major points on the map find the city fenced in by the mountains or the Tennessee River, which bisects the burg at one point into north and south sides—the north side largely residential and the south side hosting downtown proper plus the detritus of industrialization.

Once you reach the ridges you're in terraced suburbia; and on the east/southeast end of town, you're practically in Georgia. In the suburb of East Ridge, Tennessee, cheaper gas is just a mile or so away in Rossville. Before I went looking for the mysterious Mr. or Ms. Finley, I took advantage of that fact and saved a couple of bucks on a fill-up.

I found my way back to my home side of the state line and drove around for a while, exploring the ridge neighborhoods and checking the street names. Mostly I was still killing time in case Finley was at church. This was a reasonable and very likely prospect, and despite the buffet arms race that prompts area services to conclude earlier and earlier, I shouldn't expect to find anyone home until after noon, at soonest. Even this was assuming Finley hadn't joined the rest of the faithful in the mad rush to the Golden Corral.

The street number inked onto my hand read 6769. I let go of the steering wheel and glanced down to make sure, then I slowed the Death Nugget to a crawling near-stop outside a green house with peeling paint and a yard full of trees.

On the mailbox I spied a tattered 6 and a possible 9, but the remaining numbers had long since worked their way free of the black iron. But on the mailbox at the next drive I could see 6771, so it looked like I'd found it. I parked on the street, pulling over into the gutter rather than subjecting my car to the badly graveled driveway.

I was just working out my approach, trying to decide on my opening lines, when an old but well-cared-for Lincoln dragged its mighty bulk onto the rocky set of wheel ruts I'd opted to avoid. While the dull silver automobile worked its way into a docking position on the left side of the house, I climbed out of my car and shut the door, standing beside it and waiting for the other driver to emerge.

She was slender and dressed in a sharp pantsuit and high heels. Her hair was more perfectly silver than the car, and it was cropped short in the flattering, stylish way that most southern women of a certain age forgo in favor of something more easily fluffed with hairspray. She closed her own car door and cracked open a clasp on her purse, dropping her sunglasses into the bag and then finally looking up at me.

"Can I help you with something, sweetheart?" she asked, which was a fair question since I was standing just outside the grassy ditch a few yards from her front door.

"Maybe," I admitted. "I'm looking for a woman named Marion Finley."

"Huh." She looked down to her purse again and unsnapped the clasp once more, pushing past the sunglasses to extract a pack of cigarettes. "Then I guess I'll need these," she said, and though she said it with three-quarters of a grin, I didn't hear any humor in the words.

"Why's that?"

"Because it's Rhonda now. And no one who knows me by Marion has come calling in twenty years—at least no one I wanted to talk to." She looked me up and down, tapping the soft pack against her wrist. A tiny lighter popped out of the pack. She used it to gesture at the porch.

I felt like I ought to say something, so as I walked around my car to approach her I said, "I wanted to talk to you about—"

"Oh, I can guess," she interrupted. "Hell." She put the cigarette in her mouth and lit it up, never blinking or taking her eyes off me. "Now that I see you better, I can make a couple of real good guesses, in fact."

I paused, one foot in the grass and one in the air, but she waved me on. "Come on," she urged. "I'm not that kind of old lady, come on in. I'll get you a drink, if you like. Sweet tea?"

"Sure," I agreed as I followed her up onto the porch. "Tea's good."

Inside, the home was lined with hardwood floors and nicely kept furniture that would qualify for antique status in another twenty years. Two big ceiling fans spun lazily above us, and two big cats stayed just as lazily immobile on the end of the couch. One of the felines opened a sleepy yellow eye to appraise me when I came in, but the other only shuddered and yawned.

"Don't mind them," Marion said, "unless you're allergic. You're not, are you?"

"No."

"Then have a seat. Take the end of the couch if you don't mind the boys."

I did take the couch, at which point both of the "boys" raised their fluffy, wedge-shaped heads and leaned a pair of whiskered noses toward me. I held out a hand and let them get a sniff; they decided I was neither food nor foe, and returned to their apathetic repose.

In the kitchen, I heard the clatterings of cupboards and appliances, and before long Marion returned with a tall, tea-filled glass. She took the chair across the coffee table from me, and sipped at her own drink between drags on her not-quite-finished cigarette.

"You're Leslie's baby, aren't you?" She put a question mark on the end for form's sake, but I didn't have to nod to tell her she was right. "You look like her a little, more like her mother, though. She's the one who named you, I think. Your grandmother. She's the one who started calling you Eden."

I swigged gently at the tea, and the big boxy ice cubes shifted together. "How'd you know it was me?"

"Because I'm not an idiot. You're back in the news, kid. They were running a picture of you on Channel Three, talking about that crazy boy shooting the girl and thinking it was you."

"Oh. Crap."

"Naw, it was a good picture. So what brings you looking for me, anyway? I mean, more than the obvious. You want to know about Pine Breeze, that's a given. They done tearing it down yet? I'll be . . . relieved when they do. Yes, relieved."

"Is that what you really mean? You say it like it's not."

She spent a second or two too long with the cigarette at her mouth. When she moved it aside to speak, there was a faint smudge of coral lipstick on the white filter. "It's what I mean. It's a closed chapter—it's been one for me, for years. I'll feel better when it's gone to the rest of the world, too."

"It isn't gone, not all the way, not yet. It will be before long, though. They've got all the equipment up there, and a couple of the buildings are torn down. The rest aren't far behind."

"Good. Glad to hear it. You went there, then?"

"Yeah, I went there."

"Creepy, isn't it?"

The way she said it, I wondered if she knew more than she was saying. I wondered if she'd felt the same thing I'd felt out there on

113

the overgrown hills and in the decrepit buildings. I wondered if anything had spoken to her like it had spoken to me. But I didn't ask. Instead I just said back, "Yeah, it's creepy."

"You were born there. It was a mess. A big mess. The whole thing. It never should have gotten so out of hand."

"It," I echoed, again thinking of the word's corollary, *our problem.*

She caught it too. "You," she amended. "Not your fault, though. Do they treat you like it was? I hope not. Your grandmother meant well, in her own way, but I never thought she was kind. Do you know what I mean? She was looking out for her own, in the way that seemed best to her, but I thought it was too bad for a baby to be caught in the middle."

I held the tea, not drinking it, just feeling the condensation drip down over my fingers and onto the knee of my jeans. "My grandmother?"

"Your grandmother, yes. Tall woman. Angry. Furious, even. I knew her kind. Enraged at her offspring, but determined to protect them such as she could."

"Them?" I was down to monosyllables, now.

"Them, yes. All three of those girls. When the one—your mother—went off and got herself in trouble, she did it in a big way, or so I was led to understand. If the news can be believed, her mother knew what she was doing to try to keep you all away from them." Marion crushed the cigarette into an ashtray on the coffee table, briefly rousing the gray tomcat, and prompting an ear twitch in the orange one.

"But wait." I wiped the side of the glass and took a swallow of tea to wet my mouth, but didn't taste it. "My grandmother knew, then? She knew my mother was pregnant?"

"Of *course* she knew. What kind of establishment do you think I was running? Your mother was a minor; I couldn't provide her with any kind of medical treatment at all without a parent or guardian's consent."

"But Lulu said she didn't know. She said nobody knew."

"Lulu? One of the other girls?"

"My aunt, yes. She raised me, her and her husband. She said nobody knew Leslie was pregnant."

"Don't go looking all betrayed, now. Your aunt probably told you the truth so far as she knew it. She told you the important part, anyway. Neither of the other two girls knew. Grandma saw to that. She was good and vague—she stonewalled the entire family. Those other two girls were madder than hell when they found out, too."

"That makes sense," I admitted, nodding so hard I startled the tea and its melting ice. "I've never known much of my grandmother. Lulu took me when I was little. She and Dave adopted me legally at some point, but I don't remember my grandmother caring one way or another. For that matter . . ." I thought hard and made sure I was remembering right before I said the rest out loud, "I don't think she was even there at Malachi's trial, either. I could barely tell you what she looks like. She's never had much interest in me, or if she has, Lulu kept it from me."

Marion—or Rhonda, whichever she preferred—laughed. "I bet she did. I saw your aunt once, if Lulu's the one I'm thinking of, at a hearing investigating your mother's death. She wasn't supposed to be there. But she was a fireball of a thing. Spitting image of her mother, or how I figured her mother must have looked as a teenager—damn, but you all look alike. Tall and angry. And not at all intimidated by anyone, or anything. I half thought she was going to jump the table and throttle the poor man asking the questions. She was out for blood, she was. And she took you?"

"She took me."

"Then I'm glad to hear it. She made a home all right for you, it looks like. You've grown up into a tall girl yourself, and healthy looking. People may've given you a lot of grief as a little girl, but they'd think twice before it now, I bet. You're one of them, plain as day. All the women in your family, cut from the same cloth. Intractable bitches—all of you. And I mean that in the good way."

She paused to light another cigarette, and I took another draught of tea, deciding to agree that it was a compliment. "Thanks," I said.

Marion tipped her head to me. "Is this something like what you had in mind?"

"What?"

"You came here, wanting to talk to me. Is this what you wanted to know?"

"I guess. I went to Pine Breeze looking for—well, for *more*, really. I don't know much about my mother and no one wants to talk about her. And I don't know who my father is at all, but it may have something to do with my crazy cousin. You know—the one who keeps shooting at me every fifteen years or so."

"What did you find there?" She leaned forward, her forearms against her knees. "Did they ever clean that place out? When I left, the police closed the place up and called it an ongoing investigation. They wouldn't let me in after anything at all, not even a sweater I'd left hanging on the back of my chair. Damn shame about that sweater. One of those angora cardigans that looks so nice with everything, but costs so much to replace."

"If I'd've known, I would have taken a look around for you—but I don't think you'd want it back, now. It's all there, inside, but everything is rotted or rusted. I even found some filing cabinets full of stuff in one of the back buildings. There were medical records, prescriptions, people's names and social security numbers—but the place was trashed, as you might assume."

"Christ," she swore. "The board of directors kept telling me that I was going to get them sued with the way I handled things; they even tried to fire me, if you can imagine that. They tried to fire me from a hospital that the state had formally closed. I didn't have a job to get fired from. And then they went and left everything there? Idiots, all of them. They should have at least let me clean the place out. All that junk should have been shredded decades ago. It isn't fair to the kids we kept there, or to the adults they are now. Sons of bitches."

"Sons of bitches indeed."

"But you found what you were looking for?"

I shrugged. "I found things that put me on the track to finding what I need. And I found you."

"Fat lot of good I am to you, dear."

"I don't know, this is a pretty good glass of tea."

She smiled, like I hoped she would. "Then it hasn't been for naught. But I have to tell you—I don't know who your father was. I think your grandmother might have known, but I don't know if you'll ever get it out of her."

"Since she's dead, that's a pretty safe bet."

"I'm sorry to hear that. It's as I told you: she was trying to do right, even if she didn't go about it in the best way. I got the feeling she didn't know her own children very well at all, and it confused her and made her mad. I hope your aunts learned that—and they learned to forgive her for handling Leslie the way she did."

I didn't know how to answer that, so I didn't. I don't know about Aunt Michelle, but Lulu hung on to her grudge with a death grip, and I don't think that grip eased up any with my grandmother's passing.

"But I do want you to know, I liked your mother. She was an old soul, as they say sometimes. Older than her years. She was a child, yes, but she was a wise little thing, and she knew she'd screwed up. Even though she was shut away there, out in the hills, she never acted like she was a prisoner. I think she felt better for being there, as strange as that sounds. Like she was relieved to be free of the drama." Marion finished off the tea and the cigarette in two separate breaths.

"Thank you," I said, since nothing else seemed appropriate.

"Thank you for what?"

"For this, all of it. You told me more about her in a couple of paragraphs than Lulu has ever managed to share. She doesn't like to talk about her, or her mother either."

"Oh, you're welcome, then. And don't hold it against your aunt; it hurts her to remember, that's all. Leslie was . . . Leslie was something else." She rose from her seat to take both of our glasses into the kitchen. "Pine Breeze wasn't the happiest place to be. It was someplace that kids went when the rest of the world didn't know what to do with them anymore. It was a place where kids went to cry."

Marion retreated to the kitchen, and I heard the glasses clink into the sink where she set them down. "But Leslie was there, and I liked her, because she could still laugh."

III

Next night, after spending an evening with a couple of friends who knew their way outside the city better than I did, I came home with a resolution to leave. Marion was a neat lady and I appreciated her time, but she'd given me everything she knew in a couple of paragraphs. If I was going to get any real answers, I was going to have to head south and hope for the best. I did not anticipate that Lulu would let me do this without a fight, though, and she was unprepared to disappoint me. She was waiting at the door when I pulled in; it was late, but not so late that she could pretend the sound of my car had roused her.

"You've been drinking." I made it a statement, though I wasn't certain until I got close enough to smell her. It was worth noting aloud, because it wasn't something she did too often when she knew I'd be around. I'd been out most of the night, and Lulu knew better than to wait up for me. I couldn't figure out why she'd done so now.

"So've you."

"Not much. Just a little wine to go with the conversation."

I think she knew I was baiting her, so she made a point of not biting. "Dave's in Atlanta, and I got bored," she said instead. "And I'm not feeling too hot, so you never mind what I have and haven't been swallowing. I don't owe you any explanation."

Usually she wouldn't have asked, but that night curiosity got the better of her.

"Where've you been?"

"Walking to and fro upon the earth."

"No dice, Job." Lulu's sharp even when she's hammered. Sometimes I think it's cool, and sometimes I wish she were more easily impressed. This time her response was hard, and it utterly lacked any saving cushion of humor. I was immediately ill at ease; her tone was crying for conflict, and that was never a good thing.

"Where were you at? And what are you up to?"

I had no reason to lie. I'd already decided I was leaving, anyway. I was glad I'd found Marion, but she had only told me that there was nothing for me to learn there in the valley. It had taken me a couple of days to come to terms with it, but once that difficult truth had settled in, the rest of my course was as clear as it was peculiar.

"I was out with Jamie and Drew," I said, "but that's not half as interesting as what I was up to this weekend. I went to Pine Breeze. It wasn't that hard to find." I took a hard breath and stepped past her. I went down the hall to my room without looking back, then gathered an overnight bag and started packing it with clean underwear. Socks followed suit, and a clean pair of jeans. Lulu trailed behind me and stood in the doorway, one arm lightly hanging on the frame in a gesture that had become very familiar to me.

"Where do you think you're going?"

"Macon," I responded without looking up from my bag. "Now are you gonna ask what I think I'm gonna find?"

"No. You're looking for *Tatie*." She spit the last work out, adding contempt to the pronunciation. Tah-*tee*, she says it, and even though that's the way it's supposed to be, it sounds like a curse, or something like despair. "You don't really want to find her. You don't really want to go to Macon."

"Okay," I agreed. "Then maybe I'll go to Highlands Hammock."

I would almost swear that the blank stare Lulu gave me was genuine. She's a good liar—maybe a better one than I am, but I don't think she's *that* good. "Where?" she asked, and my confidence faltered. I've been wrong before and bluffed my way free, but if you're wrong with Lulu, you might as well fold. She'll have won before the next words are out of your mouth.

"Highlands—Highlands Hammock. It's in Florida."

Her forehead did not uncrinkle to hint at enlightenment. "Where in Florida?"

I was forced to confess that I didn't know. "But I've got a map in the car. It can't be that hard to find."

"Who's in Florida that you think you need to talk to?" Again, I didn't think she was messing with me. If she really knew something about the place that I didn't, she should have gone into politics with that poker face.

Shit. All right, then, it was time to bluff; but once again I didn't know the answer. "Tatie could tell you, if you'd bother to ask her." Like Mr. Spock used to say, "Never lie when you can misdirect."

"Tatie would as soon see us dead as tell us anything useful."

"Sort of like you?" It flew out before I could stop it. Old patterns die so hard. I'll be eighty and she'll be one hundred, and I'll still regress to a wiseass six-year-old when she confronts me.

For a second I honestly thought she might strike me—and that would have been a first—but she held her position and straightened her back. "*Nothing* like me. That's more unfair than you know."

"Then tell me why Tatie paid for my mother to be at Pine Breeze. That would be useful, and it would set the two of you apart."

Disgust clouded her face. She shook her head. "You don't even know what questions to ask. You don't know what's useful and what's not. You're shooting in the dark, firing blind, and you think you're going to wring something out of her?"

"See—that's what I mean. Since you're not talking, I'm going to have to go ask someone else." I went on with my packing, even though I was all but done. I pulled an extra T-shirt out of a drawer and made a show of unfolding it, then folding it again.

"No." Lulu's knuckles whitened around the doorjamb. "No, don't go to her. Ask me whatever you want, but don't go there. Not after I've spent so long keeping you away from her. She'll fuck you up if she can."

I shoved the shirt into the bag and faced her then, full on, no blinking away. "Why did Leslie ask to go to Pine Breeze?"

Lulu leaned against the frame. Her temple pressed against the wood. "She was afraid."

"Of who? Or what? My father?"

"No. Not your father." She shook her head, rolling it back and forth on the frame and wearing a pink groove into her skin. "She had him wrapped around one little finger, I think. That's the impression I got, anyway. If anything, she was irritated by him. But not afraid, ever. Not that I know of."

I believed her. And if I thought she was going to tell the truth, I might as well keep asking, even if it did turn out to be too little too late. "All right then. Who *was* my father? And I want to hear more than some initial or general Caucasoid appearance you think he might have had. You've gotta know more than that."

"He was somebody's husband. Beyond that, I don't know. All I know is that he was married, and that his wife was a nut who kept threatening Leslie. I swear to you, baby, that's all I know about him. He had a wife, and she knew about Leslie. She tried to make trouble."

That may well have explained the nasty letter I'd found. "And that's why she was afraid?" I asked.

"Yes," Lulu affirmed, but her almond-colored eyes veered away from mine. "I think that's it."

In that quick dash of her glance, she lost me, and I knew for sure that this wasn't going to work. Even if she was telling the truth, it was a slanted version of it—a version that was close enough to falsehood to serve me no purpose. She was right. I didn't know what questions to ask yet, and until I did, I needed to go find someone who didn't know me well enough to lie to me. I reached back for my bag and threw in a pair of sneakers.

"We're done here. I'm going now."

"And how do you expect to find her?"

Lulu thought she had me, but I'd already thought up an answer to that one. "I bet I can find a phone book."

She didn't argue. Instead, she reissued her warning. "Don't you go to her. No good could come of it." She planted her feet apart and stood blocking most of the door. I had a feeling she wasn't half so drunk as I thought she was, but I'd never seen her desperate before and I didn't want to acknowledge her desperation now.

I screwed my courage to the sticking place and slung the bag over my shoulder. "You thinking of stopping me?" I asked with more bravado than I felt. "You'd better not try. 'Cause you can't."

She didn't take the challenge right away, but she answered me all the same. "I wouldn't be so sure of that."

"Try it, then." The longer I looked at her, lean but solid and wholly unflinching, the more I prayed she wouldn't call my bullshit.

Lulu didn't move. I wondered if she was thinking the same thing—measuring whether or not she'd be able to take me if she felt she had to. I never reached her height, but I was twenty years her junior and I was faster than she had reason to know. Lulu might have been past forty, but she could still knock the head off 'most anyone I knew. Even so, she backed down first.

"You know I've never laid a hard hand on you—not in your entire life—and I don't mean to start now. But yours is a mind that needs changing. I wish I knew how to do it, but I don't. And I can't keep you hostage here forever, even if I stopped you now and didn't let you leave.

"You're my daughter. I don't mind saying so—you're *my* daughter. Not Leslie's. And not your mythical father's, either. You're mine and you're Dave's—the closest we ever had or ever will have, and I love you accordingly. I know you've got things you think you need to get answers to, but I wish you'd take my word that you don't. There are some things you're better off—hell, you're just plain *happier*—not knowing. There's so much of that crap waiting for you that even I don't know it all, because I didn't want to hear it. I'm only going to say this once, and then I leave it to you: Don't go get involved with old Tatie."

I tried to be flippant. "You make it sound like a matter of life or death."

She snorted and slapped her hand at the wall. "Goddamn stupid kid."

Then she retreated from the doorway and half stumbled out into the hall, then into her bedroom. Her voice trailed behind her, taunting but sad. "There's more she can take from you than just your life." Her bedroom door closed, but I heard her last, bitter words.

"She knows who you really are, you know."

IV

I have a savings account that was supposed to be a college fund. Dave started it for me out of my "share" of earnings from his photographs, and it is more than sufficient for me to shun employment for a few years yet, so long as I stay living at home and don't feel the need for a Porsche. I cleaned out half of that account and transferred the rest to my checking. It was a lot of money to have at my immediate disposal, but I didn't know how much dough I was going to need for this road trip and I was determined not to come up short.

Even though it was after midnight, I hit the road. I probably should have waited, but I'm not very patient under the best of circumstances, and it seemed best to leave while I still had all that psychological momentum built up. Besides, Macon's only three or four hours south of here, provided the roadwork stays at a minimum. The state of Georgia is forever widening, repaving, and generally altering I-75 to facilitate the downward flux of northern tourists to their Sunshine State destination.

Welcome to Georgia: billboard space for Florida—not to mention a most miserable part of the world to be driving through in the middle of the night. There's nothing at all to keep you awake on either side of Atlanta, and I was wishing with each passing mile that I'd put off my quest until a more reasonable hour. Tatie wasn't going anywhere, if indeed she hadn't left years before. Lulu had shut up when I said I'd look in a phone book, so I might expect to find Tatie still in the area. If the phone book idea was a wild goose chase, my aunt would have been the first to tell me.

This trip could have waited a few hours more, but it was too late now.

My head nodded with fatigue made more potent by the rhythmic white noise behind the music on the radio, and my eyes ached with each pair of headlights that sailed by. But Macon wasn't far. I could make it. Atlanta was more than halfway, and its towering lights were growing dim out my back window. Less than an hour south from here I'd get within Macon's city limits and find a hotel. Everything would be fine.

Something dusty, something charred sage and rosemary filled my sinuses and made my sleepy eyeballs itch. At first I wondered if there was something wrong with my car's AC, but I figured out the scent's true source before I even heard the voice.

This is madness.

I didn't jump. I was too tired to be startled, or at least too tired to act on it. I raised my gaze to the rearview mirror and met a familiar pair of eyes, though not the ones I might have expected. The voice came not from Mae, who fancied herself my mother, but from one of her sisters—I knew not which.

Once, a long time ago, Lulu had said that I should ask my questions of the ghosts, so there on the southbound side of I-75, I did. "What's madness? Me doing this?"

All of it. Time, over and over changing nothing—repeating the same lives again and again, each time expecting things will come out different. They never do. It's like riding a horse in a big circle, just out front of a boneyard. You keep thinking you've gone past all those angry dead folks, but then you come up on 'em again, right where you left them, and they're still just as mad as hell to see you.

"All I'm doing is taking a trip to go ask an old woman some questions."

'Sthat all? I guess I'm crazy too, then. See, I look at you, all grown up and a woman now, and I think this time—yes, this time it has to be different. I look at you and I can't imagine how you could be the same person, there on the inside. Malachi sees it—or maybe he doesn't. I think he knows it so sure he doesn't have to see it anymore. That's faith for you, right there. It's faith when you hear the Lord talk so loud that you can't hear regular people and regular reason anymore.

An' I wish you had faith a little more. I wish your auntie's words could hold you, but I know they can't, and I know mine can't either because I know better than anyone who you really are. Your aunt said Tatie knew, and she's right—all us old folks, nearly dead but not quiet yet, we all know. And I know you'll not be stopped by us. But your auntie's right. You're not even asking the right questions. The things you think you want to know don't matter for nothing. The old woman will answer you, and she'll speak true because you're asking her nothing of value. Not yet.

Mae can call you her baby if she likes, but you and I both know you're no sweet innocent. Mae is blinded by who you are, but I'm not, and I want to see things different this time. But damned if you don't make it hard on us, going off into the lion's den like this. Damned if you don't make us wonder. Damned if you don't make us doubt what we know.

Damned if you do.

"But I—I'm not Avery, am I?" I took a second to glance in the mirror then but she was gone, vanished as surely as if she'd never been there. "That's not fair," I grumbled aloud, whapping my hands on the steering wheel. "You oughta at least stick around long enough for me to respond."

Right at the height of my indignation, I suddenly realized that my car was no longer on the road.

"I've wrecked," I gasped, lifting my forehead. It stung where the steering wheel had carved a deep dent in the flesh. I'd fallen asleep, and the wheel made a crummy pillow, but I thanked God for it anyway. In my dream state I'd wandered off the interstate and found myself puttering at a snail's crawl through heavy grass, my foot off the gas but the little Nugget engine still demanding to move forward.

I'd not wrecked, I'd fallen asleep and wandered off the road.

I'd been terribly lucky.

I sat up straight and peered over the wheel like a short retiree. Inch by inch I guided my car back onto the road and pointed it straight at the nearest exit. Adrenaline from the close call kept me alert, but even that shock of near-calamity wouldn't hold for long. It was 3:00 A.M. and I needed sleep badly, regardless of how close to my destination I'd come.

No more silly risks.

The city was near enough that I was not hard-pressed to find a major hotel chain. I left a credit card with an honest receptionist at the front desk (by exhausted accident, not by request), and tucked myself into a room last decorated sometime in the early 1980s. I hung a Do Not Disturb sign on the doorknob and fell asleep before I had time to think too hard about my gently petulant passenger. I decided to come to the conclusion that I'd dreamed her, and any message she delivered sprang from my own unconscious concerns.

Leave it to me to take the easy way out.

I slept until the next morning, though when I checked the big red numbers on the clock beside my head, it was two hours into the afternoon. I didn't much care. I took my time with a shower and getting dressed, then gathered my things and threw them into the car. Up at the main desk they returned my wayward credit card, which was good of them—I hadn't even noticed it was missing. I folded my receipt and shoved it in my back pocket as I reached for the glass doors to leave.

Something stopped me—a collection of words at the far corner of my vision, hiding behind a clear door in a small red metal booth. It was just a short phrase, a headline and a grainy photograph that captured my attention. "Police Widen Search for Twice-Escaped Convict." And beneath the bold black banner was posted an old mug shot of my maniac cousin.

I turned away from the exit and fed enough change into the slot to buy one of the newspapers with Malachi's face on it. I didn't read the article right away; I waited until I was safely alone in my car. Even then I didn't really read the story, I only skimmed it to confirm what the headline had led me to guess. He'd gotten loose, diving out of a second-story window at the courthouse during his arraignment. The police had an idea that he was headed home to Macon. And why not? Who had ever defended him but Tatie? I wondered after his parents. Had I seen them before? Had they been at his trial when I was small?

No, all I remembered so far as his family went was the wicked old Eliza, glaring at me as her nephew was led away. If his mom and dad had been there, they'd been reserved enough that I couldn't recall seeing them. But his religious fervor must have been imparted to him by someone. His parents were the most likely suspects. For some reason, Tatie didn't strike me as the religious type.

I set the paper on the passenger seat and started my car. What I'd learned changed nothing. All it meant was that there would likely be police watching the Dufresne household, which was fine by me. I wasn't breaking in, I was visiting; and if they wanted to make sure Malachi didn't get inside, I was fine with that too. So much the better. It wasn't as if he was chasing me down, for he couldn't possibly know I was on my way to Eliza's. In a way, I had the drop on him, a turnaround which left me smug.

I was less than twenty miles from Macon, and it took me less than twenty minutes to get there. I picked an exit with an abundance of fast-food places, settling on a sandwich shop where the polyester-clad employees provided me with a phone book. I found four listings for Dufresne: Eliza M., John, James-Henry and Esther, and an S. F., otherwise unspecified.

Eliza M. Her address was listed as 3112 Chiswick Lane, and her phone number was printed alongside the entry. I copied the information onto the back of a sturdy napkin and put it in my pocket with the credit card receipt. Should I call first? No. Better to land on her doorstep. Combine surprise and audacity, and see what sort of reaction it got.

I asked around the restaurant, but no one knew how to point me towards Chiswick until an older gentleman looked at the zip code. "That's a ways off from here, if it's where I'm thinking. South of town a few miles and then a few more into the middle of nowhere." He gave me directions to where he believed the road was that turned out to be rough directions indeed.

I didn't find the house until it was almost dark, and when I dragged my car alongside it, I almost wished I'd missed it. The place was enormous and horrible—a bleak, Gothic Tara. Giant trees older than Georgia's statehood crowded in against the pale wooden walls, thick and menacing guardians who would have actively discouraged visitors if only they could. Not to be outdone, the glass at every black-shuttered window was mottled, wavy, and warped as testament to the house's age and resilience; and along the wide exterior kudzu clung tight from the bushes to the storm drains and up all three chimneys, pretending to be ivy. It cast a black lace shadow against the few windows where a light was on.

A frail, stooped figure passed across one broken square of light and disappeared back into the recesses of the antebellum labyrinth.

Eliza was home.

Two shiny, dark-colored cars were parked as inconspicuously as unmarked police cars can park. Their bulk lurked partially hidden by the big troll trees, but their hoods and bumpers poked out from either side of the monstrous trunks. It wouldn't do me any good to sneak up—they'd seen me long before I'd seen them. Besides, I hadn't done anything wrong—at least, I hadn't done anything *illegal*. Why should I feel forced to sneak anywhere?

Feigning confidence, I zipped the Death Nugget around the circular driveway and stopped it in front of the door, ignoring the cop cars with conscious effort. I slammed my car door closed, making a show of the noise. See? I'm not trying to sneak or skulk. See? Just minding my own business, paying a visit to an elderly relative. Innocent as can be.

I rang the doorbell.

From the other side I heard footsteps too heavy to be hers. Two great, resounding clacks echoed as the bolts were drawn back and the door swung inward. A large man greeted me. He was too old to be middle-aged but wasn't yet a senior citizen, and he was tall enough to be staring down at the top of my head, but not so wide that he could be called fat. I lifted my eyes from his chest and planted them squarely on his somber face.

"Can I help you, madam?"

"Yes sir, you can. You can tell Eliza her niece is here to see her."

One of his bushy, salt-and-pepper eyebrows lifted as he scanned me from curly head to black-booted foot. "I think perhaps you are mistaken."

I pressed my fingertips to my chest in faux astonishment. "What? Tatie didn't tell you she had a nigger in the family woodpile? I assure you that we are in fact near and dear relations, and I think she might be interested in talking to me."

The doorman hesitated, but he did not withdraw. He recovered his composure and said, with carefully measured dignity, "Ms. Dufresne is not receiving visitors at this time. Perhaps if you were to leave a message and return, she might give you an audience at a later date. Since you are family, you no doubt know about the unpleasantness with her nephew—your cousin, I suppose. She's quite elderly, you understand, and she's not taken the news well."

It was all I could do not to laugh in his face, but he seemed perfectly nice, and being rude wasn't likely to get me half so far as manners might. "Malachi? Of course I know. I'm the reason he was in jail to begin with." I let that sink in before following it up with the rest. "*I'm* the kid he tried to kill fifteen years ago. And a couple of nights ago, too, come to think of it."

His right eyebrow joined the left one, high up in the creases of his forehead. "You're Eden?"

I propped a hand on my hip and smiled with my lips pressed together. "*C'est moi.*"

"And . . . and you want to talk to Ms. Dufresne?"

"I sure do. Last time I saw her, she made it pretty clear she had some things to say to me; I just thought I'd give her the opportunity."

He faltered, dropping his hand down the door until it fell to rest atop the knob. With his other hand, he rubbed at the wrinkle on his forehead that now threatened to swallow both brows whole. "But I don't think . . . I don't think they're . . . very nice things."

I laughed, but not too loud or hard. "You know her well, then. You've worked for her a long time?"

He permitted himself a smile, slowly catching up to my nervous good humor. "Many years. Though not as many as it sometimes seems." His arm pulled the door open and he stepped aside. "Do come in. I'll tell Ms. Dufresne you're here."

"I would very much appreciate that," I said, swooping past him and into a marvelous hallway with a lengthy Turkish carpet spread over the wooden floors. The doorman led me into the parlor—there was actually a parlor—and asked me to wait while he went up to announce my arrival. I complied, sitting on a high, velvet-padded chair at the fully stocked wet bar that gleamed brass and mahogany.

I expected the man to return and say something like, "The lady will see you now," but instead old Tatie came shuffling down the stairs alone. She was small and unfathomably old, but she held herself upright and stiff as an arrow, and she was quick on her feet. Her fingers grazed the rail for effect and not for support.

She stomped towards me, her mouth set in a straight line and her fierce blue eyes exposing no hint of senility. She did not politely stop at the edge of my 2.5 feet of personal space but pushed her way in farther, until she was right under my chin—close enough that I could count the liver spots and upper lip hairs. I did not back up, but folded my arms between us and let her look at me. Her nostrils flared slightly and she took a step away, turning towards the bar.

"You're old enough to drink, aren't you?" she asked, glancing toward the bar.

"You know I am."

"Well, I *suppose* you are. What'll you have?"

I think she was trying to convey that she never thought about me. I didn't buy it, but I let it slide. "Surprise me."

Eliza did not look over her shoulder but called out to the doorman, who had crept in a few moments behind her. "Harry, make us a couple of gin and tonics."

"Yes, ma'am."

I hated gin and tonic, but I didn't say so. Eliza glowered at me—offended, curious, and maybe just a touch amused. She plopped her little self into a green velour wing-backed chair and gestured at the one facing her. I leaned back into it, crossing my legs across the shins as though I were wearing a skirt, and not at my thighs, like a man would. Eliza noticed. She noticed pretty much everything, I was willing to bet. She dragged her eyes up and down my posture as if she was calculating a score for my presentation.

By the time we'd settled, Harry had provided the drinks and quietly retreated. A door closed somewhere down the hall, declaring that we were alone. The distant, soft click was Eliza's cue.

"So what do you think?" she demanded.

"Of what?"

"Me. This place. You came here to have a look, didn't you? You jealous and greedy mixed kids always did envy this house. You're all just sitting around, waiting for me to kick the bucket so you can go to court and try to get it."

"I wouldn't take this house if you gave it to me, and I don't need your money. I came here to see *you*." I figured I'd tell the truth until I had a better handle on what I needed to lie about.

Of course, she'd known that much already—I could tell by the way her eyes gleamed. "And now you have. Am I as charming as you remember?"

"As charming as I remember, and then some. I do remember you taller, but then, last time I saw you, I was a lot shorter. Honestly, though, you don't look any different." I was still being truthful. She hadn't aged a day, although that wasn't the compliment she took it to be, considering I'd thought she looked like a mummy when I was eight.

Eliza knew cheap flattery when she heard it, but she let slip a wry half smile to match the one I must have flashed. "You think you're pretty slick, don't you, girl?"

"Oh yes. Terribly slick." I sipped at the alcohol and tried not to grimace. It tasted like piney kitchen cleaner. "But I'm not trying to snow you, Tatie. I came here for information, not for money or to provoke you." I choked down another small mouthful.

Eliza did not appear relieved to hear this. She did not relax at all, but instead clutched her crystal glass tight and held it to her mouth. She swallowed the liquor full and deep, the way I treat wine. I watched the gulp slide down the wattle of her throat and disappear past her collarbones. She was positively skeletal, as nearly a ghost as I'd ever seen a living human being. If she stood in front of a good stiff light, I could have watched her insides tick through her parchment skin.

"You can't threaten me," she said firmly, trying to convince me that her frailty only extended so far.

I dipped my jaw enough to indicate shock at the very idea. "I wouldn't *dream* of it. I only want answers, and no one on my side of the family is very forthcoming. You're the only person who might could help me, so I've come to you."

"Hmm." She downed a little more of her drink and swirled the remaining contents of the glass with a winding of her wrist. "What sorts of answers?"

"For starters, I want to know who A is."

She jumped, almost sloshing the clear beverage free of the clinking ice and over her fingers. "What are you talking about? What A? What is it you *think* you know?"

Her reaction startled me as much as my question startled her. "I was just wondering—the A who wrote to my mother when she was in Pine Breeze. I think he must have been my father."

Eliza's shiny snake eyes glistened, but she settled back into her chair and set the glass on a small table to her left. She had misunderstood me, and she was relieved to realize it. I couldn't help but wonder what she *thought* I'd meant. "Oh. So you want to know about Arthur."

I leaned forward. "That's what the A was for?"

133

"Oh yes." She nodded hard enough to make her loose skin flap, and her voice was more earnest than honest. "And you're very correct—he was your father, if your mother was to be believed. *He* believed her, that much was certain. How'd you learn of him?"

"I went to Pine Breeze."

"Don't lie to me, child," she snapped. "Not if you want straight answers in return, like you say you do. Pine Breeze has been torn down."

"No, it was *shut* down. And it's *about* to be torn down, but it still stands—just as they abandoned it twenty-five years ago. I dug around in there until I found Leslie's files, and those files included some letters from A, presumably Arthur."

"What did those letters say?" She was on the literal edge of her seat now, our faces only feet apart. I sensed an advantage, but I didn't want to press it too hard or reveal too much. I leaned back again and took another swig. It was easier to imbibe after two-thirds of a glass, but not much easier. I'd still rather drink turpentine.

"Mostly that he missed her, and he wanted her to leave Pine Breeze. He wanted her to move to a facility closer to him. He also complained a lot because she wouldn't write him back."

"Is that all?"

"Basically."

She retreated too, distrusting my slippery word but sinking against the winged chair back and exhaling. She polished off the rest of her drink in one quick upward tip of the glass.

"So, who was he?"

"Arthur?"

"Yes, Arthur. Who was my father?"

Her cheek twitched, poorly smothering a smile. "You won't like the answer."

I rolled my eyes. "You know, people keep telling me that—no matter what questions I ask. I'd rather know something unpleasant for certain than wonder after the truth for the rest of my life. Please, Tatie."

She rose and set her glass on the bar, empty except for the half-melted ice cubes stacked on the bottom. Then she moved to a bookcase laden with old volumes and accented with family photographs. She pulled one of the pictures down, and handed it towards me. I obliged her offer by standing and crossing the room to meet her, taking the photo by the frame and staring at the man and woman within.

"That's Arthur. And the woman beside him is—"

"His wife," I guessed.

"Yes. You knew already?"

"That much Lulu told me."

"And what else?"

"Nothing," I confessed. "All she said was that he was married."

"Did Louise tell you that Rachel was a lunatic?" She didn't wait for me to respond, so I didn't have to fib. "Oh yes, that woman was a basket case. One of those holy rollers who can't keep her nose out of anybody's business. I never liked her—not from the moment I met her. Always had to know way too much about every little thing. Asked a lot of questions—rude ones. Then when Art went and married her, well, that did *not* make me happy. Not at all. Rachel cared way too much about things that weren't her concern. Small wonder he turned out the way he did."

Her apparent swing in topic confused me. "Arthur, you mean?"

"Huh? No. I mean Malachi."

She said it casually, though she watched me closely from under shuttered lids. She wanted to see my reaction as the realization blossomed that I was wistfully holding a snapshot of Malachi's parents. I tried not to swallow too hard, and I made my face a mask, refusing to give the evil old crow her satisfaction as I stared down at the man who must have fathered me and my homicidal nemesis both.

He was average enough in appearance, light brown hair and eyes more green than my hazel ones. I searched for any likeness we might have shared and found only a similarity in our slouched posture. Just about anyone could see that I favored my mother's family; Lu had passively passed me off as her child for years. But Malachi favored our father strongly. I now knew where he'd gotten his sharp cheekbones and rectangular chin, as well as his bird-thin bones— a gene that had passed me by entirely. I glanced at Eliza and realized she had the high cheeks too, though age had hung her skin from them like curtains from a rod.

"How do you feel about *that*?" she asked, prodding for the carnage she felt she deserved.

"I'm not sure," I said. I shook my head, pretending to toss my hair over my shoulder and out of the way. Mostly I wanted to do something that didn't involve looking over at the smug old battle-ax again. "It doesn't matter, really. Where could I find him?"

"Up the hill under a stone. He killed himself in 1979. She's still alive, I think, his crazy wife, but she's long gone. I haven't seen her in twenty years. She left Malachi here one day for his summer vacation and she never came back for him. Last I heard she joined some crazy cult church out west, but I couldn't tell you if that was right or not. It wouldn't surprise me, anyway."

I tapped my knuckle against the picture frame, working up the fortitude to face Eliza without wanting to punch her. "So he's dead."

"Thoroughly."

"And Malachi is my half brother."

"Yep."

"As well as, somehow, my cousin. I mean, since you're my aunt, with a couple of 'greats' tacked on. And Avery was my grandfather. And he was *your* half brother. That definitely makes him a cousin too. This is . . . damn. This is messed up." For one nasty second I remembered and cringed from a moment of grade school shame.

"Well, it's complicated, yes—but when you say it that way it sounds strange."

"It *is* strange," I insisted, and I felt dumb for feeling like I needed to do so.

"Not so much." She retrieved the photo from my hand and put it back on the bookcase. "Modern families are complicated things. Siblings, half siblings, stepparents, stepcousins, what have you. You can't pick who you're born to, that's for sure. I'm fortunate that way; I'm a *legitimate* Dufresne, the name is mine by right. I didn't have to steal it from anyone."

I was suddenly defensive. "No one in my family calls herself a Dufresne anymore—or hell, no one ever did, that I know of."

She looked like she wanted to argue with me, but after thinking about it for a second, she didn't. "And thank the Lord for it," she said, still gazing at the picture. "What name did you end up taking? I can't recall."

"Moore. My mother's."

"You mean your grandmother's married name."

"Whichever." It then occurred to me that it wasn't my immediate family she had in mind. Since she'd done her best to provoke me, I decided to return the favor, or at least to try. "Your half brother was the son of a slave, and he took the Dufresne name, didn't he? Otherwise you wouldn't be worried about anyone in my line having it."

She wheeled around, face brimming with hatred, but her words were mostly level. "My family never kept any *slaves,* girl. If you knew more about your own birthplace you'd know that. Nobody around there kept *slaves.* An' Avery, he had no right—the name wasn't his. My father tried to be kind, and you see what it got him? You see what it got *me?* A line of illiterate, money-grubbing, mixed-breed cousins who feel entitled to everything that's mine. And here you come, into my own house. Into my own house through the front door, goddammit. I thought you might be different. I thought I saw in you . . ." She stopped, teetering at the edge of saying more but resisting, regaining her balance.

"What?" I pushed. "What did you think you saw?"

"Someone else."

I was about to lose her if I wasn't careful. "Tatie . . ."

"Don't you call me that. Don't you call me that, ever."

Perhaps a hasty subject change would distract her enough to calm her down. I needed to nudge her attention in some other direction; I needed to remind her of someone else she hated so she could forget how much she despised me. Given Eliza's nature, I figured just about anyone could serve that purpose.

"Why did you pay to send Leslie to Pine Breeze?" I asked, throwing my mother in front of her, giving her someone else to be angry at. "If you wanted her out of your hair there were cheaper places she could have gone to have a baby in secret."

It worked, at least a little. She shrugged one bony shoulder and scanned the room for something. "That's where she wanted to go." Her eyes settled on what was left of her drink.

"What damn did you give?"

She ignored me for a second, returning to the bar and to her glass. Eliza reached under the counter and pulled out the bottle of gin. She dumped it straight over the remaining ice and took a hearty gulp. "I didn't give any damn, and that's the truth. I went along with it because of Arthur—and because I couldn't stand the sight of his wife, who hated your mother so much. It was worth paying to keep Leslie out of Rachel's reach just to keep her angry."

"You're not really so vindictive."

"Oh, the hell I'm not." Tatie lifted the glass to her lips again, killing nearly half the drink. Her crinkled eyes slipped sideways, peeking at the door. "I wonder when he'll get here," she murmured.

"Who?" I asked, then I recognized what a silly question that was, so I answered it myself. "Malachi?"

"Well, yes, Malachi. The police are right. He's got nowhere else to go. He'll come here in his own time. And when he does, I'll be sure and tell him he just missed you."

"You know they're waiting for him right outside? They're parked out in the trees. They'll catch him if he comes here."

Eliza's confidence was disconcerting. It made me wary, and it made me think she knew something the rest of the world didn't. "I doubt it," she said. "I know they're there. They can sit and wait till Jesus comes again and they won't get my boy. Of course, even if they do, they won't keep him long."

"Yes, he rather has a gift for escape, it seems."

"A gift. That's a good way to put it." She was pensive now, or the alcohol was finally seeping its narcotic way into her bloodstream. "It *was* a gift, though I can't make him understand it. I believe Indians think madness is a gift, too. His mother . . . his mother, she . . ." Eliza took the drink and wandered back to her chair.

"Did she write letters to Pine Breeze? I found one I think she might have sent."

"Probably. I don't rightly know. God knows she wouldn't have told me about it, but she probably did. It sounds like something she'd do."

"The letter kept calling Leslie's baby 'he.' She thought I was going to be a boy?"

"I guess." She shut her eyes for a few seconds, then opened them again. I didn't trust her fatigue, but then she *was* over a hundred years old and apparently drank like a camel.

I didn't have to ask it. I already knew. "She thought I was Avery. She's the one who convinced Malachi of it."

Eliza was instantly awake again. It was that name, Avery. It stirred her every time I said it. "She was crazy. Crazy to think that."

"Why *did* she think that?"

"I don't know," she said, but I felt like she was being stubbornly untruthful. "I don't know how she got it in her head. I told you, she liked to dig in things that weren't her business. Arthur told her his family history, and she took it and went crazy with it. I suppose Louise told you the story, or you would've asked by now."

"Yes, she told me."

She closed her eyes again. "People used to frown on me because I never married or had children, but I've seen what mothers do, and I want no part of it. Avery, he . . . Avery might not have been so bad if his mother hadn't been a witch. She did it to him. She made him what he was because she hated us, and she wanted him to hate us too. She wanted him to hurt us, because she hadn't been able to. She made him into a monster. A *sorko*. That's what they called him. It's what he called himself, too. Wore it like a badge of honor. Lord, but he hated us all, and she's the one who inspired it."

Can't hardly blame her, I thought, but I kept it to myself. "And Malachi's mother wasn't any better. You've seen a lot of bad mothering in your time. I don't guess I blame you for not caring to have offspring."

"Don't you ever have children either. You've got it too, you know. I can smell it on you."

"Excuse me?"

"I said, girl, I can smell it on you. You're a witch like he was, and his mother."

"I'm certainly not."

"You are. I can smell it. An' I don't need Avery's damned book to divine it. I smelled it on your mother too. All the women in your family, just about. There's a smell to them, and once you've whiffed it, you never mistake it for anything else. Witches, every last one of you."

"Look," I insisted, sitting forward in the chair again. "I don't know the first thing about Wicca, or voodoo, or anything like that. I wasn't even raised with any of the more ordinary kind of church-going, so I sure don't know what you're saying."

"I don't mean a religious witch, you silly child. I mean that you've got shining. Everyone knows you talk to ghosts. You and Leslie both. Probably Louise too. All of you. And there's a smell to you. Avery told me, he said, 'You can always know one by her smell.' And boy, was he right."

I tried not to sound *too* interested when I pounced on the implications, but it was hard to keep the curiosity out of my voice. "I didn't know you ever actually met Avery. Why don't you tell me about his book. Lulu said something to me once about a book, but I don't remember what it had to do with anything."

She ignored me, or she didn't hear me anymore. "I might think that's why Rachel settled on you so hard. She knew your mother was a witch. And Malachi'd heard about you and the ghosts and he figured the worst. That might be it, right there. It's not such a far jump for a mixed-up head to make. Hey—do you hear him?"

"What?"

"I asked you, 'Do you hear him?' He's coming up now. He'll be here soon."

"Tatie?" I asked, using the title again because I didn't know what else to refer to her by.

Despite her prior admonition, she didn't object.

"Huh?" Her eyes were still closed, as if she were on the very verge of sleep. I'd never reclaimed my chair, but was still standing by my father's photograph. I left it on the shelf and approached her, crouching down almost as close as she'd first come to me. This sad bundle of wrinkles and bones was my only real link to the truth, and she was passing out before my eyes. But there were things I still needed to know. The aerosol smell of her Aqua Net hairspray made my nose itch, but I drew even closer, until my mouth was almost at her ear.

"It's not true, is it?" I asked, balancing on my toes and listening hard.

She sighed and shook her head just slightly. "Sure it's true. He killed them all three, and the baby girl with them. His boy, by one of the other women, that was your granddaddy. That's why there's still this whole line of you, coming after my money. But your other

141

aunt, she's got no children, does she?" Eliza cracked an eye open and stared at me from it.

"No. No children."

"Good. Then you're the last of them."

But she'd answered the wrong question. I asked it more directly while I still had her attention. I wanted to draw my face away from hers but I couldn't. It might have broken the spell, and the right question had not yet been aired.

"Tatie," I tried again, "It isn't true, is it? I'm not Avery, am I?"

Despite my best efforts, my words carried a tinge of fear that made her smile. I loathed myself for requiring this weird, uncomfortable intimacy, but what else was I to do? Lulu said Eliza knew, and I had Eliza talking. She might not be telling me the truth, but she was at least giving me something to chew on.

"Malachi thinks you are," she finally responded.

"What do *you* think?"

"Doesn't matter. So long as Malachi believes you are. You're the last, and when you're gone . . ." Her words petered away. Her slitted eye closed and she exhaled, long and warm so close to my face. Then she drew in a shallower breath and her body drooped, her head lolling against the chair's winged sides. Her wrist went limp and the remaining gin and water dripped onto the floor.

"Tatie?"

She did not reply.

I stood and stretched, leaning my back to crack the kinks out and returning to the photo. I turned it over and pried the frame loose to remove the picture, fully intending to cut Rachel out of it at a later date. I deserved one picture of my father, didn't I?

When I turned around to leave, Harry was standing in the doorway. He must have seen me take the picture, but he said nothing to indicate that he planned to do anything about it.

I waved at the softly snoring old woman in the chair. "She fell asleep."

Harry nodded. "I'll see to her."

"Hey, Harry?"

"Yes, ma'am?"

"There's a cemetery near here, right? A family plot?"

"Leave to your right, out of the driveway. Go up the hill—you can't miss it."

"Thank you, Harry."

"You're welcome, ma'am. Ma'am?"

"Yes?"

"She wasn't too hard on you, was she?"

I grinned, clutching the picture to my chest. "Nothing I couldn't handle."

6

Up the Road a Piece

Maybe the old coot was right. Maybe Malachi *was* on his way. I went ahead and left her there, sleeping in her oversized chair, but it wasn't because I was afraid of him. I'm afraid of some things—spiders, drowning, needles, and the like. But I'm not afraid of Malachi. He simply isn't intimidating, even with his True Faith to bolster his aggression. He hides behind God and guns, and ineptly at that. It can't have been more than luck that caused him to kill Terry. He was a terrible shot when I was a kid, and I didn't think he'd spent much time practicing his aim in prison.

It must be hard for him. He believed so firmly that he was right, and that his mission was blessed, but he failed at every turn. What did it say about him that he tried so hard? He was either very devout or very stupid, I figured. More likely a sampling of both.

I almost felt like I owed him fear. He'd worked so hard to kill me, the least I could do was be just a tad nervous. But no. I couldn't muster it. The best I could do was summon up a healthy sense of caution, and toss him a minor, grudging respect for his persistence.

Tatie would certainly tell him I'd been to see her, but I hadn't given her any indication of where I might be headed, so it wasn't as if she could point him my way. She might be able to guess about the cemetery because of my questions, but beyond the cemetery, even *I* didn't know where I was going. I was almost disappointed that my quest had ended so quickly. I hadn't found all my answers, but I had found my father. That was more than I might have expected.

As for Avery and his mysterious book, it might be better to decide that Lulu was right and it didn't matter. Let the dead who can sleep lie undisturbed.

I cast the police a backwards glance on my way out. They did not make any indication that they saw me, cared about me, or intended to pursue me. I half imagined them as uniformed ostriches with their heads in the sand: If we don't see you, you don't see us. I hoped they stayed right where they were and caught my wayward cousin-brother, if only to make a liar out of Eliza.

As for me and the Death Nugget, we headed up the hill in the dark.

The cemetery was on the right, enclosed by a low iron fence with a broken gate. I parked beside it and rummaged around in my trunk until I found the huge flashlight I kept for emergencies or for after-hours excursions.

The gate's lock could have been easily repaired, but I wasn't surprised that no one had bothered. The fence was primarily a boundary marker, altogether too stubby to have prevented anyone over three feet tall from entering; and I didn't suppose anyone was too worried about its residents trying to get out.

The graveyard was dark and silent, and held only twenty or thirty monuments that I could immediately see. Most of these could be summarized as phallic obelisks with Masonic symbols for the men and towering, virginal angels for the women. In a moneyed family grandiose markers were the order of the day; even infants who had died within a day or two of birth were graced with enormous lambs and stone lilies. Everything looked at least a century old, so I followed a gravelly path until I came to some newer, somewhat less gaudy statuary. Here were the more recent graves, with pseudo-modern slabs of granite and slate cut in nearly geometric shapes.

I shined my tube of light on each one, wincing at the reflected glare.

At the end of the row, occupying half of a married couple's headstone, I found Arthur Henson Eller Dufresne. August 3, 1945–January 11, 1979. Beloved father and husband. *And lover,* I might have added for spite, but I didn't know how true it was to say that Leslie loved him, considering she fled from him the last months of her life. Besides, it seemed unkind to speculate when I considered that half the marker was still blank, waiting for his devoted wife to join him. "Till death do us part" had become "Till death reunites us." Too bad, Rachel. My mother got him first.

I left my light trained on her name. Rachel Bostitch Dufresne. May 23, 1948, and then the anticipatory spot where her demise would be marked. I bet to myself that she wouldn't return to claim Macon as her resting place, not if she'd been gone this long. Poor Arthur. Even after he was dead, the women in his life kept running away from him.

But if I were in Rachel's shoes I wouldn't want to spend eternity next to the man who'd cheated on me twice—once with a woman and once by taking his own life and leaving me. Malachi would have been young then, but not so young that he wouldn't have had a good idea what was going on. I didn't know exactly how old he was, but I was guessing he was maybe twelve or thirteen in 1979. I was also guessing that it was around that time (or shortly thereafter) that he came to live with Eliza. No wonder he was such a nut job.

I sighed. Should I have brought flowers?

No. What would be the point? I doubted Arthur had ever set eyes on me, and I doubted even more that he would have cared that I'd come by. He was obsessed with my mother, not with me. *I* was little more than an inconvenience. *Our problem.* That uncomplimentary phrase still itched in the back of my head, hard as I tried to exorcise it. The argument could easily be made that ultimately I had cost him the relationship he had with her.

I'd been about two years old when he died. Had he ever *tried* to see me?

Not likely. If he had, Lulu or my grandmother would have guessed who he was—taking Lu at her word and assuming they didn't already know. So why was I wasting my time hanging out at a stranger's grave? I shifted my light around and watched my feet part the grass as I navigated a trail between the stones. About halfway back to the road I sorted out a separate set of footsteps crunching through the grass, moving a split second slower than mine and taking a longer stride.

I turned off my flashlight and stood still. Another voice called out. "Hello?"

Hot damn, Eliza had been right.

I didn't answer, but I hopped off the main path and set my back against one of the pillarlike monuments.

"Hello? Is someone there?" He was not shouting, not even raising his voice above a hard whisper. I did not have to see him to know I should hide from him. I doubted he was armed, but there was no sense in taking chances.

"I . . . I saw a car up by the road. Is there someone here?"

Malachi had not been to see Eliza yet, otherwise he might have guessed whose car it was. My breath came a little faster, and my heart beat a little harder. Should I head for the car? Call out? I wasn't too far from the house at all; if I yelled, the cops down the hill would likely hear me.

He stood as still as I had, nearly on the same spot where I'd been a moment before. I could have reached out and pulled his hair. He was nervous, but he was wanted by police in several states so I decided not to judge him a coward for his shaking. His shoulders were square and high, his neck craned forward, and his hands were held out and empty—not even a flashlight.

Speaking of flashlights, my own was heavy enough to brain him with if it came down to it. I fondled the metal-and-glass instrument with both hands, but did not leap out to ambush him . . . yet. I wanted to know what he was up to.

Reassured by the silence, Malachi's shoulders drooped back into the sloped posture I remembered, and his hands went into his pockets. No, he was no threat. I relaxed too, and followed him with my eyes, then with careful feet. I made my steps match his, staying a few stones back. I was not afraid of losing him. I knew where he was going. We both stopped near his father's grave. *Our* father's grave.

Even in my head, I didn't like the sound of that. *His* father, then. My sperm donor.

He sat cross-legged in front of the stone, holding his chin in his hands. I was glad he had no light—he might have noticed the freshly bent grass where I'd trampled the same spot.

Malachi ran his fingers through his hair, pushing it out of his face, and returned his chin to his palms. I half expected him to start talking, either to himself, his dad, or to God, but he did not indulge. Instead he sat there with his head cocked as if he was paying very close attention to something I couldn't hear.

Now I was annoyed with us both—me for following him and not leaving sooner, and him for sitting there like an idiot.

Suddenly his head jerked up. "Where?" he asked, his voice louder than before. He swiveled his storklike head, nose in the air. "Where?" he asked again. "I know, but . . . I can do it. But. But. Okay. Not now." Then he bolted back towards the fence, hopping over it with a spindly-legged leap and disappearing down the hill.

My eyes were wide. He had successfully creeped me out.

I shook my head and flipped my light back on, making to leave as well. The bulb flickered and sputtered, then fizzed. I knocked it against a tombstone, but this only offended it more, and it died altogether. Oh well. There was light enough to see by the moon, at least to get myself back to the car. Despite my confidence in the lunar illumination, I got myself turned around and ended up farther down the hill, away from the gate but still within sight of my vehicle. I grumbled at myself, slung one leg over the fence and brought the other down behind it, dropping my shin down on something very hard that was hidden in the grass just outside the ironwork barrier.

Cursing all the way, I sat on the ground and lifted my jeans enough to see that I wasn't bleeding so badly that I should worry. I rolled my pants leg back down and felt around in the grass until I located the source of my pain.

The weeds were high outside the family plot. In the dark, there was no way I could have seen and avoided the little stone. This was another marker, a grave set beyond the elitist dead of the Dufresne clan. I held the grass away and ran my fingers over the worn carving. With a bit of patience, I made out the inscription.

UNKNOWN SEMINOLE MAN
WHO CAME TO THE HOUSE ON
OCT 22, 1906
AND ASKED FOR JOHN GRAY
GOD HELP HIM
WE COULD NOT

Bizarre. Just bizarre.

I got to my feet and dusted myself off, then limped to my car.

Down at Tatie's, much havoc had broken loose. The unmarked cars had emerged from their hiding places, interior blue lights raging. I drove by without stopping to see if they'd caught Malachi. If they hadn't yet, I was pretty sure they would get him before long. I squeezed forth a few drops of pity for the lad and went back out to the main road.

He was my brother, after all.

Eliza had told me everything she was going to for now—not

that I could expect to get any more out of her while her nephew was busy getting rearrested under her roof. For lack of any better ideas, I returned to the hotel to pack up my things.

Dave was waiting for me in the lobby.

"Lu's worried sick about you. She called me in Atlanta and told me to come and get you." His hands were folded in his lap, an overnight bag beside him, bulging with his camera equipment. A Styrofoam cup of brew, still mostly full, steamed on the coffee table before him. He hadn't been waiting long.

"How'd you find me?"

"Called around. It's not like you were using an alias or anything, and you've got that Visa card on my account."

"Oh yeah. I forgot about that."

I sat down next to him on the white plush couch. "Next time I should come incognito, eh?"

"Wouldn't have done you any good to hide. I can't come home without you. Lu'd kill me first. I wasn't too worried for you until I started watching TV a few minutes ago. Check that out." He pointed at the screen that the night clerk was listlessly paying half attention to.

I looked in order to humor him. I could have guessed what it was without seeing the rolling captions.

A police helicopter was combing the ground with a spotlight, circling and scanning the area around Eliza's homestead. If they were still looking that hard, he must not be in custody. "They haven't caught him yet?"

"No. But they know he's there. They'll get him."

"Yeah." I should have hit him on the head when I had the chance. Lounging there next to Dave, I suddenly couldn't remember why I hadn't done so.

My uncle didn't take his eyes away from the television, so

I didn't either. "Did you find your way out there? Well, I guess you must have—since you recognized the place on TV."

"Yeah. I found it."

"How? Lu didn't point you there, did she?"

I shook my head. "Good God, no. I did it the old-fashioned way, with a phone book."

"Learn anything good?"

"Sort of. I found my father."

"Really?"

"I mean, he's dead and everything, but I found him."

"Oh." I thought he sounded relieved, maybe a bit.

I went ahead and filled him in on the evening's events, leaving out the parts about Malachi being my brother and seeing him in the graveyard. Dave grunted agreeably at the narrative, finishing his coffee while I talked. I concluded with, "And then I saw you sitting here," bringing him as far up to date as I had any plans to.

He twisted his arm around in his bag's strap, then stood with it. "Does this mean you're ready to come home?"

I hesitated, but couldn't think of a reason to say no. Even so, I wasn't ready to run off to my room, pack up, and leap into my car. My hesitation was not lost on Dave.

"It isn't safe here in town, not with that boy still running loose."

I wanted to point out that Malachi was in his mid-thirties by now, but it seemed superfluous. I wanted to insist that I stay where I was for a while yet, that I hadn't found out everything I needed to know, but nothing sounded practical or convincing.

Dave shifted his weight beneath the heavy bag, waiting for my response. He looked old and tired, his eyes sagging from concern or lack of sleep and the first starts of gray decorating his temples. He wasn't my hippie fudge buddy anymore, but he was still Dave, and he deserved more from me than ambivalence.

"I think I'm going to stay here, at least for another couple of days. They'll have Malachi before morning, and I'd like to talk to

Tatie some more if I could. She got drunk and passed out before I managed to ask her everything I wanted. And maybe I'll go back to the cemetery in daylight or . . ." I glanced down at his camera bag. "I might take some pictures, or something," I finished weakly.

"That's your call. But just so you know, Lu's gonna hurt me when she hears it."

"But you know where to find me now." I sounded like I was pleading, and maybe I was. "I'm sorry I didn't call or anything, but I'll give you my room number and I won't change locations without letting you guys know. I promise." I meant it, too.

"You should call Lu."

"If I do, she'll just yell at me. She's probably not finished from yesterday."

"She's worried. And she hasn't been feeling well. Let her yell. It'll do her good."

"I'll think about it. What do you mean, not feeling well? She was fine last night."

"She's a tough old birdie, she is. She's all right. Don't worry about her."

"You take care of her, then."

"I always do, don't I?"

"Yeah."

"Call her," he said, patting my cheek. "I'm going to head on. My cell phone's in the car. On the way home I'll let her know you're alive, but you call her too. Let her hear your voice." He slung an arm around my shoulder, squeezing me with a half hug. "Be careful."

"I always am."

"You and I both know that's not the case."

"Yeah."

He turned to leave, pausing at the door. "Good-bye. I mean it, be careful."

"Maybe I will, and maybe I won't. But I sure won't do anything *you* wouldn't do."

"Dear God," he swore. "Don't put it that way, or we're both screwed."

I was about to hug him and send him on his way when I got an idea. "Hey, Dave?"

"Huh?"

"What do you know about the Seminoles?"

"The football team or the Indians? I know they're both from Florida, that's about it. Why?"

"The Indians. And, uh, no reason."

Dave thought a moment, ignoring my lie and leaving his hand on the door. "If you really want to know, there's a store downtown called the Crescent Moon. I went to school with the guy who owns it—we ended up at UT together for a while. He's not Native American himself, but he dabbles in the culture. He could help you out, maybe. His name's Brian Cole."

Of course. Leave it to Dave, the Answer Man. I should have known he'd have the right connections. "Brian Cole at the Crescent Moon?"

"Yeah, it's one of those incense-smelling New Age shops. Tell him I sent ya. I'd try to think up some directions, but since you've become such a master of the phone book, I'll trust you to figure it out on your own."

"Yeah, I will."

Only after he was gone did I begin to feel tired. It had been a big day, and it was getting late—at least late enough that an independent retail shop would not be open. I retreated to my room and turned on the TV, trying to find a local channel that wasn't covering the manhunt at Eliza's. They'd catch him, I knew they would; but I didn't really want to watch it.

I gave up and turned it off, then hit the lights as well, still not knowing what I intended to do in the morning.

My dreams took a strange turn that night.

I often dreamed of the ghosts, and of the sticky swampland

that had haunted my childhood. Frequently enough I heard Mae's quiet crying or her sisters' warning pleas, but that night the voice was different.

It was not vague, or tearful. It was not begging, or demanding. It was simply calling.

Come home.

In my sleep-choked state, I tried to interrogate the speaker with half-formed questions. "Who are . . . ?" "Where is . . . ?" "Why do . . . ?" I tried to remember the name on the stone. "John Gray?"

Come home.

As in my youth, I saw the book again, sitting on the table beside the vials of powders and syrups. I approached it slowly, like struggling through tangible fog. I needed to see what was inside. I needed to look in the back. I put out my hands and touched the dry leather of the binding. It crackled beneath my touch, as though it were alive or on fire. A fine yellow powder that was not dust covered my fingertips. But the hands were not mine—they were not my fingertips. They were different, bigger or smaller or older or younger, different. I couldn't see them. I couldn't feel them. I began to panic.

"I can't feel my hands," I blurted out, fumbling with the book.

You don't need them here.

"I don't . . . I *do* need them. Everywhere." The book came open to a crinkly page covered with formulas and drawings. I think the sketches were plants, or trees, or roots; I saw words I didn't recognize: *Korombay, diggi, sibitah kaaji* . . . but the numbers ran together and I couldn't sort them out from one another. "What is this?"

You should know.

"But I don't." I lifted the pages and pushed them over to the left, ten or twenty at a time in order to reach the back cover. "What is this? What is this?"

The speaker was chanting, softly but with increasing volume.

Asi goun goun ma . . .

Asi goun goun ma . . .
Asi goun goun ma . . .

One more page. I held it between my thumb and index finger. "What is this?" I turned it.

Violently, a giant black bird flapped out, up towards the ceiling, then back down to peck at my head. I shrieked and dove away, shielding my face with one arm and trying to close the book with the other. I slammed the covers together but the bird did not stop its assault. I waved my arms, trying to push it away and meeting the feathery pressure of strong black wings beating the air around me.

You can't put him back now. He knows you're here.

"What is this?" No. Not the right question. "Who? Who is this?"

Laughter. *You said a name. John Gray. How much do you know, after all?*

I sat up, sweaty and cold. Calmed to find myself in my hotel room, I reclined against the pillows and panted until I'd caught my breath. I opened my eyes again expecting nothing but the ceiling fan.

Willa was standing above me, a knife in her hands aimed down at my chest. *Not this time, you don't!* she growled, plunging the blade down through my ribs.

I gasped.

It was then that I truly awakened, wet with fear, clutching the blankets around my neck. I hunkered into a crouch, leaning my back against the headboard and rocking myself back and forth like a child.

7
The Right Tree

I

When day broke, when light crawled under the heavy hotel curtains and spilled onto the floor, I was finally able to sleep a few hours more. Otherwise, I spent the night angry and afraid, curled in a rag-doll bundle with the covers up under my ears. Who did these ghosts think they were, harassing me like this?

I got up feeling drained and unhappy, and a shower did little to take the edge off of my misery. By way of distraction, I took the phone book out of the nightstand and looked up the Crescent Moon. The day clerk at the front desk supplied me with fuzzy directions that got me downtown all right, but then lost me. I had to stop at a gas station and get more directions, and thereby learned that the day clerk had been off by miles. Lovely. Once I did get to the correct block, parking was tricky; but the Death Nugget is small and I can parallel park in two flawless moves, so the situation remained manageable despite my grumpy frame of mind.

The Crescent Moon was just as Dave implied—thick with incense smoke and light with imported fabrics. Candles of every color were grouped in clumps according to their scents: musky and exotic, floral, perfumey, and simply decorative. Along the back wall were rows of specialty books on everything from feng shui to natural childbirth. Silver wind chimes tuned to friendly minor keys tinkled when the door fell shut behind me.

"Peace be with you, little sister," greeted the man behind the counter. He was maybe fifty, with a Walt Whitman beard and a straw hat that had feathers in it. "Can I help you with something?"

A large brown dog ambled slowly out from behind the counter. It stretched with a mighty grunt and came to sniff my legs. "That's Bo. He'll just smell you and leave you alone unless you start petting him—and then he's yours for life. He's real friendly."

"He sure is," I said, scritching the dog's scruffy head and ears. He thumped his tail against the counter and leaned into my thigh.

"Some folks don't like dogs, but I don't understand it."

"Bo seems real nice," I said, and I meant it. I'm more of a cat woman, personally, but I'll not begrudge anyone a fondness for a good old mutt.

"Are you Brian Cole?" I asked.

"Oh yes, yes, I am," he nodded, unsurprised that I knew his name. "What can I do for you?"

"I'm Dave Copeland's niece, Eden. Dave said you might be able to help me out."

"Dave? Well, I'll be . . . how's that old son of a gun doing? Good, I hope?"

"Same as always. Indecent, dishonest, and up to no good."

Brian laughed. "That's him, all right. I'm glad to know he's well. And what can I do for you today, little lady?"

Where to start? And how to phrase it? "See, I was going through some old family things and I kept coming across these vague references to places in Florida—maybe places having something to do with the Seminole Indians, or a guy named John Gray."

Brian's eyes went wide. "Whoa, there—John Gray? You want to know about *him?*"

"Um, I guess so."

"That's a tall order of trouble right there, sister. You're not thinking of getting involved with a group like his, are you?"

I waved my hands in a hearty disavowal. "Man, I don't know the first thing about him. There's just a rumor that some cousins of mine were wrapped up with him, and I wanted to know what he's about—that's all."

"Whoa," he said again, this time as an exclamation and not a suggestion. "Whoa. Not anyone on Dave's side, I hope?"

I shook my head. "This is on my mom's side, a couple of generations back. So he wasn't a real nice guy, huh?" I said suggestively, trying to prompt him to say something more helpful than "whoa."

"Hold on a second." He held up a finger and stepped over Bo, who had flopped down beside me and was all but lying on my left foot. "I've got a book over here that—yeah, hold on. I got it."

He went to the rack and pulled out a volume entitled *Occult America*. Checking the index in the back, he selected a page and let the book fall open to a full-page black-and-white photo of an older man in Native American dress. His light, loose-fitting cloth tunic was decorated with small, ornate bead patterns and woven feathers, and his hair hung in long braids tied up in suede strips. But his skin was quite dark, and his nose was broad, not arched. I traced his full mouth with my fingernail.

"He's black," I announced the obvious. "Why's he dressed like that?"

"His father was a Seminole. Couple of hundred years ago there was a freedman's colony outside of St. Augustine, on the northeast coast of Florida. It was a popular destination for runaways and free people of color alike."

"Why? I thought most runaways headed north."

"Back then Florida was more old-Spain than slaveholding

Dixie. The Spaniards were fairly tolerant as long as you went through the motions of being Catholic, and the Seminoles who lived nearby were friendly with the Africans. The free colony was destroyed when the British made a move on St. Augustine, but at any rate, there was a great deal of intermarriage. That's where John Gray came from."

I turned the page and scanned the text. Brian summarized and paraphrased behind me.

"John made a nasty mix of his mother's Hundun and his father's native ways. No one knows how powerful he really was, but between his magic and his charisma he gained a small cult of followers who called themselves Graysmen. Eventually the Spaniards had enough of him—he was accused of killing a priest or something. Who knows if it was true, but they hunted him down for it and killed him in 1840."

"That must have been a blow to his followers."

"Yes and no. They stayed in a loose alliance for some time after his death. When are you thinking your family members might have been involved with him?"

I had to calculate a rough time frame. It took me a second. "Maybe twenty years after the Civil War. Maybe the 1880s or '90s. I'm not sure."

Brian's head bobbed quickly to the left in a half shrug. "I don't know when they officially disbanded—or even if they ever did, honestly, but they were being harassed by the police as late as 1882. A round of them got hung for witchcraft, of all things. Of course the official charge was something more ordinary, but everyone knew why they really got them."

I leaned forward against the counter and pressed my chin into my palms. "But why? Why after all that time? What did John Gray promise them to make them keep his memory alive so long?"

"What everyone who wants a cult promises: eternal life."

"I hate to harp on the obvious, but he *died*."

"He was killed, yes, but he hadn't told anyone that he *personally* could make them live forever. He had this idea he got from his mother; there's some potion, or formula, or powder, or something, that a true wizard could concoct. Unfortunately for him, he never managed to get the right combination of ingredients mixed up. The trouble was, most of his recipes called for plants that grow in Africa, so he was forced to substitute. It's not quite the same thing as swapping apple juice for sugar, I don't imagine."

"But his cultists believed he'd work it out?"

"They were certain of it. He'd demonstrated his powers with smaller miracles. Other spells—spells that made you stronger, faster, smarter. Spells that could make you invisible, or give you the power to see other people's dreams. He claimed he could astrally project, and walk through solid objects."

"So, what you're saying is that he was a charlatan."

"Don't assume that so fast. In his mother's country there's a long tradition of *sorkos* who have demonstrable supernatural abilities. Anthropologists took a shine to them in the early 1970s, and there were several studies published on the subject of African tribal occultism. Fascinating, really."

"Hang on—what did you call them? *Sorkos?* I know that word. Where was she from, John Gray's mother? Was she from Niger?"

"I think so. Yes, I think that's right. Is that where your cousins were from?"

"Yeah." I turned the next page. It featured another photo of Gray, this time with a woman.

"That's Juanita, his wife."

"It says she went mad when he died."

Brian shook his head. "She didn't go mad. She knew good and well what she was doing when she cut off his hand."

I jumped as if the gentle fellow had punched me. "His . . . his hand? Why would she do that? Why would she . . ." I was stammering, but I couldn't make my tongue straighten out and work right. "Why would she cut off his . . . his hand? That doesn't make any sense, it just doesn't."

"Calm down, child—I swear by the goddess—calm yourself down. There's no need for it, now. Whatever's gotten you? Yes, she cut off his hand, but she waited until he was dead, if that's what's worried you."

I braced my elbows on the table and took two or three measured breaths, avoiding his eyes until I'd shrouded my own. "It's just the way you said it." I spoke carefully, trying too hard to sound light. "I thought you meant it was while he was alive. Yeah, that creeped me out." I shuddered, and the shudder was real enough to satisfy Brian, but I could tell he felt I'd overreacted.

"He was dead. No doubt for it. Juanita wanted a relic to work magic with. She took his left hand off clean at the wrist, she did. It was easier than taking just his ring finger."

"His . . . why would she want his ring finger?"

"Magic. According to his hodgepodge theology, the fourth finger of the dominant hand is the power finger. It's the only finger in African cult lore that has no name. So long as she had that piece of him, there was the possibility she could raise him again. Fortunately—at least for the members of the holy order that hanged her husband—she came down with smallpox and died before she could wreak too much havoc."

I didn't really want to know, but I couldn't stop myself from asking. "And the hand?"

"Disappeared. She wasn't really strong enough to do anything with it anyway; Juanita was more of a hanger-on than a priestess. But for a long time there were serious fears that someone else might make a go of it. Eventually, John Gray and his crew were pretty much forgotten."

I shifted uncomfortably. "That's not surprising. It's been an awfully long time."

"No, not surprising, but possibly dangerous. The time's not quite up yet. Soon, though."

"How do you mean?"

Brian turned another page. "It's not yet been one hundred and sixty-five years. That's the longest his soul can stay tied to earth close enough to come back—before passing all the way over to the other side, that is. Once that anniversary has passed, he's gone for good."

"So it's this year?" My math was never the best, but I knew I had to be close.

Brian returned to the book and went to a page we'd already passed, dragging his finger down the page until it stopped on the date John Gray had died. Apparently he wasn't much good with numbers either, because he then reached for a calculator in a drawer beside the cash register to confirm my calculations. "Yes. This year. September twenty-ninth."

"That soon?"

"Yep. About a week and a half from now and the world will be quite safe."

"That's . . . reassuring." Only a week and a half away. "Quite safe" was just around the corner.

"You don't *look* too reassured."

"I'm sorry," I said, but then I felt stupid for apologizing. "I'm not sure why it makes me feel so uneasy."

"Probably because it's not past yet. You're just showing good sense."

I grinned, trying to make it look real. "Thanks."

He patted me on the back. For a minute I thought he was going to call me "little sister" or "little lady" again, and I might start laughing despite my unease. "Don't worry about it so much. John Gray's dead, and so are all his children. There's nothing more to fear from the likes of him."

"You're right. I'm sure you are," I lied, for he was too kind to argue with.

As thanks for the information, I went ahead and bought the book and some incense that smelled sweetly of vanilla and jasmine.

"Take this too, on the house," he said, handing me a tiny velveteen bag about the size of a strawberry. It was soft and blue, and inside it was tied a mixture of herbs and powders that might have been cinnamon and sage. "It's a gris-gris."

My confusion turned to mild skepticism, but I accepted the gift. I didn't have any lucky charms, and perhaps this one would do me good. I took it with the same apathetic optimism with which I swallow the occasional vitamin—it can't hurt, and it might help. "Thank you so much for your time."

"No, thank *you*—for your company. And take care of yourself, miss. Tell your uncle I said hello. Tell him too that he should make his own way out here before long. I haven't seen him in ages."

"I sure will tell him," I promised, "and thanks again."

I left the shop clutching the brown paper sack with the book, incense, and gris-gris. My car was parked outside, so I opened the passenger's side and set my purchases on the seat before venturing into the street.

Though it was well past lunchtime, I couldn't detect much in the way of hunger pangs. I was too distracted by the wealth of new information to worry about food. I paused before a newspaper rack and read the date on the right-hand corner. September 18. Eleven days until John Gray was thoroughly sent to rest, even by his own religion.

No one remembers him anyway, I told myself. *This is ancient history. There's no one left alive to try to raise him—as if it could even be done.* I'd seen plenty of ghosts, but nothing of the resurrected. And I'd certainly not seen anything like a man dead for a century and a half brought back. It was more than I could imagine. There would be nothing left of him to raise.

A street or two down I saw a sign for an International House of Pancakes, and promptly changed my mind about whether or not I needed to eat. I retrieved my new book from the car and started walking, certain I could find something fruity, syrupy, hash-browny, or milky to ingest. IHOP had never failed me yet.

Amidst the clinking silverware, clattering plates, and bustling of waitresses, I read on in the glossy, hard-backed book while I waited for my blueberry cheese blintzes. September 29, 1840. John Gray was dragged from a ceremony by a group of Spanish monks who wrapped him in chains and hung him from a tree outside the Castillo de San Marcos in St. Augustine, Florida.

September 29.

A week and a half. But why should it worry me? The nearness of the date was a good thing—I was so close to being beyond fear. Why did this affect me so much? Because I'd dreamed of his hand? I shook my head, knowing I could not clear it. My connection to John Gray was more distant than I could imagine. It was distant enough for me to live without fear, and for me to ignore the superstitions of the long, long dead.

Still, I continued to read.

"The monks tried to persuade Juanita Gray to surrender John's hand, but she refused them. He'd given her no children, she argued, so she needed a piece of him to keep for memory's sake. According to Gray's beliefs, it was a drain on a *sorko*'s power to have progeny, as it disseminates his blood and diffuses his power. It is said that when a man in later life decides to become a *sorko*, he may decide to kill his children and/or his grandchildren in order to reclaim his blood, that he may retrieve and increase his power."

I'm no relation to Gray, I reassured myself. *And all of his followers have been dead for generations. No good reason on earth to be concerned. None at all.*

My food arrived. I closed the book and ate.

When I was finished I was fat-feeling and tired, so I returned to the hotel for a nap.

I was awake before she called. When the phone rang I didn't even have to guess.

"Lu?"

"There you are," she said, with relief and malice both in her voice. So she was still angry that I'd gone—no big surprise there. I thought I heard something else too. She sounded tired, or ill. Dave had said she wasn't feeling well; he'd said there was no reason to worry.

"Are you okay?" I asked anyway, and she snorted a reply.

"Yeah. I'm okay. What about you? Are you finished molesting the dead yet?"

If she was going to be short, I would too. Distance makes the heart grow braver. "Not yet. I'm going back to the cemetery later, I think. And then who knows what trouble I might get into." I stopped myself before I took it too far. "While I've got you on the phone, what do you know about John Gray?"

"What do *you* know about him?" she countered, coughing or clearing her throat, I couldn't tell which. It wasn't the best of all possible retorts, and this weak response worried me almost more than the cough.

"I know about his cult. And I know about Juanita, and how she cut off his hand. I know how it's in that book," I bluffed, fairly certain I was okay to do so. What other hand could it be lurking inside the back cover of the tome in my dreams? It was too tempting a conjecture to let me accept that it could be some other, less significant, odd body part.

She didn't argue with me, but she didn't exactly pat me on the head and give me a gold star, either. "Good for you."

"Lu, you don't sound good."

"I feel good," she croaked.

"No, you don't." She was definitely not herself, and I could have sworn by the tone of her voice that she was lying down.

I heard a rustling that suggested she'd shifted the phone. "I'm only tired. I'm allowed to be tired, once in a while. Everything's fine, and I just need some rest."

"Don't you lie to me." I wasn't sure why, but it was terribly important that Lulu be all right. My unease was mounting in my chest until it threatened to cut off my air. I found something awful and ominous in her lack of fortitude, and there was a number rolling through my head that I didn't like. Eleven days. All the logic, reason, and sanity in the world couldn't kick that thought loose and shoo it away.

"Lulu, don't lie to me. Are you getting sick?"

"No, I'm not. I said I'm only tired. Now are you ready to come on home? Come on, they're having a funeral for that girl Malachi killed. It's tomorrow morning; you should go."

"We weren't friends," I said, a little too fast to be as casual as I wanted to say it. It was true, we weren't friends, but it sounded bad when I put it out loud like that. She was dead, and I knew her. The gravitational force of a southern funeral dictated that I attend, but there were few things I'd rather do less. I could safely bet that the media would be there, and it was an even safer bet that some damned fool with a microphone would want a word with me. I'd had about enough of that the first time Malachi struck, and I didn't want to go through it again.

"She's dead, and you were there when it happened." She stopped blessedly short of pushing on to the most obvious point—that it was practically my fault she'd died. "Come on home anyhow."

"I'm not done yet."

"Get done. Then get home."

I wandered to the window, phone in hand, and pushed the curtains aside. "I will. But I'm not sure when. Not yet anyhow." Outside, it was growing dark. I hadn't realized I'd slept so long. In the parking lot, a streetlamp kicked on with a sputter and a hiss.

"Come back tonight. It's not so far. You can make it by nine or ten if you hurry, and I know the way you drive. You always hurry."

"Not tonight." I held the curtain back and watched the fluorescent beams bounce off my car's fresh wax job. Just then, something moved.

I started.

"Tonight!" Lulu insisted. "Get back here tonight! They've not caught Malachi yet, girl. Don't you be hanging there, waiting like a sitting duck for him to come after you."

"No one's sitting around here duck-style, Lu," I insisted, but I barely heard her admonition. I was almost certain there was someone lurking behind my car. I'd only seen him for an instant, but that moment was enough to reveal a tallish woman or a shortish man in a long, dark-colored coat. A head and hunkered neck rose barely above my trunk. He or she (he, I suspected) was checking my license plate.

"I've gotta go," I said, letting the phone fall from the side of my face and dropping it into the receiver. I let the curtain slip back into place and twisted the dead bolt.

Inside my overnight bag I kept a marble-handled knife with a blade too long to be legal in most states. It wasn't a utility knife like the serrated folding blade I'd taken with me to Pine Breeze, but it looked mighty intimidating all the same and it was weighted more nicely for holding. An old friend gave it to me as a birthday present, and I took it with me nearly everywhere, so I guess I did have a lucky charm of sorts, before Brian handed me the gris-gris.

I always kept the thing razor sharp and shiny, and when I was feeling like a more nervous soul, I kept it on my belt. I unfastened the latch to my pants and slid the holster onto the black leather belt I wore mostly for decoration, then buckled myself tight again. I unsnapped the sheath's guard and let the knife ride free, ready to be whipped into action if such was called for.

I ducked low beneath the window and lifted the curtain enough to peek back out at the lot. The shady form was nowhere in sight, but, then again, I didn't think it cared to be. Maintaining my crouched position, I reached for the lock and, as quietly as possible, I released it. I grasped the handle and pulled it down slowly, waiting for the click.

With a yank and a shove, I opened the door, still nearly on my knees.

Nothing.

No one jumped inside, no one reached for my throat.

Nothing.

I craned my head around the corner. No one. I stood, knife now in hand, hand discreetly hidden halfway behind my back. I braced my feet apart and let the doorway frame me, wide open and vulnerable . . . sort of. The knife's handle was warming under my fingers. I opened and closed my knuckles around it, clenching for the best grip.

"Hello?" My breath was steady, though my pulse came hard. "Whoever you are, get the hell away from my car."

No one answered.

I might have gone on, following up the order with a threat or two, but just then a large black sedan turned into the parking lot. It crept over the yellow speed bumps that hazarded the asphalt, signaled with a flashing left blinker, and pulled into the empty space next to the Death Nugget. I held a hand up to shield my eyes from its blazing headlights. I'd almost decided to retreat to the comfort of my room when the lights switched off and the back right door opened.

Eliza Dufresne emerged, short and crooked, from the shiny black vehicle. Harry offered me a shy half wave from the driver's seat, but he cut the engine and remained where he was.

"Girl," Tatie addressed me. "Girl, I want to talk to you."

"Go on." I made a show of sheathing the long blade at my left side. Her eyes widened a touch, but she didn't ask about it.

"I want you to come on back to the house with me."

"Do you, now?" I smirked and leaned against the frame, neither in welcome nor in refusal. "When'd you get bit by the hospitality bug?"

"Girl, I think it'd be a good idea if you did. I don't think you're safe here. Come on back to the big house with us."

She couldn't be serious. "Thanks, but no thanks. I'll take my chances here."

I do believe Tatie wanted to stomp her little feet in rage, but she bit it back. "Girl," she said it as a growl this time, "you come on back with me now. I can let you have one of the big old guest rooms. There's plenty of space for you."

"As I said, ma'am, thank you, but no. I'm already settled in here, and I'm not of a mind to leave."

"Dammit, girl, you come on!"

"No." I liked this game. This was fun.

"And why not? I'm offering you family privileges, an' here you are being an ingrate."

I couldn't hold my smile back any longer. "At least I'm not trying to milk you for your money like the rest of them mixed-breed illegitimates who want family privileges. Thank you kindly, Tatie, but I'm staying here."

Her wrinkly arms folded together, pulling a cable-knit sweater more tightly around her shoulders. "How come?"

"How come?" I repeated after her, still laughing on the inside with disbelief at the absurdity of it all. To be tactful, or not to be tactful? I went with the latter. "Because I don't trust you. No offense intended."

She nodded as if we'd reached some minor understanding, and it was good. "None taken. But since we're speaking plain, tell me why not."

"Because so far as I've heard, they've not yet caught Malachi. And I think you mean to hand me over to him if you can." I didn't really know if they'd caught him or not, but I figured she'd contradict me if I was mistaken.

"Well, that's not right. I'm not about to hand you over to him."

So he *was* still out there and Lulu had been right. Chattanooga considers Macon nearby enough to be a source of local news, so it wasn't surprising that she'd heard. "Well, *I* don't know that. Hell," I added, "for all I know he just followed you and he's planning to come for me once you're gone."

"That's not the case," she insisted.

"I'm afraid I don't believe you, Tatie. I'd love to be friends, what with us being family and all, but I don't believe you're as interested in that prospect as I am. If you want me at your place tonight, it's not because you've suddenly found your manners. You tell me why you really want me there, and I might think about it a little harder."

She shifted, tapping her feet and twirling her fingers in the sweater. She was getting cold. I was too, for that matter. If she didn't make her point before long, I was going to have to choose between inviting her inside and shutting the door in her face.

"You can't stay here tonight, girl. You and I know it's not safe."

"You're stalling. Besides, you and I know how little you care about my safety."

Her shoulders slacked and she quit bothering the buttons on the sweater. "If you must know . . ." she began, but then stopped.

"Oh, but I must," I prompted.

"Lord. It *is* Malachi, but not what you think. I swear, that boy's lost his religion now."

I laughed outright—practically in her face, which must have made her mad enough to boil. "Only just now? Christ, lady—what do you think he's been up to all this time? He's been as mad as a hatter most of his life, and you're only just now deciding it's so?"

"Never to me!" she shouted, raising one gnarled fist. "*Never* to me! He's never put a hand against me, and I don't know what made him now, but the boy's lost his senses this time, and it just frightens me all to death. I can't stay in that house now, not all alone."

"What about Harry?"

"He's not so old as me, but he's an old man still and my nephew's a young one with murdering on his mind. I tell you, child, I'm just so frightened it sends my heart trouble."

Curiosity got the better of me. Even though I knew I might not get the truth, I couldn't keep myself from asking, "What did he do? Did he attack you?"

"He tried to choke me! He held his hands against my throat and would've killed me if Harry hadn't hit him with the poker from the fireplace."

"It seems to me like you and Harry are doing just fine without me. You ought to give Harry more credit. In a pinch, it sounds like he's got your back."

"But what if Malachi comes back?"

"Harry can whack him with the poker again," I suggested. "Last time it worked so well that you're not dead yet."

I think she wanted to say "please," but the word refused to pass her lips. Instead she launched on with her begging, disguised as commanding. "Girl, come on down to the house with me, won't you? I want someone else in the house, and there isn't anyone else who can come. You can pick whichever room you want, and Harry can make us supper."

"Now, Tatie, that doesn't make a bit of sense and you know it. The one thing in life Malachi wants is to see me dead, but you want to invite me in to keep him away? You're a daft old woman, and I'm not going to hear this anymore." I made like I was going to shut the door, pretty sure by now that she wasn't going to let me.

"Eden," she choked out my name in two soft syllables. "Come with me, won't you?"

"Lady, I'm no one's bodyguard."

Down at my feet something glistened. I kicked at it with the toe of my shoe. It rolled off the sidewalk and down over the curb, away to the gutter. Three or four more of the gleaming, rolling things were scattered about near my door. Some kind of beads. Harmless enough, but they hadn't been there when I'd come back from eating. They could have belonged to anyone, of course. No reason for me to be alarmed. They were only beads. Black and red, scattered across the walkway.

"Eden, what do I have to do to get you to come with me?"

What was it about those beads? An old jingle ran circles in my head, or perhaps it was a whispering hint from one of the ghosts—I couldn't be sure. *Red and black, friend of Jack. Red and yellow, kill a fellow.* True of snakes, at least, but I couldn't see it as a sign. To go with Tatie would only be to invite trouble, and I knew it.

"Eden?"

"Yes?" I stared back at her, pretending I'd not been distracted.

"Well? What do I have to do to get you to come?"

I looked down at the beads, and back at my hotel room. I listened hard, but heard no warnings or prohibitions from the grave. Something was up, but whatever it was, my ghostly guardians must have felt I could handle it. Besides, even without Eliza's fussing, I wouldn't have felt safe in that motel another night; and I'd be lying if I said I wasn't curious to know what she really wanted. I didn't believe for a moment that she was scared of Malachi, not any more than I was.

"I don't know." I sighed, knowing I ought to know better. "Do you have cable?"

"Cable television? No. No, I don't. The old TV barely picks up the locals."

No big surprise. "Then just say 'please.'"

"That's all it'd take?"

"That's all."

"All right then, please follow us home. And be sure you don't leave that knife here."

"Don't worry," I told her. "It stays with me."

II

She gave me a room on the second floor with a window that overlooked the front yard. The portal was flanked by immense, heavy draperies that hung down from cast-iron café rods and tied back with gold cords. I let them fall closed, sealing myself into the place with only the light from the bedside lamp.

The bed itself was tall, nearly waist-high against my torso, and covered with a light duvet warm enough for winter, but not so heavy that it'd cook the sleeper in summertime. My duffel bag was perched atop the overstuffed pillows leaning against the thick, darkly varnished headboard. The antique board rather uncannily resembled a huge wooden tombstone, carved with deep swirls and lilies; it lacked only an epitaph and the requisite dates to cross that fine line from tacky to the macabre. I wasn't sure I'd be able to sleep in it at all, but truth be known I didn't plan to sleep anyway. Not in this house, much less in that bed. Even if Malachi *were* safely in police custody, Tatie had many secrets, and I was willing to bet she kept them within arm's reach.

Specifically, I had a feeling she knew about that book with the stolen hand. Perhaps it was intuition, but it was possibly something more independently minded. Either way, I had little upon which to base my suspicions. I'd inferred from our previous conversation that she'd had more contact with Avery than one might have thought, and she was therefore only one degree removed from John Gray himself *if*, as I was by then fairly certain, Avery had joined him at his Florida coven. It wasn't much to go on, but it was better than nothing.

I'd been instructed to make myself comfortable and then return to the main dining hall for supper. I didn't think Harry would be able to top IHOP, but by then it had been a long time since I'd eaten and food sounded good.

Tatie Eliza was already ensconced at the head of the table when I arrived. An ice-filled glass of sweet tea and a white china place setting signified my seat at the other end. Harry had laid out more silverware than I was likely to use all day, but I knew roughly what fork went with what dish, so I wasn't too afraid of looking like a fool.

Harry pushed the swinging door to the kitchen aside with his thigh and brought forth salad and rolls. I reached for the outside fork and munched on the greens without speaking. Eliza did the same.

Since I was uncertain what would offend her and unwilling to make myself appear ignorant, I wondered privately where Harry ate and whether or not he'd care to join us. No doubt it was profoundly improper for the manservant to join the family, but when the family was reduced to one lonely old woman, what did propriety matter? She couldn't have been so dead set on formalities as all that; after all, she did have a colored girl sharing her table. Her parents would do barrel rolls in their coffins if they knew.

"Tell me," I eventually broached, determined not to eat in silence. "How did it happen—what Malachi did to make Harry take a poker to him?"

She chewed pensively at a wedge of tomato before answering. "He raised a hand to me. That boy raised his hand up against his own flesh and blood."

In the name of good manners, I refrained from pointing out that I was his own flesh and blood as well and he'd made a fine tradition of raising a hand to me for fifteen years. "How cowardly of him, to attack a woman of your . . . health."

"Yes. Cowardly."

"But why did he attack you?"

The kitchen door opened again and Harry carried in the main course of rice and grilled chicken. I set the salad fork across the remains of the greens and reached for the next piece of silver in line. Harry was either a fabulous cook or he knew one, for everything was fantastic. I'll never say he topped Lulu, but he gave her a run for her money.

"I hope he didn't hurt you," I said, taking a bite and allowing Eliza time to elaborate.

She shook her head. "No. He just made me mad. Got his hands up around my throat before Harry heard the commotion and came to help me."

I tipped my head toward the kitchen door. "Harry's quite a useful guy. You should give him a raise."

"Listen to you—talking money at the table. Not sure why I'm surprised; I know who raised you."

Rather than get us both riled by defending myself, I tried to drag the conversation back to the most obvious topic. She was playing nice, for *her,* anyway. She might let something slip if I played my own cards right. "That's neither here nor there. But what did you— I mean, what I meant to ask is, what *happened* to make Malachi come after you?"

She took another bite and her own sweet time replying. "He was asking after some book. He wanted some old book and he thought I had it, and I don't. I guess God was wrong on that one."

"God?"

"You know. He thinks it's God what tells him to pull those stunts he does. But if it were God, He wouldn't be wrong. So it's not Him."

"That's sound enough reasoning." God might not be his official copilot, but that didn't mean Malachi wasn't hearing voices. No one knew that better than I did. I went ahead and feigned ignorance. "What sort of book was he looking for? A Bible or something?"

"No, not—well, yes. Something like that. More like a journal." She jammed another mouthful of roll between her gums and started lying as she chewed. "I don't know, really. I don't know what he thinks I've got here." She swallowed and spoke more plainly. "But he's wrong. He could turn the place upside down for all I care, and he wouldn't find a thing like what he was hoping for. I told him so, too, but he didn't listen."

When supper was through, we folded our napkins and left them on our plates. I followed her into the "sitting room"—a cozier version of the parlor—where she asked if I cared for a drink.

This time I declined, but she pressed the issue so I admitted that despite our previous imbibing of spirits, hard liquor was not my first choice of beverages.

"What do you take, then?"

"Not much of anything," I admitted, "except the occasional glass of wine."

Her eyes perked. "Red or white?"

"Red, if you have it."

She clapped her hands together and actually smiled. "Honey, I've got a whole cellar full, though I don't think there's anything drinkable up here, since I don't ever take much myself. I hear it's good for your heart, but at my age there's only so much care you can be bothered to take, and I'd rather have the gin. Let's go down to the cellar and see what we can find. Harry!" she hollered, and he materialized at her side. "Go on, get us a light. We're going downstairs."

"But, ma'am, I—"

"You'd rather we go down there in the dark? Is that it?"

"No, ma'am. Of course not. I'll be back in a moment."

Harry's obvious reluctance was clue enough that Eliza might have more than sharing spirits on her mind. "You really don't have to go to all this trouble just for my nightcap. It's getting late, I should turn in anyway. Don't make him do that."

"Balderdash. It's nothing. We have a wonderful collection downstairs, and no one ever drinks a drop of it."

Harry returned with two long black flashlights that could have been siblings to the one in my trunk. Eliza and I each accepted one and tested the buttons.

Harry behaved obediently, but he was clearly displeased. "Would you care for me to accompany you?"

"We won't be down there long," Eliza said offhandedly, or at least trying to sound like it.

"Then perhaps I'll join you."

She paused, but decided against arguing. "Suit yourself."

He tagged behind as we prematurely clicked the flashlights on and started down the hall. Eliza took the opportunity to give me a running commentary on the history and particulars of the ancestral family home.

"This house was built by my grandfather, Frank Wilcox, in 1804. He made his money on cotton and indigo, and he retired here with his family. My mother was his only daughter, and when she and my father married, my father joined her here. I was born in this house, and Lord willing and the creek don't rise, I'll die here too.

"During the War Between the States, it was all nearly burned except that my father was a Freemason, and the Yankee general spared the place. He said he couldn't burn a brother's house, which was dandy except that it wasn't outside his morals to burn a brother's barn and steal his horses. But the house survived, and us with it. We always do. Except now, I guess. Once I'm gone, and Malachi's gone . . . well, we're the end of this line."

For a moment she stooped, and it seemed that the light was too heavy for her old hands. Harry reached out, offering to take it, but she wouldn't let him. She straightened and pointed the light down the lamplit corridor. Her voice regained its vigor. "Well, I'm not gone yet, and neither's he. We're not done yet."

Along the hall we all three trod quietly on the long runner that graced the wooden floors with Oriental themes. Our footsteps made barely a dull patter and they did not echo behind us. I was acutely aware of the quiet immensity of the house, and I felt very small beneath the weight of all the years and bricks. This was my family home too, but I did not imagine I would ever feel welcome. I was subject to Eliza's displeasure, and she was the very incarnation of the house's spirit. So long as she lived, and possibly longer, it would not be happy to have me.

The hall turned and made a dead-end at a door, the Oriental rug stopping just short of the crack at the bottom. Eliza reached into a pocket on her sweater and pulled out a set of keys on a big brass ring. The keys clanked and clattered together as she held them up one by one, comparing them to the hole beneath the doorknob and trying to recall which one fit.

"Really," I said uncertainly, "I appreciate your effort, but this is too much trouble. Please, don't worry about it."

"Nonsense." She tried a long black one that looked more like the key to a gate than a door. It wiggled and scraped, but did not turn. She put it aside and reached for another. "Wine's made for drinking, and it's just collecting dust down there. I'd like to bring up a few bottles anyway, and now's as good a time as any. You got something better to do? No, I didn't think so. I already told you we don't have cable. Here we go. This is the right one, I'm nearly sure of it."

Indeed, the mechanism within the slot creaked and clicked and the door slid back in halting inches. Harry leaned against it and forced it to open completely. He shined his light down the stairs and over the shelves down below as if he were checking for something, sweeping the light for unpleasantness.

"Oh, hell, Harry, there's nothing down there but maybe a rat or two." Eliza stepped past him onto the first stair, then turned to me and lifted her shoulders in an explanatory half shrug. "You do what you can about the rats, but in a place this big you never get them all. As long as I don't see them upstairs, it doesn't cost me any sleep to know they're here."

"Nor should it," I murmured, following her sloping back as it shuffled fearlessly down into the cellar.

Harry brought up the rear, taking care to prop the door open behind us. I liked him better and better all the time. He came down after us, fretting his hands together as if he feared some great calamity.

"Some of this wine is over a hundred years old, I imagine," Eliza continued her narration. "Since my father died, it's just sat here. He was the one who bought it and stashed it here. Every now and again someone will give me another one for some reason, and I just drop them all down here. Sometimes I used to bring them out for holidays and the like, when I had more family around, but mostly the bottles just stay here and turn themselves to vinegar. It's such a shame, it is. I'm glad you mentioned wanting some, I really am. It gives me an excuse to bring some of it up, even if that does mean we've got to go down here for it first."

At the bottom of the stairs, the floor was flat stone and mortar, and the air was at least ten degrees cooler than the warmish upper floors. Four or five rows of wooden racks extended deeper than our flashlights, each shelf lined with black and green bottles gleaming dimly beneath a furry layer of mold and dust.

I rubbed at my nose, trying to shake away a sneeze that was working its way through my sinuses. I held it back, but the uncomfortable trace of a tickle in its wake left my head congested and achy.

Eliza was taking her time, wiping at labels with the back of her hand and crunching her eyelids together, trying to read in the semi-darkness. "Damn it all," she cursed, wiping at her eyes. "I need my glasses. Harry, would you go grab them for me? They're on the nightstand by my bed."

"Ma'am . . . I'd rather not leave you down here—" He glanced at me, hesitating to add "alone." I honestly couldn't tell which one of us he didn't trust—me, or the hundred-year-old biddy squinting at the wine bottles. Either fear would be fair, so I didn't take any offense to it.

"Harry, you get on out of here," she ordered mildly. "I just need my reading glasses. It won't take you a minute. Or do I have to go up all those stairs again and get them myself?"

He groaned a sigh and turned to scale the stairs. "No, ma'am. I'll be back shortly."

A rectangle of light blossomed above when he opened the door, then shrank to a sliver as he let it fall behind him. He was careful not to let it close all the way; I watched him wedge something between the door and the frame to keep it braced.

"I'll only be a moment," he called. Neither of us answered, so he left, his hasty footsteps evaporating above us.

"Silly man," Eliza muttered, fondling a particularly old-looking bottle. "Look at this, would you? It was fermented before I was born."

But I was looking into the recesses of the cellar, aiming my light down the rows and seeking the back wall but not finding it. How deep did this place go? Did it run the entire length of the house, or even farther? I looked up above and saw only the bare ceiling supports. No electrical fixtures. Probably no electricity. Something scuttled along one of the rafters over my head. I saw a slim tail whip back and forth, then vanish with a pitter of claws on wood.

"Eww," I complained.

"Don't pay them any attention. I told you, they stay here and don't bother me if I don't bother them. Hey, girl. Come and take a look at this. I wonder if it's any good. Do you know anything about wine? It all gets better with age, doesn't it? Unless it goes to vinegar. Isn't that right? Would it taste good after all these years?"

"No, I don't . . . I don't know anything formal. All I know is what I like." Another rat scooted along a parallel beam. Then a third. I thought it strange that they were running towards us and past us.

Tatie's assurances aside, I didn't like it. As Eliza continued to demand my attention, my suspicion grew.

"Would you just come here a second? Look at it. I'm telling you, this is older than I am. Don't you even want to take a look?"

I didn't move, I only shined my light in her direction, aiming at her midsection so I could see her clearly without blinding her. "How can you tell?"

"What do you mean, how can I tell? The date's right here beneath the name of the vineyard!" She poked the filthy label with one agitated, bony finger.

"Then why'd you send Harry up to get your glasses?"

She froze, her grip tightening on the bottle.

Something was definitely going on. I figured when I came that the pretense was likely false, but now I was absolutely certain she was up to no good. I backed slowly towards the stairs. "Why did you really send Harry away? You wanted me alone down here—what for?"

She hesitated, nearly fumbling with the bottle before she found her brashness again. "You've got a screw loose, girl. I can read the date because it's printed real big. Here, come and see it. Come and look for yourself, if you want to."

"No. I don't think I will." The back of my leg bumped against the bottom stair. Still keeping her in my sights, I began to slowly ascend. "I think I'm going to go get my things and leave."

"What? Why? What's spooked you so bad? This is ridiculous."

She was stalling me, but I was letting her. What if she was right? What if I was making a mountain of a molehill? "I shouldn't have come here. This was a bad idea."

"How so?"

"Because I think that you're—"

Right then the door opened quickly, flooding the stairs with light. A slim figure cut the brightness for a fraction of a moment before the door slammed closed behind him, but it was long enough for me to see the danger. I jumped away from the stairs as Malachi crashed down them, falling the last of the way and nearly flattening Eliza in the process.

She pressed her back against one of the shelves and let out a cry of anger, but not surprise. "You were supposed to be down here already!"

He didn't have a gun this time, but he brandished a long black nightstick. Not for a second did he turn it to his grand-aunt, and she did not shirk away from him. We all knew he was here for me.

About that time Harry returned, probably having heard the commotion of Malachi's bumbling entrance. But the door was locked behind us, and Eliza was holding the keys in her sweater pocket. The manservant began to beat against the door, abandoning protocol and calling both our names. I doubted he'd hear if I called back, and there was nothing he could do anyway, so I saved my energy for the lunatic in front of me.

I beamed my light directly into his eyes and he flinched, but lunged forward. I ducked away, swinging the sturdy flashlight and connecting it with his head, but only barely. He caught my hand and I twisted it free, kicking against him with the toe of my weighty boots as he brought his weapon down from above.

The nightstick missed my head but caught my shoulder, and it hurt like hell. He raised it up again and came in close. I braced myself against the side of the stairs and shoved him away with both of my feet, though I had to drop my light to do it. Something inside it cracked. The bulb went out as it rolled around on the floor.

Now Eliza's electric torch was the only illumination, and she was wielding it too erratically to do anyone any good. Malachi could hardly tell where I was, and I could hardly see where he was coming from.

I pulled my knife out of the holster on my belt, fully intending to use it if I had to. My legs are strong and they ended in a pair of army surplus boots, so I let them serve as my main defense; no woman in her right mind puts her arms up against a man's upper-body strength, even when the man in question is a skinny twerp. That skinny twerp was holding a heavy weapon, and I wanted that weapon to stay far, far away from me. So long as I kept moving, my defense worked. My mad brother was forced to stay at a distance far enough away from me that he couldn't land a good blow.

Unable to see me clearly or to get past my kicking, he started swinging wildly, slamming the stick into anything that was holding still. This meant he mostly missed me and caught the rack at my side, which was fine with me, but not so fine for the old wood rack. After he'd given it several solid blows it broke with a splintering crack, followed by a series of resounding clanks. Bottles of wine were dropping down to the stones and wandering heavily about in awkward ovals. Malachi stepped on one and staggered, falling into the pitch darkness somewhere between the shelves, then retreating to regroup.

Harry was still beating on the door, harder and more furiously than before. The knocking stopped, then became a hard lunge. I wished him nothing but luck, but that door was old and stout, and I didn't think he'd be able to break it.

Eliza turned her flashlight on me. I saw only her silhouette behind the beam, but I could make a good guess about where she was. If I could reach her, I could possibly use her as a hostage and bargaining chip.

Good idea, but it came too late. Malachi had pulled himself together. His shoes scraped on the gritty stones, then he launched himself boldly into the air. It didn't do him much good. He landed chest-down on my knife. It sideswiped his collarbone and sank through muscle, splattering my face and neck with blood.

Malachi howled and leaped back. If I hadn't held the knife so firmly as it unsheathed itself from his body, he would have yanked it away with him. Once it was free, blood flowed warm and slick down my hands. I'd hurt him badly, but I wasn't sure if it was enough to keep him from coming back for more.

"Malachi?" Eliza was showing the first signs of concern, or possibly impatience. "Malachi, did she hurt you?"

"Yesh . . ." he said it with a slur that promised shock was on the way. "But I'mall . . . right. I'mallright." He shuffled to his feet.

Eliza permitted herself a moment's glance at him, removing the light from me to reveal her nephew clutching his dark-soaked shoulder. He raised one hand to shield his eyes. "Not at me, Tatie," he pleaded, and she remembered herself. But by the time she'd sent the beam in search of me once more, I'd fled to a safer spot behind the stairs.

"Where'd she go?" Between his blood loss and his incompetence, Malachi was growing frightened.

Eliza tried to comfort him with overconfidence. "She's not gone far, boy. Here. Take this—" She held out the light. He wavered forward and took it, but he held it like he wasn't sure what it was for. "And go *find* her," his aunt demanded.

He nodded and swung the light around, but he overestimated how far I'd gone. In truth, I wasn't more than two or three steps from my original position, but I was shielded by the jagged underside of the stairwell. My dark clothes and huddled body blended well into the debris I found there—empty barrels and crates stuffed with insulating sawdust.

Malachi wobbled deeper into the cellar—farther away from me—while Eliza began to feel her way along the wall in search of the stairs. I no longer heard Harry's pounding up above and I prayed he hadn't given up. If he couldn't open the door from outside, that meant I'd have to get the keys from Eliza and do it before Malachi came after me. In the near-complete dark, I didn't think I could wrangle the keys away and successfully find the right one before he returned.

"Where're you?" Malachi did his best to sound commanding, but I hoped he didn't seriously expect me to answer. He swiped the shelves and racks and cases with the flashlight to no avail. I crept sideways, trusting the military castoffs to give me quiet traction. They worked wonderfully, for neither of my adversaries heard me. I peeked between the boxes and watched Malachi's back retreat as he worked himself farther away.

Eliza had found the staircase. I heard her slipper tap against the bottom step and feel its careful way upwards. There was a rail bolted fast along the wall. She grabbed it and held, and the old bolts grinded against their rust-filled holes but stayed. Slowly she began to find her way up as Malachi found his way towards the back of the large room.

He must have been losing blood fast, for he was faltering more by the minute, slipping in puddles of his own making. He was bound to collapse before long; perhaps I could simply wait him out.

Of course, if I let Eliza reach the top of the stairs, she would open the door and then . . . and then maybe I could throw her back in and lock them both within. If Harry confronted me I could probably take him too—or at least get away from him if I had to.

I hoped it wouldn't come to that. I liked him, and I'd hate to have to kick his ass.

Eliza was two or three steps up now. Her featherlight feet trod uncertainly onward, gripping the rail with all her weight. It groaned beneath her but it held. Anyone heavier and I'm sure it would have given way, but she was shriveled and dry, and probably fell short of a hundred pounds with rocks in her pockets.

I tried to estimate how many stairs there were altogether. I put my hands above my head and felt the underside of the incline. Each step was about a foot deep and high, and we'd come down at least twenty feet. I needed to wait until I heard her reach for her keys. Any sooner and she'd not have time to open the door before I got to her; any later, and she'd have time to lock me in with Malachi.

Then again, perhaps that wasn't the worst-case scenario. Surely she wouldn't leave him down here to bleed to death . . . would she? Well, I wouldn't have sworn to it, but I suspected she wouldn't do it on purpose. She'd have to come down there *sometime* and check on him.

Malachi was maybe fifteen yards away now, moseying aimlessly between the ceiling-tall cases. He was running low on blood and adrenaline, and it was making him slow. I saw him stagger and it made me bold. I emerged from beneath the stairs and trusted the darkness to keep me from Eliza's eyes. She was too intent on finding her way up to look down for me, and I was nearly beside her feet when we all heard Harry return.

His voice was muffled through the door, but it carried well enough. "If there's anyone right behind this door, you need to stand back."

"Harry? What are you doing up there?" Eliza yelled in her harshest tone.

185

"Get away from the door, ma'am," he said.

"I'm not at the door yet," she replied with petulance, and that was all the permission he needed to open fire.

Two consecutive shotgun blasts rocked the door, the second one sending it flying nearly off its hinges. I almost whooped with joy before I remembered that Harry wasn't necessarily on my side.

Eliza toppled back down to the bottom, which wouldn't have been far for me, but was hard on a woman her age. She collapsed against an empty barrel and sat there grasping at her throat, trying to recover her breath.

With the door open, light spilled across the stairs and my position was revealed. Although he was drenched with a blackish stain from his shoulder to his knees, Malachi found his second wind and began to run straight at me.

I clambered over to the stairs, tripping over the wheezing Eliza in the process, and ran head-on into Harry in his descent. Our eyes met over the shotgun which was pressed between us, and for a moment I was frightened enough to think that Eliza had armed reinforcements. Then he saw Malachi below us and shifted the gun to aim both barrels at him.

Malachi made a hasty reassessment of the situation and ran the other way, into the darkness at the back of the cellar. Harry pushed past me and prepared to make a chase, but then hesitated beside Eliza.

"He's down here somewhere," I said as much to myself as to him. "And he's hurt—I don't think he'll get far."

"He'll get farther than you might think," Harry answered. "He knows the back way."

As if to illustrate his point, somewhere in the shelves a creaking of hinges sang out and the halo of light that had indicated Malachi's position went cold. A door of some sort fell shut with a bang that rivaled the shotgun reports, and then all was quiet except for the soft, panting breaths that heaved from Eliza's chest.

"Where's he gone?" I asked, still standing stupidly, midway up the stairs. "How'd he get out of here?"

"There are ways in and out of this labyrinth of a house that even I don't know. Once upon a time it was a stop on the Underground Railroad, though it pains Miss Eliza here to know it. But trust me—in this house, there's *always* a back way."

That was the first time I'd ever heard him say her name, and there was venom in it, even with the polite title before it. He turned to me and his voice retreated to an apology. "I never saved her from Malachi. She came into my quarters and announced he'd been here, and that he'd tried to hurt her but she'd gotten away. That's when she told me she wanted to go get you."

"Why did you let her lie to me?"

"She thought you wouldn't believe her unless she said I'd helped. I'm sorry about all this. If I'd known what she was really up to I would have never let her go to you. I mean, it doesn't catch me altogether unaware, but I didn't think she'd let it go so far as this."

Eliza coughed and opened her angry little eyes. "I'm not dead, you know. Or deaf."

"Too bad for us," I said, descending the stairs and stopping at her feet. "Did you really think that would work?"

"You fell for it just fine."

"I most certainly did not. I was curious enough to play along. There's a difference."

She laughed, sharp and staccato. "You don't want me to believe you'd have come here if you thought Malachi was waiting for you?"

"Sure I would have. I half expected it. And in case you hadn't noticed, Malachi has never been the most effective assassin. I hope you don't expect me to believe you thought he could kill me? You even knew I had a knife. Was that only to give me a false sense of security, or are you as fed up with your crazy nephew as I am?"

"He'll get you yet." She scowled like a television villain, but she didn't answer further. There was little else for her to say.

"No, I don't think he will, Tatie. But I got *him* pretty good. He's going to need a doctor, and soon. He can't go on bleeding like that and expect to live very long. Harry, perhaps we should call the police, or maybe even an ambulance, since I'm feeling charitable. If they do another helicopter run over these grounds—"

"Not yet." He came forward and lifted the gun from its position at his side, raising it until it was nearly in Eliza's face. "We're not finished here."

We all held still and stared back and forth at one another. Harry's arm was steady and the shotgun did not waver.

"Harry?" I couldn't believe it. "Harry, what are you doing?"

Eliza didn't believe it either. "Get that thing away from me. What do you think you're doing?" But something about the way she asked it hinted she already knew the answer. She was not as shocked as she let on, that much was apparent.

"Come on, you two," I broached, trying to sound as light as possible. "What's all this about? Harry, I know you don't need that." He didn't need it unless he was going to whack her upside the head with it, anyway. I hadn't seen him reload, and he'd used both shots on the door. I had to assume that Harry was well aware of this, but the odds were better than good that Eliza didn't know enough about guns to know he couldn't shoot her if he tried.

He ignored me, and kept his eyes and the business end of the barrels on the old woman. "Where's the book, Eliza? What did you do with it?" he asked calmly, coolly.

She tried not to flinch. No, she didn't know he was out of ammo. The way her eyes fixated on the end of the barrel said as much. "There is no book."

"You know that's not true as well as I do. As well as Eden does. Eden, why don't you refresh her memory. She's quite old. Perhaps she needs a good jogging."

I couldn't believe what I was hearing, except that I knew I was watching him menace her with an empty shotgun. I took this to mean that he didn't really intend to hurt her any, though the temptation to jog Eliza's memory with the back of my hand was almost more than I could resist. But no. I restrained myself. "It's filled with ritual magic," I offered a verbal jogging instead. "There's a dried-out hand mounted inside the back cover. It used to belong to a guy named John Gray. Your brother was a big fan of his."

"I don't know where your stupid book is. I'm a God-fearing Christian, and I don't have your crazy magic book."

"God-fearing Christian—like hell." Harry said it before I had a chance to. He ran a hand through his hair and let out a grunt of frustration. "I've spent eight years combing this place—every inch of it— and I've found enough to know that you're no God-fearing Christian, but I've not yet found that book. And you *have* to have it. There's nowhere else it could be except somewhere in your possession."

"Eight years," Eliza spat. "Yes, eight years that I've trusted you. And this is what I get for it? You would betray me over some stupid book! A stupid book that doesn't even exist," she added, sticking to her story.

"People are dying because of that stupid book!" he shouted back at her, bringing the gun within an inch of her nose. "People are dying and you know it! Don't talk to me about betrayal—and for God's sake, don't talk to *her* about it." He pointed at me and I waved, wiggling my fingers.

"You don't know what you're talking about. And you don't know half of what you think you know." She hauled herself to her feet and stared defiantly up at him, ignoring the enormous shotgun. "Get out of my house," she directed, lifting one gnarled finger and gesturing up at the stairs. "You too—" She bobbed her head at me. "Both of you, get out. I'm through with the both of you."

But Harry was done following orders, and he was the one with the weapon. "No. I don't think we will."

"Actually," I interjected as unobtrusively as I could, "I'd rather like to be on my way, if that's okay with you. She says she's finished

with me, and that's fine. I'd like to be finished with her as well." I
didn't blow his cover by following my request with, "And besides,
that's not loaded anymore," because, hey—he was frightening Eliza,
and that was all right by me.

"Don't go," he said, but it rang more like a request than a command. The gun was still trained on Eliza, but his eyes met mine
sideways. "Stay and help me look for that book. You may not know
it, but your life depends on us finding it."

I stood still and thought about it for a second. He knew how to
get a girl's attention, that's for sure. "What do you mean?" I asked,
not wanting the answer but probably needing it, regardless.

He waved the gun towards the top of the stairs. "Bring her up
and let's get her secured. I'll explain while we start hunting."

Eliza's eyes were a dare, but I met them anyway. "You heard the
man," I said. "Let's go. Get those little legs moving."

"And if I refuse? I don't think he'll shoot me, and I don't think
you'll hit me, either."

"If you refuse, then you'll look mighty strange slung over my
shoulder like a gunnysack. And don't think for a second that I won't
do it. For that matter, don't be so sure I wouldn't hit you. If I were
you, that's not a bet I'd take."

She sniffed, then stuck her nose in the air and started up the
stairs once more.

Harry was waiting for us at the top.

III

Harry affixed Eliza to one of the dining room chairs with an exten-
sion cord. I watched from the other side of the room, still uncertain
what I should make of this shift in alliances. He did not speak until he had her wrists and ankles tied, and then it was to offer her one
last chance to be helpful.

"Tell us where the book is."

"No. I don't know what you're talking about."

He wadded up one of the cloth napkins and held it up to the side of her face. "Is that your final word on the subject?"

"Yes."

"Fine." He stuffed the napkin into her mouth and strapped one of the curtain ties around her jaw to hold it there. "Then you'll at least be out of the way."

"Harry, I don't know . . . we've got to let her go sometime, and she's going to run straight to the police. I don't need that, Harry. I really don't."

"She isn't going to the police," he assured me. "She can't tell them anything about us without her harboring Malachi coming into it. And she *has* been harboring him, you can bet on that. Furthermore, you can bet she'll continue to do so once we're gone. He's gone off to lick his wounds, but he'll come back. He's got nowhere else to go."

"But he's hurt. Maybe badly. Didn't you see him when you came downstairs? He's bleeding like a stuck pig."

"I'm sure his *God* will take care of him," Harry said with a sneer. "Malachi always comes back. Surely you know that better than anyone. You're probably right, and he probably didn't go far, but that doesn't mean they'll catch him—even if we called the cops ourselves, right this second. They hunted around this place all today and all yesterday and couldn't turn him up. He'll hide as long as he has to, and then he'll be back for more trouble."

"He does seem to have a knack for it," I admitted, shuffling my feet and trying to ignore Eliza's evil, beady eyes.

"He's getting some kind of help," Harry admitted, "but I'm pretty sure it's not God who's feeding him information."

"Then who? Or what?"

He put his hands on his hips and stared up and down around the dining room. "Couldn't say. But right now, believe it or not, Malachi is not the worst of our worries. We've got to find that book."

"Yeah—about that book—you said my life depends on us finding it. I don't suppose you'd mind elaborating on that point, would you?"

Harry quit scanning the walls and floor and met my eyes with what appeared to be genuine concern. "It's very hard to explain. And I don't want to frighten you."

"Oh, good grief. Try me. You'd be surprised what I understand, and besides, when you mentioned my life was on the line you officially entitled me to an explanation."

"Yes, you do deserve one," he agreed, but he wasn't ready to fill me in yet, so he didn't. "I've checked the servants' rooms quite thoroughly, and I'm almost certain she hasn't hidden anything in there. She'd be more likely to keep it closer to herself anyway, and the places that I haven't been able to search have been those she spends the most time in. Let's start in her bedroom, shall we?" He finally paused to acknowledge my narrowed eyes and firmly set lips, and then sighed. "And I promise, I'll tell you everything I can while we look. But the most important thing of all is that we find it, and quickly."

I agreed to his terms and followed him up a flight of stairs into a hall. We passed several bedrooms that were furnished, but clearly unoccupied; and at the end of the row was Eliza's room. It looked much like I would have pictured it, had I bothered to give the subject any thought. Her bed was a giant four-poster canopy, and the vanity and dressers were made to match it. Old-style oil lamps were mounted on the walls, casting a flickering warmth across the maroon-and-ivory furnishings. Across the room on the far wall there was a window, but I couldn't imagine that it had been opened any time recently. The room was stuffy, smelling of medicine, dust, and dried flowers.

"This is where she lives?"

"Yes," Harry said. "And the book must be here someplace."

But I heard the doubt in his voice. "You aren't certain?"

He rubbed at his forehead, then at his eyes. He was not old, not in comparison to Eliza, but he was older than the folks who'd raised me. I might have guessed he was a well-preserved sixty, and those decades showed, but he was not at all fragile. He'd handled himself as well as a younger man when Malachi had posed a threat. I wondered who he'd been and what he'd done before coming into Eliza's service.

I would have asked him directly, but in the course of the explanation that finally followed, he answered everything well enough.

"You're right. I'm not certain the book is here—or more accurately, I'm quite terrified that it's not. If it isn't, then I've come all this way and spent all this time for nothing. And it may have cost . . . a great deal."

"How so?"

Harry reached for a corner of the bedspread and gave it a yank. Once the covers were off, he began to root around between the mattresses. I took his cue and started opening drawers, sifting through cream-colored girdles and stockings.

"I'm not sure how to begin," he said.

I insisted on the cliché. "Try the beginning."

"Which one?" He threw up his hands. "Or whose? You already know of John Gray, it would seem, and that is the *very* beginning. Sort of. You know how he died?"

I shut one drawer and opened another. "I know he was hanged for witchcraft."

"Yes, that's brief, but it's correct. On September twenty-nine, 1840, four priests from St. Augustine's church went out under cover of darkness. They carried with them rope, pistols, and the Word of God. John Gray had been waging a war against the clergymen, testing his powers even to the point of killing two of them, though it would have been impossible to prove."

"Why?"

"Because he was using black magic. He'd first practiced on ordinary people—on people who'd angered or offended members of his community. But as he grew stronger he began to play games with the Church as well, sending his ghosts and his devils to haunt, to torment, and even to commit murder. It could not be tolerated, but it could not be stopped without putting a permanent end to Gray himself; so four brave men took on the danger and went after him. Two went into the camp and dragged him out, and the two others were waiting with a coach to spirit them away. They took him to the town square and hanged him before his followers had a chance to retrieve him.

"But then came another beginning. Gray's wife cut off his hand before he was buried, intending to raise him from the dead."

"Juanita," I said.

"Yes, Juanita. She was a Spanish colonial woman who had fled her family to marry him a few years before. She took his hand and then they buried him, leaving his body to await the promised resurrection. When the priests learned of this, they dug him up and burned the rest of his remains, just to be on the safe side.

"I think they can hardly be blamed for their caution, for even once Gray was gone, his cult lived on. His followers became a pestilence to the community and were routinely run off or hung. Thankfully, none of them were so strong as their first martyr had been. At least, not at the time."

He retrieved a bundle of papers from between the mattresses and paused, hoping he'd found something of import. But upon a quick examination, he dropped them onto the nightstand and continued his quest and his story. "Now, Eden, tell me—what do you know of Avery Dufresne?"

Ah, here was the connection. "I know he was Eliza's half brother, and that he was considerably older than she is. He had a child who was a great-grandparent of mine—or some such. The relationships confuse me. I'm not sure how it all fits together."

"The relationships *are* convoluted, that much is true. Avery married Mae Jones and they had at least one legitimate child together, but Avery packed up his wife and her two sisters and headed south with the whole crew, and they were never seen or heard from again. However, the middle sister, Willa, had given birth to a child some years before that was believed to have been Avery's as well. This child remained with relatives when Avery and his harem took off. That was James, who was your mother and aunt's grandfather. But Avery also had another child by another woman, back before he met your grandmother. From that came a line of cousins I suppose you are unaware of."

"You're right—I thought we were pretty much it. You seem to know an awful lot about my family. Did you know who my father was?"

"Yes, but it was hardly my business to tell you, now was it? And it has become something of my job to know. That's where another beginning comes in—and don't worry, it works its way back around to Avery. I'm not going as far off topic as you think."

"Okay."

About that time Harry gave up on the bed and turned to the wardrobe against the far wall. In it were rows of old-fashioned dresses and skirts, jackets and robes. He pushed them aside and pulled them out a few at a time, examining them and then tossing them on the undone remains of the bed.

My luck wasn't any better. I'd made my way through all the dresser drawers and had decided to try her bathroom. "Go on," I said as I opened the narrow door. "I'm going to check in here, but I can still hear you."

"Very good. Yes, it was another beginning. And this thread of the story I think will be mostly news to you. After Gray was dead and Juanita was raving out in the swamps about bringing him back, the threats began. At first they were vague and without any substance, but gradually they became more specific. Gray's cult was determined to avenge him, and they began by bringing about the deaths of the four men who'd collaborated in his death. One by one they died of agonizing, lingering illnesses, and after each death Juanita would leave behind some token claiming responsibility. The day each man died, a bloody swatch of cloth cut in the shape of a man would appear nailed to the door of the room where he passed on. No one ever saw anyone deliver this calling card, and no one ever heard the nails being pounded in. But everyone knew who was responsible.

"Then, one after another *other* members of the clergy began to die as well. The group was nearly down to nothing, and those who remained either fled or lived in terror. Just when they thought St. Augustine's church might close forever, a smallpox epidemic seized the city, and although many perfectly ordinary, decent people died, so also did Juanita Gray. Thus, the mysterious deaths ended. When the plague had passed, it seemed as though all had returned to normal.

"Then, roughly around the time your grandfather Avery fled Tennessee, things began again. By then the church had been restocked with a fresh supply of God's servants—in fact, most of them had nothing at all to do with Gray's killing, if they even knew of it at all. But within a month, three died; and a month later, two more. It was then that we received the warning."

"Uh-huh," I said from the bathroom, and the indistinct syllables echoed off the grayish ceramic tiles. The room was clean, but the fixtures likely hadn't been updated since they'd been put in. Although it seemed in no way large enough to hold the missing book, the medicine cabinet appealed to my nosiness and I opened it, swinging the mirror aside.

Harry prattled on from the master suite. "One morning a priest found a letter tacked to the confessional. It said, in short, that John Gray would never die, and that there remained one hundred and fifty years to retrieve him. His followers had found a new leader, and together they were conserving and concentrating their powers. And when Gray returns and his vengeance becomes complete, neither the church nor anyone within it will remain standing."

"Heavy threat," I called, reaching inside the cabinet. Mostly it was filled with the ordinary sorts of things an old lady would have—prescription medications, a pair of nail clippers, some eye drops, and some cotton swabs—but also there were two slim glass bottles stopped with corks.

"It was no idle threat, either. The church tried to keep an eye on the doings of Gray's cult, but it was a difficult task. Not only did they live out in the woods but they were a tight-knit group with a tendency to kill anyone who asked too many questions about them. The information we *do* have has taken one hundred and fifty years to accumulate, and it has cost more than a few lives."

"So they—this cult of John Gray's, I mean—it's still up and running? There are still people who are trying to bring him back to life? I thought his body was burned. What are they planning to raise, a cloud of ashes?" I held one of the glass bottles up to the light. The label was a piece of notebook paper that had been affixed with Scotch tape. "Half of this at a time," it read. Sure enough, the bottle was about half-empty.

"Yes, something like that. This is why it's taken them so long to get their act together, and this is where the threat to you comes in." In the next room, Harry quit digging through Eliza's things and came to stand in the doorway. "Tell me," he said quietly. "Your aunt—the one who raised you. How is she doing?"

I set the odd little bottle on the edge of the sink and turned to face him. "What do you mean, how's she doing? She's fine."

"Are you sure?" His hands were twisting at one of Eliza's slippers.

"Of course I'm sure. What are you getting at?"

He put his eyes and the shoe down on the floor. "This cult, or these people in it—they believe that to have children is to dilute their power. The more children, or the more descendents such as grandchildren, or even great-grandchildren, the less life energy is available to them."

"*And?*"

"And, those cousins of yours I mentioned?"

"*Yes?*" I gripped the porcelain sink behind me and sat against it. I did not like where this seemed to be going.

"They're . . . they . . . their line was much like yours—it was not a large branch of the family. But all of them, beginning with the oldest and working down to the youngest—the farthest from Avery, that is . . . all the blood relations. They're all dead."

"You're lying." My head was growing light. "There's some mistake. You don't know I was related to those people. You can't possibly know that."

"Eden, we've been tracing your genealogy since before you were born." Harry could see from my expression that it would take more than words to convince me, so he muttered, "Hang on," and shuffled out of the room.

My mind was racing so hard I barely noticed Harry leave. When he returned, he silently handed me a scrapbook. I took it grudgingly and began flipping through it, only to find pages and pages of obituaries. By the time I reached the last two entries—a little girl, Cora, whose forlorn pose in her grade school picture could have doubled for one of mine; and my own grandmother—my eyes were teary enough that I could barely read. But still I protested. "These people all died of random diseases. There's nothing here to prove there's any connection between them."

"The cut-out cloth men came in the mail. There is no mistake."

"There *is* a mistake. Nothing is wrong with Lulu, and nothing's wrong with *me*."

Harry held out his hands, palms out and fingers up, trying to calm me or keep me back. "Listen to me, Eden. Someone has tapped into Avery's energy line and is drawing his power. He was the only one who was ever strong enough to attempt the magic needed to resurrect John Gray, and whoever this is will certainly need every ounce of it he can get. You and your aunt Louise and her younger sister are the last remaining descendents. Only a few days remain before the gateway closes and they lose Gray forever. *That's* why we have to find that book. Without the book, they have nothing—not the power to harm us nor the power to resurrect him. They can't raise Gray, and they can't hurt any of you."

I pivoted and slammed the cabinet closed, then planted my hands on either side of the sink. The mirror splintered, leaving the image a fragmented, bug's-eye view, but I could still see Harry's tragic, haggard reflection in the mirror. His gray eyes were blood-shot and tired, but his jaw was set. He ran a hand through his salt-and-pepper hair.

"Don't you understand, Eden? Before I came to Eliza, I was Father Harold Frazier. If they bring Gray back, we're all done for. You, your aunt, and me too. I'm a member of the order they've targeted. They're coming for us all."

I looked down and turned the faucet handle. The pipes squealed and hissed, then finally provided a tepid stream that grew hot as I held my hands under it. "You're off your rocker. You ought to be out there with Malachi. The two of you could talk about God all the livelong day. I'm sure you'd have a fabulous time."

"Eden, you can't ignore this. It's too close now."

Steam was rising from the sink, and the water was hot enough to scald my hands, but I held them under the nozzle anyway. The broken mirror went damp and muted with white fog just the way I wanted it, and after a minute or two I couldn't see Harry's pleading eyes boring into the back of my head. "It isn't true," I said, reaching for the soap in order to validate my use of the sink. "It just isn't true."

"I understand that your aunt has been in ill health of late."

I wheeled around and hurled the bar of soap at his face. It landed against his forehead with a wet smack before bouncing out into the bedroom and sliding to a halt against the wall. "You shut your mouth."

"Call her, then," he insisted, wiping bubbles out of his eyebrow.

"Maybe I will!" I stomped past him towards the hallway in search of a telephone, but I'd barely left the room when Harry called out.

"Eliza doesn't have long distance. Use my cell phone." He withdrew a small black phone from his trouser pocket and held it out to me. "Take it. Call."

I snatched it away and began to dial, my fingers slipping on the rubberized buttons. I should've rinsed better.

No one was answering at home.

My fingers started shaking. Small slivers of white were stuck beneath my nails, rendering anything I touched a bit soapy. I messed up Dave's cell phone number twice, then managed to dial it correctly. I wrapped both hands around the receiver and pressed it against my aching head.

"Dave?"

"Eden, where have you been? I've been trying to call you for hours!"

"I'm—I'm sorry. Something came up and I left the hotel, but I'm all right," I couldn't help but notice Dave's voice was half an octave higher than it ought to have been. "What's the matter?" I asked, even though I surely wouldn't like the answer. My chest, throat, and ears began to congeal into one solid lump.

"Lu dropped tonight when we were out to eat. She's in the hospital. They don't know what's wrong with her. We were just eating at that Italian place, and she ordered a glass of wine, and I went to the restroom, and when I came back the waiter was trying to bring her around. She just fell over in the booth, and I don't know what's wrong with her. No one will tell me anything—"

Dave rambled some repetitive combination of the same phrases while I sank against the wall, clutching the slippery phone. Slowly I dropped to my haunches and put my head on my knees while I listened. I concentrated on a worn spot on the carpet. I focused on it *hard*.

"Dave, what was it? They must have told you something." I was talking into my own lap, refusing to look at Harry, who had come to lean against the doorframe beside me.

"They don't know. They're saying it was just fatigue, or exhaustion, or whatever, and they're running some tests and keeping her overnight. That's just their expensive way of saying they don't know."

"Did she come around at all?"

"For a few minutes. Long enough to argue with the doctors that she was fine, then say something completely nonsensical and pass out again."

I stared down at my feet on either side of the worn spot, rubbing and shuffling on the carpet, playing idly with the edge of the rug. "What'd she say?" I whispered.

"Oh, it started out okay—she wanted me to call you. But it was what she wanted me to say that was all-out confusing. She said to tell you to find the man and save yourself. But that doesn't make any sense at all, does it? Does it?" In the background, all the static noise of a hospital came through. I heard a muffled name gargle across an intercom, and the rolling wheels of gurneys. It made my uncle sound all the more alone.

Bitter, hot tears welled up in my eyes. My nose filled up and made my voice all soggy. "I've got to go."

"Eden?"

"Dave, I've got to go. I'm going to take care of it."

"What are you talking about? Do you know something? Dammit, what was she talking about? What do you mean, you're going to take care of it? What are you going to do down there? And why don't you come home, like she asked you to in the first place?"

"I've got to go. But I'm going to take care of it. You tell her to hang on, and I'm going to go get him. You tell her when she comes home from the hospital, I'm going to be waiting for her at the door."

I pressed the "end" button. It disconnected us with an electronic blip, and the lights behind the numbers went dim. Harry reached out as if he meant to touch me in comfort, but I drew away, holding his phone out to him and lifting my head.

"Okay. You win. How do we find this goddamned book?"

IV

I spent the next hours sick at heart, tearing through Eliza's house in a frantic search. Together, Harry and I turned every room inside out—we emptied cabinets, we broke plates, we dumped silverware onto the floor. We dragged out all the liquor bottles and tapped around in the wet bar, seeking any small hollow place. We went inch by inch along every wall, feeling each crack with the tips of our fingers, hoping to stumble upon some hidden spring or button. We lifted aside all the rugs and pressed the toes of our shoes into the floorboards, seeking some loose part that might come away.

We found nothing.

In the end, we returned to Eliza's bedroom and scoured it once more before dropping ourselves to rest on the floor against her bed. By then it was nearing dawn. Both of us were exhausted and despairing, knowing that for once in her century-long life, Eliza had been telling the truth. She didn't have the book.

"Then where could it possibly be?" I asked, fully aware that Harry didn't have any better idea than I did.

"Anywhere. Nowhere." He was fidgeting with the papers he'd removed from between her mattresses. I could now see that they were letters, in envelopes. They made me think of the bundle I'd pulled from the files at Pine Breeze.

"What are those? Besides the obvious, I mean."

"These?" He held them up. "Nothing. They're all empty. Just empty, old stationery. Some of them are postmarked as far back as fifty years ago. Look at this one—July twelve, 1956."

I took one from him and examined it for myself. Yes, it was empty, but I had a feeling it wasn't "nothing." The one I held was made from the same cheap paper as the one I'd found in Leslie's file. The handwriting on the outside was even the same. And so was the postmark: Highlands Hammock, Fla.

"Harry, what's in Highlands Hammock?"

"Where?" He looked at the postmark. "In Florida? I don't know."

"Is it anywhere near St. Augustine?"

"No, not really. If it's where I think it is, it's considerably farther south, towards the Everglades. Now that you mention it, I think it might be a state preserve of some kind. Why do you ask?"

I told him about Pine Breeze, and about what I'd found during my excursions. "Come to think of it, the letters are out in my car," I added. "You wanna see them?"

"I'll take your word for it."

Something about the handwriting intrigued me. I held the envelope up to the light and watched the paper glow. Something about it. Something . . . I'd seen it somewhere else. I climbed to my feet and started towards the bathroom.

"Where are you . . . ? Oh," Harry said, seeing my destination.

"No, I'm not going to use it, I want to check something." I opened the medicine cabinet again and reached for the bottle that'd caught my attention earlier. The brown glass containers were where I'd left them, so I retrieved them again and held the labels up next to the envelopes.

A perfect match.

"Hey, Harry, check this out." I returned to the bedroom with the bottle in one hand and the envelope in the other. "It's the same on both of these."

"So?"

"So whoever prescribed the dosage on *this* stuff also addressed *this* envelope."

It took a few seconds for the truth to dawn on him. "But that envelope was sealed and mailed in 1956, and I know for a fact that that bottle arrived in the mail last week." Then he shook his head. "No, but that doesn't necessarily mean anything. Eliza's over a hundred years old—it's reasonable to think she has friends of a comparable age. Especially if they're in Florida."

"Possibly," I conceded. "I guess there are a lot of old people in Florida." But I couldn't help but think my deduction was more significant than coincidence.

"There's no return name on the envelope—is there any signature on the bottle?" Harry asked.

"Uh-uh." I unstopped the cork and took a whiff of the greenish liquid that sloshed inside.

Damp grass. Slimy bark and moss. A memory receptor fired in the back of my brain, but not hard enough for me to tell what the scent reminded me of. I could only recognize that it was familiar; I couldn't have said what it was or where it came from—except that it had apparently come from Florida, maybe someplace near the Everglades. It certainly smelled like a swamp in a bottle, that much was sure.

"What is this stuff? You said you know she got it last week; does she get it often?"

"About twice a month she gets a package, addressed just like these letters. When I asked her about it, she said it was an herbal remedy for her rheumatism that she orders from a doctor down there."

"This is no doctor's script." The letters were heavy and precise, though not refined. Whoever had printed them was working slowly, and laboriously. Perhaps he or she couldn't read very well. I was willing to bet it was a man, for the letters had a masculine quality to their square-edged straightness.

"No, it isn't. But it's never done any good to argue with the woman, as you can well imagine." Harry sat on the edge of the bed and shuffled through the letters again, furrowing his brow into deep creases. "Do you really think this is important?"

"It might be. We could ask her."

"She won't tell us anything, not now that she's been tied up in a chair all night. You thought she was uncooperative *before* . . . I'll bet we ain't seen nothing yet."

I stared down at the bottle, swishing its contents around into a whirlpool. "You're probably right. But she's all we've got. This time, how about you let *me* do the asking?"

He shrugged and rose, reaching his hands behind his shoulders and cracking his back. "Be my guest. You can't possibly get any less out of her than I did."

Downstairs in the dining room, Eliza had fallen asleep. Her curly white head was tipped forward, her chin resting on her breastbone. Her chest expanded and contracted just enough to lift and lower her face, still blocked by the gag. I was merely inches away from feeling sorry for her until Harry removed her gag and she shot awake and started yelling.

"You scalawags—both of you dirty goddamned carpetbaggers— I'll see you both dead! I'll see you both gutted and stretched and dead on a rack before I'm gone, do you hear me? I'll kill you myself, with my own two hands! I'll—"

Harry popped the saliva-soaked rag back into her mouth and let her gnaw on it in muffled rage. "I told you," he said to me. "She's not going to be of any use. We may as well turn her loose and make a run for it."

"I'm not going to run away from a little old lady," I said, jaw set firm. "I'll smack some manners into one if I have to, but I'm not going to flee from one. It's undignified."

"What do you plan to do, then?" He said it with a hint of warning that implied, all threats aside, he would prefer that no actual manners-smacking took place.

I positioned myself so that Eliza could stare me down all she liked. I wanted her to look at me. I wanted her to remember how much she hated me, and my mother before me. There was a chance I could use that fury to my advantage.

"Eliza, who's your friend in Florida?"

She stopped squirming and gnashing her teeth against the rag. Her eyes shrank to tiny, mean slits, and she slowly shook her head back and forth.

"Okay," I said, "that'll work. I'll just ask yes-or-no questions and you can shake your head. That'll work fine."

At that, she threw her nose into the air and stared at the ceiling. I might have expected as much, but her refusal did not daunt me. I could get a knee-jerk reaction out of her, and that was something. It was more than "nothing."

I decided it was safe to act on my assumption that her correspondent was male. "Tell me, Tatie. Your friend in Florida. You've known him for a very long time, haven't you? We found some stuff in your room that tells us you've known him for fifty years, if you've known him a day."

Her eyes didn't release their death grip on the ceiling, but she didn't huff as though I'd said something stupid and wrong. Her hands had instantly gone into hard-knotted fists where they were strapped to the armrests, and it was not because she was tied inhumanely.

"Is he a family member?"

Nothing. Not even a twitch at the corner of an eye.

"This swamp water he's sending you, it's some kind of medicine?" She continued her steadfast policy of nonreaction, so I wiggled the cork loose and smelled at it again, squinting down the neck of the bottle. "I have a hard time believing that. And you take this regularly?"

"It's for her rheumatism," Harry reiterated without enthusiasm. Eliza pivoted her head just enough to glare over at him instead of the ceiling, then permitted herself a half nod.

"I don't buy that. Not for a second."

"This conversation can*not* go anywhere, Eden. She's not going to tell us anything." My coconspirator was growing tired of the games, or possibly just tired. Lord knew I was beat like an old rug. I would have given anything to lie down in the big bed upstairs they'd assigned me earlier, and go to sleep as I ought to have.

But there were bigger things at stake than circles under our eyes. "Eliza, what would you do if I threw this out? Flushed it down the toilet? Would you care?"

Her head jiggled ever so slightly, signifying the negative.

"Not at all?"

She did it again, more firmly. Harry was wrong. Whatever the vial contained, it was important enough to Eliza that she wanted me to think it was useless. If it had really been something ordinary, she would have left her eyes on the ceiling and kept her head stationary.

"All right, then, maybe I'll just dump it down the sink in the kitchen." I left her immediate vision and walked towards the door.

Eliza shrugged, and by all appearances was unconcerned. She didn't even try to see what I was doing. Either she knew I wasn't going to do it, or she knew she could easily get more. Or I supposed she might be bluffing. Perhaps it ran in the family. I hesitated. Or maybe Harry was right and the foul-smelling stuff was inconsequential. Hmmm. So many possibilities. There might be a way to tell.

I returned to Eliza and stood before her again. Her eyes were tilted skyward once more, and they did not come down to meet me. "Herbal stuff. Folk medicine, huh? Then I bet it doesn't have anything more interesting in it than saw palmetto and mud. Maybe I'll just take a drink of it myself."

That got her attention, but she didn't seem sure how to react. She was reluctant to give too much away; she refused to struggle against the bonds or try to call out, but she clearly had something on her mind. She brought her eyes off the ceiling and looked at me again.

"Well?" I held my breath and put the bottle to my lips.

"*Urngh*—" she grunted. "*Urngh urgh.*"

I stopped, and pulled the gag out of her mouth with two careful fingers. The rag was soaked with drool and I didn't want to touch it. "Yes?"

She didn't start screaming again, which was a relief; in fact, she didn't say anything at all.

"Well?" I waggled the bottle before her. She blinked, but kept quiet. I'm not sure what I wanted her to say, but whatever my expectations, she disappointed them. "All right then, bottoms up."

She gasped as I poured a mouthful of the stuff past my teeth.

I would have gasped too if it wouldn't have meant spewing the brew all over the place. Eliza's herbal medicine tasted as vile as it smelled. I swallowed with force so quick that it made my throat hurt—but the pain was more tolerable than the taste so I couldn't complain. The stuff burned going down, boiling all the way to my stomach where it simmered and stewed.

"What on earth is *in* this shit?" I asked, more as a rhetorical statement than a genuine question.

Despite the limited progress I'd made in Eliza's interrogation, Harry was not happy. "You shouldn't have done that. She probably doesn't know what's in it any more than I do, and it might be . . . bad for you."

"Oh, please," I wiped my tongue around my molars, trying to scrape away the fetid flavor. "Anything a woman her age regularly drinks can't possibly be that harmful. See? No ill effects. It's disgusting, but I'm sure it's harmless." For emphasis, I threw my head back and took another deep, hearty swallow—this time taking care to plug my nose to dull the assault on my taste buds. To my surprise, this second swill left the bottle close to empty. Hard to believe I'd ingested so much of it. Hard to believe anybody could.

Eliza finally broke her silence. Her voice was strange, soft, and unhappy. "You shouldn't drink that."

"Why? Is Harry right? Will it hurt me? I know you don't care, so be sure to try a different approach when you answer."

"No. I don't care if you *choke* on it. Look at yourself, guzzling down a sick old woman's medicine that you stole from her cabinet. I need that to live, and you don't need it at all. You're young and strong, and you are killing me with every drop you drink."

"That's not much of a deterrent. If anything that makes me want to hunt down every bit of it you've got in the house and run it down the sink." I wiped at my mouth with one of the napkins that had not been used to plug Eliza's mouth. I couldn't have downed another sip if they'd held a gun to my head. How she'd been drinking it in such quantities for years astounded me. "You've got a lot of faith in this stuff."

"It's strong medicine. I need it."

"But you can get more. Harry said you get a new shipment about twice a month."

"I don't know if I'll last until the next one comes." She was afraid. I saw it in her eyes, in her floppy jowls, and her quivering mouth. I looked down and saw there was enough "medicine" left for maybe another smallish dose. I looked up at Eliza.

In that moment, she and I understood each other for the first time. We both understood that I had leverage.

"You really do need this, don't you? Or at least you think you do."

"Yes, I do need it."

"Then tell me where you get it from, and I'll leave you the last bit."

"You already know. I get it from a friend in Florida."

"Who?"

"No one you know." As she made her curt replies, she was watching me intently. Even in her fear, she was curious. She was expecting something, but what? What could the stuff possibly do to me? My stomach was sloshing and queasy, and burned in a place or two where the liquid rolled against it, but I did not feel any different.

Not better, not . . . worse.

"Satisfy my curiosity." My voice came louder than I meant for it to. "Who lives in Highlands Hammock?"

She balked, or stalled. God. We *were* related. We used all the same tricks. I wondered if I was so transparent when I tried to manipulate people. Surely not, or I'd never have gotten anywhere in life. "No one lives there. It's just a swamp. It's a park. Nobody could live there, even if they wanted to."

"Maybe it's an alligator that sends you this medicine, then. Or a musk . . . rat." I wanted to be cocky, but it was coming out wrong. I almost giggled. "A muskrat. I don't even know what one looks like. They're something like possums, I bet, but they live where it's wet. I guess. I don't know. . . ." I let it trail off.

With one hand, I reached behind me and pulled out one of the dining room chairs. I meant to take it casually, but instead I dropped onto it like a stone. My legs were going numb, and after them my arms and hands.

"Eden? Eden?" I dimly saw Harry rush to my side and take the bottle from my hand, but I didn't feel his touch on my shoulder or the pressure of his fingers moving mine. I only saw Eliza's wicked blue eyes, though they were not regarding me with triumph. They were still sad, and a touch angry.

"What . . . is . . . this?" My tongue felt like Silly Putty. I couldn't maneuver it around my palate. I was weakening by the moment; but I desperately assured myself that I must not be dying, or else Eliza would be laughing some horrid laugh. My fright forced the words together faster when I repeated them a second time. "What is this?"

Surely I was right. I could not be dying, for in those frigid eyes I saw only resentment when she replied. "My magic."

And then the room went dark.

Completely black.

Eliza was gone, and Harry was gone, and though the long table and the chairs and the plates and silverware had never been cleared away, all of these things were gone.

My stomach had stopped hurting, though, and that was nice. I could breathe again, and that was nice too. I could still taste the concoction in the back of my mouth, clinging to my tonsils and refusing to slide down all the way, and that was not so nice. But I was no longer afraid.

Not at first.

Not until I began to see that although Harry and Eliza were no longer with me, I was not alone in this new darkness. Beside me, behind me, around me, and above me, there was movement. The fast kisses of displaced air tickled the hairs on my arms and on the back of my neck until they all stood at attention, waiting to be touched.

"Hello?"

A match was struck.

In that brief flare I saw the sketch outlines of a face, but the face drew back as the flame caught a wick. Now there was a candle, and there was some light, but I still could not see my company. The face and its owner had retreated to a corner away from the candle, which seemed to have been lit for my benefit.

Against the wall leaned a man, tall and broad of shoulder, with his arms crossed and his head down. His skin was not as dark as Dave's but not as light as Lulu's or mine. His hair stood out in a curly halo that cast just enough shadow to obscure his face in the half-light, half-dark where we met.

I waited for him to speak, but he did not. Instead, he pointed at the candle—no, he pointed at the bottle beside the candle. I stood, and was glad to note I once more had the use of my legs. I picked up the bottle and read the label.

Drink me.

"But I already did," I said to the man in the corner.

"Yes, that's why you're here, baby." Every word was rich and low, and charged with energy. Each word, falling coolly into place in a resonant line of displeasure, made me more uncertain and more afraid.

"Where am I?" I didn't know what else to ask.

He did not move. I did not even see his jaw line rise or fall when he replied. "Here with me. You're not supposed to be. You're not who I thought you were."

"You expected Eliza?"

He nodded. "You're not supposed to be here, but here you are. May as well make the most of it. You're on your way to find me anyway. You're on your way home to me."

"Who . . . who are you?"

He shifted his weight and uncrossed his arms, then passed along the wall like a shadow until he stood before me. In his left hand he held the bottle. I'd not seen him pick it up, but when I looked over my shoulder at the candle, the medicine was missing. He held it out to me, label forward so I could read its command again.

"But—but that's how I got into this mess," I argued weakly. "I don't want to drink anything else unless I can readily identify it."

His right hand was on my throat.

Just like that. So quickly I didn't have time to start, or scream, or fight. I tried to push against him but his body was like flesh-painted steel. Even with my feet against his pelvis and my nails digging into his forearm, he took no notice. I could not help but think that he was not really there at all, not in any way that I could fight him. I was in his world, one way or another, and at his mercy—if he had any.

His wrist shifted, providing me with the two options of letting him crush my windpipe or leaning my head back. I leaned back. He slipped two of his massive long fingers up around the joints of my jaw the way you force a cat to take a pill, and he poured the liquid down my gullet.

The last thing I remembered before waking was that it was not like the first brew. It was almost sweet and not half so bad, which didn't make it good, but I didn't gag on it, either.

"What are you doing to me with this stuff?" I gurgled as the room started to fold in upon itself.

I'm getting you ready for it. I'm making you strong.

8

In Search of Lost Time

I awakened alone in my own car, in the passenger side. Brilliant lights were shining down into my face, though it was clearly night-time. 9:03, according to the dashboard clock. I blinked a dozen times and wiped at my eyes, then opened them enough to realize that my car was parked beside a gas pump, and that I was beneath the neon and fluorescent advertisements of a large truck stop. The dense, sharp stink of gasoline crept up my nostrils and made me dizzier still than I already was.

Harry's face appeared at the driver's-side window. He juggled with a bag and my keys, opened the door, and climbed in beside me.

"Doughnut? Or chips? Soda? I thought you might be hungry when you woke up."

I stared stupidly at the bag, and at Harry. Food. Yum? "Give me a minute," I mumbled, adjusting the seat belt to wear a new and less painful groove into my shoulder. At least he'd thought to strap me in. "Where are . . . how long have . . . what . . . ?"

He removed a candy bar and set the brown paper bag with the extra food on the floor at my feet. After locating the drinkholders, he set his soft drink aside and put the key in the ignition. "Well, let's see. You've been asleep all day. I took your car because if I'd taken Eliza's she would have probably reported it stolen and then we'd really be screwed. I went back to your hotel, paid for another night so *I* could get some rest, then put you back in the car and started out about two hours ago."

"I slept through all that?"

"Yes, and all this while I've been toting you around like a sack of potatoes. Allow me to add that you're heavier than you look."

"Thanks. Lotsa muscle. Meat on my bones, or something." I squirmed in the seat and rolled my head and shoulders back and forth, trying to crack my neck. It didn't work. The stiffness remained, and so did my bewilderment. In the near distance I saw a stream of steady headlights that suggested an interstate. The presence of half a dozen other gas stations and fast-food stops supported that assessment, and furthermore hinted that we were at an exit. "Where are we?" I asked, hoping to learn something more specific about our location.

"Somewhere in south Georgia. I don't think we've hit Tifton, but we will soon."

"Why . . . why are we driving through Georgia?" I asked, though the obvious answer was "To get to Florida," because that's really the only reason anyone ever drives through south Georgia.

"Because it's rather hard to get to Florida without doing so," Harry confirmed. "Well, unless you're coming from the west. Or unless you want to go many hours out of your way. Or I suppose you could swim for it. But in the interest of efficiency, we're taking the direct route."

"Why are we . . . oh." Yes, the letter.

He cleared his throat and looked both ways before he pulled out towards the interstate and into the merging traffic. "I didn't have any better ideas, and you seemed pretty sure there was something important in Highlands Hammock. I thought it might be worth a chance to see. Actually, I thought I'd head for St. Augustine first. There's a whole library full of reference materials at the church. Perhaps we can find a good starting point there. It's not that far out of the way, anyway. Just a few hours."

"Oh."

I couldn't complain. His plan was as good as anything I could have come up with, maybe better. I didn't tell him about the man in the dark room, for fear he'd assume it was a dream or my imagination. Instead, I rode beside him in silence for a time, trying to get my thoughts to line up in a row. It half worked. I had a half plan hatching, and a half idea of what might be going on farther down south than I'd ever been before.

Never before? Could that be right? No.

Even as I turned the thought over I sensed it couldn't be. I was born and bred in the Tennessee mountains, on the banks of the river that runs through the rocks, but I knew somehow about green-gray mud and stubby cypress knees. I knew the rotting stench of an alligator's hole and the way the dull, curly moss hung down from the tree limbs to trail lazily in the water. I knew . . . I knew many things I shouldn't have. Things I didn't learn from the Discovery Channel or from Hollywood.

And strangest of all, I thought I knew who was waiting for me. I just didn't know what he wanted.

9

Unbearable Lightness

We arrived at St. Augustine around midnight, and the city was completely quiet.

I was tired of being asleep, and I was happy that we'd soon be out of the car. I don't like long trips unless I'm driving, and I wasn't feeling well enough to demand that Harry hand over the keys. My stomach lurched with every bump we took, and my eyeballs rocked about in my skull, settling on strange, small things, but refusing to focus on the road in front of us. It was better to let him act the chauffeur, especially considering that he knew where we were going and I didn't. And then I could continue to sleep off and on, with the seat leaned as far back as I could get it, and my head lolling every time I nodded off. It's a terrible way to doze, and it left me cranky and restless, itching to get free of the vehicle.

By the time we hit the city limits, I was desperate to stretch my legs, but Harry refused to pull over, even for a bathroom break. We were almost there, he insisted, but the church was down farther towards the old part of town near the fort. It was not terrifically far from the lion's bridge.

My groggy interest was ever-so-slightly piqued. Visions of shining armor and billowing flags filled my imagination. Knights and such. Or possibly pirates, and gold. "There's a fort? And lions on a bridge? Cool."

"The Castillo de San Marcos. The Spanish built it in the 1600s to protect the settlement from the British, and it worked, too. The town burned a few times, but the fort was only occupied by the English for about twenty years. Considering that Spain had it for a couple of centuries, it's a pretty good track record. The church is down the street a couple of blocks towards—towards the shrine. We'll be there in a minute."

"And there are . . . lions? I like lions." This sounded like the sort of place a Leo could make herself at home.

"Statues, dear. Not real lions."

"Oh." Disappointed but still determined to stay awake, I pressed on with the questions. "What shrine?"

He waggled his fingers towards the window and said something vague about Mary and milk. "There's a shrine, with a big metal cross. It marks the first place in the New World where Christian mass was ever held. But we're not going quite that far down the coast."

"Too bad. That sounds like it might be . . . uh, informative."

He tossed his shoulders in a quick shrug. "Yes, well, next time we're passing through I'll be sure and run you by the gift shop. You can get a mug, or a candle, and feel terrifically blessed, though unless you're Catholic, I'm not sure why you'd be interested."

As we drove through the narrow streets, still brick in places, I was strongly reminded of a Mardis Gras trip I took to the Vieux Carré in New Orleans, except that the trimmings were all Spanish instead of French and there were no drunken partyers stumbling along the sidewalks wearing plastic beads. Old stone storefronts with overhanging balconies graced the curbs, and the sense of antiquity was undeniable even in the dark.

This had been a colony for fifty years when the settlers at

Jamestown arrived a few states north, and that realization threw my sense of historical perspective askew. Despite what the New England snobs think, *this* small city is the oldest European civilization in America—or the oldest consistently occupied one, as I would later learn. Anglo-centrists be damned.

When we stopped at a streetlight, a man in full Spanish military silver was perched atop a big brown horse beside us. He shifted his weight in the saddle and the joints in his armor clanked and ground together. A sword hung by his side, down close to my window, almost tapping against the glass by my cheek. The horse snorted and swung its huge head my way, then whinnied and flipped its mane. Its rider wrapped the reins another loop around his wrist and nudged the animal with his heels until it loped into a trot.

Long after they'd disappeared down one of the side streets I could still hear the heavy, metallic jostling of the armor and the resounding clunks of the horse's shoes on the pavement. Harry did not act as though he had seen them, or at least he wasn't paying any attention.

Rather than jump to ghostly conclusions, I tried to be nonchalant. It might have been my hyperactive imagination, after all. Or—another thought crossed my mind. "Hey, Harry, do people run around in costume here, like in New Orleans or in those, um, historic places?" I asked. "Like they do at Jamestown," I added, since that was the only one I could think of off the top of my addled head.

My companion nodded. "Oh yes. All the time. Much of the old city is a state park. There are many living history exhibits—they do historical reenactments and the like. You can even take guided 'ghost' tours now. It's ridiculous."

"Oh," I sighed, relieved. Then it wasn't just me. I hoped.

Along a rooftop a woman in long, full skirts was pacing back and forth, holding a lantern. Even as far away as we were I saw the light casting warped shadows across her face, illuminating her in orange streaks and bursts. One of her hands was clenching the lantern's ring and the other was holding a shawl snug across her shoulders. Although she was moving back and forth, wearing a path on the roof like a tiger in a cage, her eyes never left the east.

"Harry?" I said, pointing a finger up at the lonely woman as if to ask about her.

He glanced out the window. "What? Oh, the roof. Yes, a lot of the older houses have long balconies like that. It's called a widow's walk. Sailor's wives would wait up there at night, watching for the ships to come in from the ocean. There's more than one tragic tale of husbands and lovers who never returned."

"I can imagine." But I preferred not to.

I wanted to ask if he'd seen the woman in the shawl or the armored conquistador, but I stopped myself short. He said it was normal to see people dressed up. He said this was a state park and it happened all the time, so that's what I was going to believe was going on. But after midnight? On deserted streets? There was no one to watch and appreciate the historicity of it all. Were these people paid, or were they fanatical reenactors? In Tennessee they call some of the Civil War buffs stitch counters because they insist so particularly upon attention to detail. Surely this was more of the same. Yes, surely.

I held my tongue. If Harry had seen them too, then all was well. If he had not, then I was seeing ghosts again, which was rarely an indication that good things were to follow.

Judging by the yellow of the opposing traffic lights, our red one was about to change. I peered back up at the balcony for one last look, but it was vacant. Either she'd gone inside or . . . or she'd simply gone. I quit straining against the seat belt and rested my head on the back of the seat. The light switched to green and Harry took his foot off the brake and pressed it against the gas. We were the only vehicle in sight, and it was strange for me to hear the reverberations of my own car's engine humming against the stone and stucco storefronts. Down at the end of the next street I saw something like a tower with a bell rearing up into the low skyline, and I thought with relief how close we were to the church. Yes, almost there.

Then my heart lurched up past my tongue.

"*Harry!* Oh my God, *stop!*"

He slammed both shoes down onto the brake and we left a short, smelly trail of black rubber on the pavement. But we did it—we stopped just before we hit her.

Yes, there she was.

The woman from the roof, standing in the middle of the road. I didn't see the lantern; she must have put it down. Both hands were now holding her shawl against her chest. "What? What?" Harry sputtered, knuckles white around the ridges of the steering wheel. "What was that for?"

Oh no. My previous relief evaporated. "You don't see her, then?"

"See *who?*" He was panting, legs still stretched taut against the floorboards, holding the brake and clutch down as far as they would go. "What are you talking about?"

I turned to him, waving my hand towards the road. "Right there—in the street! Oh, dear God—please tell me you can see her. Please don't tell me—"

She smacked her hands against my window and I cut myself off with a shriek.

"*Donde es*—?" I caught that much, but the two years of high school Spanish I slept through hadn't taught me enough to understand the rest.

The woman pounded her hands against the glass and shouted her question again.

"Drive, Harry! Get us out of here!" I begged, but I was nearly in his lap and he couldn't reach the gearshift. I covered my eyes and shook my head. "Lady, I can't help you. I'm so sorry—I can't help you."

"Who are you talking to? There's no one there, Eden," he

insisted, but his voice was not steady. Whether or not he believed me, he shoved me back into my seat and obediently pulled the car forward, leaving the specter behind. I peeked into my side mirror and saw nothing, but when I turned around to look out the back she was still there, eyes wild and forlorn, standing at the intersection and watching us leave.

"What . . . Eden, what was that, just now? Are you all right?"

"Then you didn't see her."

"See who?"

"It doesn't matter. You didn't see her."

Quickly, though gradually, more figures congealed into solid shapes and walked the streets beside us. Women and men, children, even dogs and the occasional rat. Horses and carts and soldiers and seamen. One by one they appeared. A few gave us second, confused glances; but most ignored us or seemed oblivious to our presence. They did not move when my car approached them, they merely parted for us to pass and formed again as though we'd never disturbed them.

I put my face down into my hands. "They're everywhere, Harry."

"Who? Who's everywhere? What are you talking about?"

Shaking my head, rubbing my eyes, I could not answer. "Please just get us to your church." A church, any church, sounded safe. Any refuge at all would suffice.

"We're here now. This is it. I'll park around back."

I didn't raise my eyes until the car had stopped, and then I saw no one but my traveling companion.

The night was too dark for me to see much of the building—as near as I could tell it was the same pale beige-gray stone as many of the city's older structures, but with huge, pointed-arch doors affixed to black hinges. Harry climbed the four or five stairs to the doors and dropped a heavy iron knocker against the wood. His summons thudded deep inside, and with its thick echo came footsteps.

After a series of clacks and booms, one of the giant doors

retreated and a small bald man adjusted his thick brown glasses, all the better to squint at us with. "Yes, can I . . . Harold? Is that you?"

"Why so surprised, Marcus? You knew I was on my way."

"No, I'm not surprised. I'm delighted, you old fool—it's only that we weren't expecting you so soon. You made this poor child ride all night then." He beamed us both a giant smile and swung the door back with a flourish. "And you must be Eden." Marcus took my hand and squeezed it, then shook it—also with a flourish. "It's so very nice to meet you, dear."

"Likewise." I tried to return his warmth but I was tired and flustered, and I still felt woozy from that concoction of Tatie's I'd been dumb enough to drink. It was all I could do to stand erect and feign lucidity, even though I'd felt so restless while I was inside the vehicle.

"Oh my," he fretted, "you don't look at all well. Can I make you some tea?"

Tea? Tea was good for what ails you, or so some dim recollection suggested. "Tea. Um, okay. Thank you. Yes, that would be nice."

"Or perhaps something to eat? Would you like something to eat?"

I shook my head. "No, no thank you."

He pressed on, unsatisfied that tea would be greeting enough. "Are you sure? Even something light? I could make you some toast, or open a can of soup? You look so pale. You really should have something. Come on—I'll make you something. Anything you want, and I won't take 'nothing' for an answer."

Harry rolled his eyes but allowed himself a grin. "Marcus, she's exhausted. She said she'd take some tea, and I think she's humoring you at that—now let her be."

"Well then, fine, if that's how it is. Would you prefer to lie down? We've made you up a room, and I hope you'll be comfortable. I've found some things that might be of interest to you both, but we can catch up in the morning if that would be better. There's little enough we can do tonight as it is."

But he'd gotten my interest up, so I reminded him I'd first take some tea before retiring.

"Oh good." He smiled even bigger. "I so much wanted to show you the birth record we found."

"Birth record?"

"Yes, for the little girl. But do come on back to the kitchen and I'll fill you in."

We followed the bouncy man past the sanctuary and down a hall until we reached a set of wooden double doors. "A few of us still re-side in the old monk's quarters," Marcus explained. "It's rather like a dormitory back here. I apologize for the state of disrepair, but four-hundred-year-old buildings don't care to be remodeled for plumbing and electricity. We're working on getting it brought up to date right now, but you'll need to be careful. There's scaffolding and tools everywhere you turn. I hate to see it done, really. I honestly feel like we're gutting the place, but the present pipes and electrics were installed in the 1930s, and they're rusting and rotting out the walls. It's the ocean air, I suppose. Wreaks havoc on them. Best thing we can do for the place now is to tear it all out and start fresh."

"This church is four hundred years old?" I asked, disliking the quiet clip of our feet down the empty corridor. At least I prayed it was empty. Merely knowing its age made me want to close my eyes and be led through it. I'd seen enough ghosts for one evening.

"What? Oh, well, not really. Well, part of it is. The original structure was built not long after the Castillo, but it burned a time or two and was put together again. But back here, where the hous-ing is—most of it is original. This was a mission, you see."

"It's bigger than it looks outside."

"Oh yes, yes it is. Quite large. We're backed up against the sea wall, sort of. You only see the very front from the street. Come this way—the kitchen is over here."

The kitchen was enormous. Its ceiling must have cleared twelve feet, and the interior appeared to have been cut from one single block of rough, light stone. A large, half-oval niche in the wall staked out a fireplace so expansive that it could have cooked my car, and the floors were flat stones held together with a brownish grout. Elderly appliances, not one of which could have digitally displayed the time, sat against the walls and on the counters. The most advanced piece of equipment I saw was an avocado green coffeemaker next to a chipped porcelain sink filled with empty white mugs.

In short, it looked *exactly* like it had been built four hundred years ago and was remodeled in the 1930s.

Marcus lit a burner on the gas stove and filled a teapot, setting it atop the flame. "Hold on a moment," he said, setting two mugs down before us on the table beside the old fireplace. "Let me go get the papers. It's very exciting. I think we might have a lead!"

With that, he skipped from the room, returning just in time to pull the kettle. While we waited for our tea to steep and fiddled with the sugar, Marcus removed the contents of a manila envelope and carefully laid them out before us.

"Here we are," he squeaked. "You're not going to believe this. We wouldn't have found it at all, except for the courthouse in Sebring has put all its records into a computer. We sent out feelers as far south as the Everglades, and a lucky thing we did. Look here." He withdrew a black-and-white photocopy and set it between me and Harry. "I think we found them, I really think we did."

The copy was not a very good or clear one, but it was sufficient. What we saw before us was a deed made out to Avery Dufresne. The exact location of the property was listed as a set of numbers I didn't understand.

Marcus was more than happy to clarify. "It's out there near Sebring, in the middle of the swamp where they've put the state park. Whoever is trying to raise John Gray may be there yet. This is just one acre in the middle of nowhere, on what's technically government land. But it's mostly dense cypress swamp that's virtually unnavigable. I'll bet they could safely hide several people there—maybe even a small coven."

I fiddled with the photocopy, staring down at the formal scrawl of Avery's name which had surely been put there by a bored public official. No, it was not Avery's hand. Down below, on the line marked for a signature, there was a large solid *X*.

"He couldn't read or write," I said, though to hear it aloud was strange.

Marcus shook his head. "He could read some, at least. And there's some evidence he may have learned to write later on. It's hard to do research on much of anything if you're illiterate, and from what we can tell, this man did *loads* of research."

"Research?" I pulled the second sheet of paper out from underneath the first. My hands were shaking and it was almost hard to read but I forced my fingers still and stared at the page. "What was he trying to research?"

"Eternal life," Marcus breathed. "Some seek it through God, others take a less reputable path. Avery was trying to re-create a potion that John Gray had told him about, but some of the ingredients he needed are hard to get your hands on this far from the Congo."

"The Congo?"

"Well, I don't know if it was the Congo, exactly, but you understand what I mean. To work the magic, he needed a wide assortment of plants and animal viscera. Since it was an African recipe, some of the ingredients were tough to come by, and Avery had to resort to some substitutions. I think he headed south seeking a comparable climate in hopes that the flora and fauna might be similar to what he required. If it weren't for the fact that Mae wouldn't go, I've often thought Avery might have found his way back to the Dark Continent."

"Not a bad theory," I admitted, scanning the second document. "But I can imagine that the recipe would have to be quite specific. What's this one? Is it the birth certificate you mentioned?"

Marcus hesitated. "Yes. I mean no. Something like that. That record is mostly interesting because it tells us that he still had at least his wife with him for a while after he came here. She was pregnant, and she had a difficult labor. Avery took her out of the swamp and to the nearest church a few miles away. The nuns cared for her, and this is a record of their visit. They paid for her medical care with three white chickens. This is the receipt, with a note of explanation."

"There was a child?" Harry took the paper from me and read it for himself. "I didn't know there was a child. Was it a boy or a girl?"

"It doesn't say." Marcus shrugged. "What does it matter?"

"What if that child was the beginning of the coven that's at work now? Hey, what if . . . well, what year was this—here it is. 1898. This child would be about Eliza's age, were he still alive. Do you think this guy might be Eliza's contact down here? It would certainly make sense, they would be what—cousins? Something like that."

"That's a reasonable thought," Marcus agreed.

I'd only barely heard them talking, and I didn't realize that Harry was asking the question of me. He repeated it, and I still didn't answer. "Eden, do you think this child might be Eliza's pen pal?"

I said, mostly to myself, "It was a girl."

Both men offered me blank, perplexed stares. "How on earth do you know that?" Harry asked, his eyes scanning the paper again. "It doesn't say that on here. It only says that the woman gave birth."

"It was a girl," I insisted quietly. "And they named her Miabella." They went quiet. "How do you know?"

"She was his pretty one. That's Italian, though, isn't it? I wonder where he heard it."

I stood and went to the teapot Marcus had set back on the cool burner, looking more to avoid them than to pour another cup. They let me stand without protest, but talked behind me in lower tones as if I'd left the room or I couldn't hear them.

"Harry, is she—I mean, is Eden—is she like the rest of them?"

"I think so. If she says it was a girl, we may as well believe her."

"But a name? I don't see how she . . . unless she's considerably stronger than the rest of them, I don't see how she could possibly know that. Even the other one, the girl on the other side of the family—the poor little thing who died . . ."

"I don't think it's just that she's stronger. I think it's more than that. I think . . . no, I'm not sure enough to say it."

"Say it anyway."

"If this girl, Miabella, is still there and in contact with Eliza, then maybe—"

Without turning around, I cut him off. I rallied every ounce of energy I had remaining and shaped it into my next words, trying to sound ordinary. Trying to sound rational and confident. Not altogether failing, but not succeeding as well as I would have liked, either.

"It's not her. Whoever it is that's been sending mysterious potions to my batty old aunt, it's not that baby. She's dead. She's been dead for years." I reached for the teapot, but when I extended my hands they were badly quivering, so I pulled them back and crossed them against my chest. I stayed there, facing the stove, probably looking somewhat stupid to the two men behind me.

"Eden, are you all right?" Harry asked it, and I heard a chair scoot away from the table.

"Yes," I lied. "I'm fine. Don't worry about me. I'm just, I'm just not feeling well. Still. I mean, from sleeping . . . from sleeping in the car. And my stomach was upset anyway when we started."

"Would you like to go lie down?" Marcus's voice.

Behind him I heard Harry whisper a sentence or two that contained the word "poisoned." Oh yes, the draught of sickly drink. Now that they mentioned it, I *had* felt strange ever since first I sipped it. Somehow I managed to disagree, though I didn't care enough to argue. Eliza's brew was no poison. It was something more . . . helpful. I hoped.

"Would you like to lie down?" Marcus asked again.

This time I nodded. "I would, yes. I think that would be good."

Miabella.

"Yes?" It was my own voice. Who was calling? And who was I to answer?

Miabella.

"Yes."

Harry joined in. "Eden?"

"Yes. Yes, I'm all right." But I wasn't, not really. My hands, crossed against my chest. I held them out before me to watch them shake, and they were not my own. They wavered before me more distant and hazy than any oasis. And they were covered with blood.

"Harry?" I said in barely a whisper. "Harry?"

He was beside me then, an arm around my shoulders.

My hands were not my own.

They were covered in blood.

I swung around, pressing my crimson-smeared fingers against Harry's chest, but the gore wouldn't wipe away. "Do you see it?" I demanded, holding my palms out for them to inspect. "Do you see? It's his, it's Malachi's. I can tell. It's so close to mine. I can smell it. Tatie's right, there *is* a smell to us. . . . I must have done it—or maybe, maybe I haven't done it yet. Don't you see?"

"See what?" Marcus was baffled and frightened, but he wanted to help. "Is there something wrong with your hands? Give them here."

"Yes, they're—" I looked down at them again, just to make sure. "They're all . . . they're all . . ." The blood remained, and it might have spelled my cousin's name, with such certainty did I know its origin. But how? And why?

Then I saw, in a long, neat line, heads bowed and hands folded together, a string of brown-robed monks file solemnly past the door behind Harry and Marcus. Each man held a strand of red and black beads with which to pray, and every hooded face was pointed toward the stone floor. I counted five, ten, twelve. The thirteenth monk paused in the doorway, lifting his face to stare directly at me. The red and black beads hung limply from his hand, wrapped securely around his knuckles.

You will not make them see. He said it in Spanish and I understood perfectly, though I could not have explained how. *They are not like us. They call you a witch, but we would have made you a saint for your gift. And it is a gift, though you don't think so now. Your hands are clean, child, for you died blameless in the eyes of God.* He turned away from me then, and rejoined his fellows in line.

When I looked at my hands once more, they *were* as clean as if I'd only just washed them, and even beneath my fingernails there was no trace of red. "I don't understand."

Harry and Marcus still hovered, Harry with his arm nearly supporting me and Marcus fluttering at my side, desperate to be assigned some useful action.

"I'm all right," I said, ducking woozily out of Harry's grasp and swatting at his arm. "Stop grabbing at me. I'm all right. But—but I need to go lie down, or just close my eyes for a while—there's too much, there's too many people here."

"Too many people?" Marcus stood astonished. "You haven't seen a soul except for—"

"Stop it. Don't say it like that." I put my hands over my face and then faced them both again. "You don't understand at all. You understand even less than I do, so I don't know what help you're going to be."

Harry summed it up with one word. "Ghosts?"

"Yes, ghosts. Ghosts, spirits, *souls* . . ." I emphasized the word for Marcus, who was very nearly cowering away from me. "What's the matter?" I asked him. "What is it? Surely you knew; you two seem to know just about everything. You knew that I see ghosts, didn't you?"

"Y-y-y-yes, but I didn't know you could see them . . . here. I mean, we have them here?"

"You're joking! In this city? Has no one ever lived here before, or died here either? You said it was centuries old, do you think there's no trace of that? Good Lord Almighty. They're everywhere."

Across the room a fire blared to life in the stove corner and a large pot appeared, tended by a man who held the iron lid with his hands wrapped in rags. He dropped a long wooden spoon down into the simmering brew and gave it a stir, eyeing me with a half smile. I smelled chicken stock, runny and pungent with curry. I wrinkled my nose.

Yes, it's very strong, he said in that impossibly lucid Spanish, *but the curry will keep them from tasting that the meat is not so fresh. Will you be staying with us tonight?*

"Yes, I'll stay the night. But only the night. In the morning we have to go."

Harry nodded. He and Marcus were both trying to see who I was talking to, but to no avail. "That was the plan all along. I promise, first thing we'll go and find this place, and these people. Then we'll head away in the morning."

Again he spoke softly to Marcus and again I heard the word "poison."

I'm getting you ready, the dream man had said. *I'm making you strong.* But what sort of strength was this, that now all the undead crowded me close, when before it was mostly the three sad women. I did not like this kind of strength, and I was not at all happy to have it. I was exhausted and angry, and I wanted only to close my eyes and leave them that way for a very long time.

I let Harry and Marcus lead me to the room where I would spend the remains of the night, and fell into bed without even washing my face. I lay staring at the ceiling, half gasping, half choking. I couldn't look anywhere without seeing *them*. Some of them were monks, and occasionally I would see a conquistador or an Indian, but they wandered the halls and the rooms as though they were yet alive. It was more than enough to keep me from sleeping.

All night long they passed my door, a strange cavalcade of brown hoods and copper-skinned locals. Sometimes there was prayer, and sometimes there were loud words, but more often I saw only the silent ones shambling past without a sound. They were so perfectly real at the edge of my vision that I could not say who was living and who was only an echo of the dead. Surely there could be no sleep with such company.

Besides, I was so worried about Lulu that it was making me even sicker to my stomach. I'd have an ulcer before this was all over, but I didn't dare call—I could only assume the news would not be good, but she was still hanging on. Of that much I had to keep faith.

There was no other option.

She could *not* die.

But to guarantee that, I'd have to find Gray's cultists, and quickly.

I must have dozed, though, for I did not hear the door open and the man come into my room. Just like the rest, when I rolled my head to see him, I could not tell if he was among the living or dead. He was dressed in a robe like the one Marcus wore, but his head was covered and his face concealed by shadow.

He ducked his head, bowing gently and folding his hands. "I understand you are not feeling well. Harold thought you might wish for something to aid your sleep." His voice was nearly a whisper, low and soft, and it invited confidence. It implied that he was alive, and that I was secure. Although I couldn't see him well, I got the impression that he must be a very old man beneath the cowl.

I didn't respond except with my stare, and he seemed embarrassed, or maybe he was only polite and reserved.

"I . . . I have a tonic here, if you'd like."

"Okay."

He fed it to me like I was a baby, propping me up with a pillow and spooning the drink into my mouth. I took it obediently, even willingly. I wanted nothing more than to sleep deeply enough to keep the ghosts away, and even though the tonic was bitter, I had the strangest feeling that it could only help.

By the time I'd taken the last spoon, I was already losing con-
sciousness. I wanted to thank the monk, but the words were thick
in my mouth.

He removed the extra pillow from behind my head and pulled
the covers up under my chin with a grandfatherly tuck. Then he
held his hands above me, in a blessing, I suppose, and murmured
something I didn't understand—a Latin prayer, I thought. But the
last words I heard were understandable enough that I suddenly remembered where I'd heard his voice before. But by then it was too
late to cry out.

He took my hand in his.

You're on your way back to me.

Oh yes, soon you'll be home, child. And you'll be mine once again.

10

Gone South

We arrived at Highlands Hammock State Park in early mid-afternoon after another six-hour drive. While the map showed that the area of the park was quite large, the official entrance was barely more than an outbuilding, a sign, and a small parking lot. Though there were several other cars, we didn't see any people aside from the woman in the ranger's station who gave us our pass. She suggested that we register to camp, as the park closed at sundown each day, but after a quick consultation, Harry and I declined the invitation. Some cursory scouting was in order before we stormed the place, and besides, neither of us had any burning desire to camp in the middle of a swamp unless it was absolutely necessary.

If Harry was right, the main road ran fairly close to where the land in question must be, out on the south side of the preserve. According to the maps from the rangers' station, one of the catwalks extended far enough down to possibly come near it as well. We decided to hike the trail like ordinary tourists first, and then return later for a closer, less legal look.

I wasn't happy with the delay, but Lu's life—and likely my own—depended upon our success, so we forced ourselves to proceed with caution. I stalked along the path behind my companion, who stared into the surrounding water as if it were tea and he might read the leaves that floated on the murky surface.

A two-by-four boardwalk on stilts disappeared back through the trees, and we climbed up on it to follow.

The narrow wooden path was raised above the water, but only by a few disconcerting inches. I could have dipped a toe into the scum without any trouble, but something about the smell of the place prohibited it. The air was heavy with the scent of rotting, soggy wood, and of other things decaying where the alligators had left them to soften and stink. Overhead the sky was almost blotted out by the interlacing branches of the tall cypress trees strung with fuzzy gray moss, and it was difficult to see deeper than twenty yards into the woods, so thickly did those black trees grow.

Just beneath the slime of the water, small and large things moved. Maybe snakes, maybe turtles. Maybe amphibians larger and more sinister. Across the top of the algae, mosquitoes and other light bugs zipped and buzzed.

The wet swamp world was alive with green, damp motion, and it was *hungry*.

Harry and I walked the path in silence until we'd gone more than a mile through the stifling, dank forest, each of us wishing we'd thought to bring a bottle of water. We were both sweating ourselves into dehydration by the time we reached the boardwalk's end. It simply stopped in a cul-de-sac turnabout, refusing to take us any deeper. We stood on the edge and shielded our eyes, smacking at bugs and hoping to see some sign of habitation.

There was none. The trail did not go far enough. We'd been quite miserably wasting our time.

"Let's go back," Harry proposed, as if we had some choice in the matter. "We could rent a canoe over near the rangers' station, and we could maybe use some wading boots too. And a couple of canteens.

And if we have time, we can try our luck along the road before it gets too dark."

"Okay," I agreed, since there was no other action to take. I was frustrated because I knew we had to be close, but there was no practical way for us to safely navigate the oily, chest-high water. If the snakes didn't get us, the bugs would take us apart like winged piranhas.

Off to my right, closer to the walkway than I would have preferred, a pair of round yellow eyes revealed a larger danger. The gleaming pair lifted out of the muck, followed by a long snout and a protruding set of nostrils. I saw nothing else of the alligator, but from the size of its head it must have been at least eight or nine feet long, though this was admittedly just a guess. The end of his nose wasn't two feet away from the platform, and the platform wasn't six inches above the water. I didn't have to be any good at math to work out the danger. Were alligators good climbers at all? Could they jump? This one didn't deign to answer my questions; instead, he sank away into the darkness from which he'd come.

"Yes, let's go back." I took the lead, stepping lively but quietly.

Harry had seen the gator too. "Supposedly if you move in a zigzag motion, you can outrun them. It has something to do with their center of gravity, I think."

"That's very reassuring, Harry. Thank you so much for that bizarre piece of information that might or might not save my life in the frightfully near future."

"Anytime."

Harry and I beat a fast retreat back towards the park's entrance, accompanied by the clomping of our shoes on the boards and the incessant whines of the stinging insects. When we reached our starting point once more, we took turns swilling tepid water from a stainless steel fountain. The great state of Florida didn't see fit to refrigerate the drinking fountain, but the water was wet and we were thirsty. I tried to ignore the yellowy flavor of sulfur and dirt and swallow it without tasting, but this was not possible. I gave up and gulped, then stood upright and dragged my forearm across my chin to wipe the last drops away.

Along the side of the station was posted an enormous diagram of the entire park, complete with topographical markers and indications of where the ground was solid and where there was only water. A sign indicated that there might be more such source materials inside.

"Why don't you go on without me?" I suggested, picking up a couple of official park pamphlets. "You go get a canoe and some other things, like you said. I'll be here inside the station looking over this stuff."

"Hmm, yeah, that would be all right. I'm just heading back up the road, and I won't be gone long. So I guess that would be okay. But *don't leave*," he admonished, wagging his finger at my nose.

"Where would I go?" I wasn't trying to dodge his command, as I had every intention of staying put. But Harry was unsatisfied, so I nodded and shrugged. "I won't go anywhere, I promise."

"Okay then. I'll be right back."

"Righty-o."

He left in my car, the Diabolical Death Nugget. I stayed, just like I told him I would, and I returned my attention to the information at hand.

If the government's park service could be believed, Avery's spot of land was somewhere in the gray area between swamp and forest. I guessed it would be just barely on the forest side; it's hard to stake a claim in four feet of water. I pressed a finger against the map and traced out the swamp, mentally noting the spot where it joined terra firm enough to be technically called land. It looked like Harry was right, and that point was within a mile of the two-lane road that runs alongside the park. The map featured tiny numbers along the road's green line—mile markers, according to the legend in the corner. There was one right next to the spot where I'd put my finger.

I squinted.

On the Plexiglas that covered the wall map, there were scratches and fuzz that made it opaque in places. I stared harder, sadly failing to focus on the tiny notes beneath. Was it mile marker 11? Or was that a 17? I couldn't quite make it out. I brought my face closer, until my nose was almost touching it. I could smell the plastic, and something tart, like bug spray.

Eleven. I was almost sure of it. I cocked my head. Yes, it was definitely an eleven.

A flicker of color flashed, a reflection in the shinier bits of the mostly clear covering.

I almost had time to turn my head before he hit me.

Something hard slammed into my skull, and my skull slammed against the shield, sending broad spiderweb cracks across the board. I ducked, or rather I conveniently fell to the ground, missing the next blow. I was stunned, but not unconscious yet. My ears were ringing and silver-white static flared before my eyes, but I could still see Malachi rearing above me.

I held out my hands to push him away but it wasn't enough. He was using a nightstick again, or a flashlight, or something else black and extremely hard. He brought it down on my forearm and pain blasted up to my shoulder. I struggled to uncross my eyes and defend myself, but the bell chorus in my ears and distracting bolts of pain forbade it.

He swung again.

I tried to catch it, but I was too dazed to do more than deflect his next strike. I kicked at his legs, and missed the worst of his next wild plunge. It clocked me between my shoulder and neck, hurting me, but not putting me out.

It took one more solid swing to do that.

It thwacked my head, just past my temple. I ricocheted off the wall and flopped onto my back, staring up at the white, white sky, watching a large bird with gangly legs fly up towards the sun. Then my brother-cousin's face loomed into my vision, and there was nothing else.

I awoke to darkness, and there was a humming, rumbling noise all around. I was cramped, my arms ached, and my head was throbbing, but I was awake. It was more than I'd had any right to expect. I shifted my weight and realized why my arms were sore; they were tied haphazardly, but tightly, in front of me. My ankles were bound as well, but not so snugly.

I winced and stretched out.

No, I could not stretch out. My back and feet had already reached the limits of my confines. Hmm . . . I was lying on something hard, but with enough give to bounce a bit. All was black, but as my eyes adjusted I could see pale threads of light here and there.

Despite the ache in my cranium, my cognitive powers crept slowly back to me.

I was in the trunk of a car. The lump beneath me was a spare tire. The surrounding noise was an engine—a big engine from the sound of it, maybe a V8. The trunk was pretty roomy for a trunk, though that was a weak guess on my part, not having seen the inside of enough trunks to make a fair comparison. Perhaps I was in Eliza's vehicle, the one Harry used to drive. That was as good an answer as any as to how Malachi had scared up transportation. No way of knowing from inside. No sense in dwelling or wondering yet.

First things first.

My hands. I wrestled with the bindings for a few seconds, not feeling enough slack to work with. My feet, then. Luckily I was wearing black sneakers I'd removed from my own trunk before we'd gotten to the park; I could have never popped off my boots so easily. But one after the other I pried my shoes free, then without too much trouble I slid my feet loose. I lifted one knee up to my chest

and put my heel against my wrist restraints. My toes are almost pre-
hensile, but in socks they weren't much good. I put my leg back
down again and began to feel around, reaching for my shoes and
wrenching them back on, shoving my foot against the wall to jam
my heel into place. I might have to run through the swamp, and I
didn't want to do it barefoot. It would be bad enough to do it with
tied hands.

Okay, *think,* I ordered myself.

But this is easier said than done when your head is marked with
swelling goose eggs and your arms have patches of sprawling bruise
that you don't have to see to believe.

I was in a trunk. There might be tools. Something metal I could
use to cut the ropes. I searched unsuccessfully for a bit, then discovered that the lining of the trunk had been lifted out at some point
and the raw metal of the car's frame was exposed beneath. In lieu
of any better ideas, I began to rub my wrists against it, and I was
satisfied to hear the gentle, slow sawing sound of fraying fibers. I
held my arms to my chin and felt the groove I'd worn through the
rope. It would work, provided I had enough time. I had no way of
gauging how fast the car was going, but it seemed to be making
steady progress down a well-paved road.

Nothing to do but try.

After a minute or two the top wind of rope snapped and the
knots slacked. I writhed myself clear and lay there, triumphant but
fuming. Great. Now what? He was taking me somewhere, but God
knew where, to do God knew what.

I'd find out soon enough.

The car backfired, and smoky carbon monoxide filled my nostrils. The humming engine coughed, and more noxious fumes
flooded the trunk. I covered my nose with my sleeve, but it wasn't
enough to keep the burn away from my eyes.

We were slowing down.

The car lurched and heaved, and the pavement subsided to a

slurping crunch as we pulled off the road. I floundered for something heavy to use as a weapon but found nothing. The car came to a complete stop and the engine was cut off. My time was running out.

I reached for the ropes that had held my feet and wound them loosely back into place, then did likewise to my hands—not actually restraining myself, but giving the appearance that I was still tied.

The driver's door opened, then closed. Squishy footsteps worked their way alongside the car. They paused. Another vehicle was coming. I heard the distant roar and rush as it approached and slowed down.

"Do you need any help there, buddy?"

"No, no, I'm okay. I just pulled off to make a phone call."

"Oh—all right. Have a good day."

"You too."

The other car drove away. Malachi did not move for a moment. His heart must have been beating as hard as mine, but I had little sympathy for him. In a moment he was going to open the trunk and then . . . and then what?

The key clicked and twitched in the lock. The trunk lifted. I held as still as I could, facedown with my hair spilled across my shoulders, trying to look as helpless and unconscious as I possibly could. My hands were tucked beneath me, so he might not notice they were not tied with his original handiwork.

He must have been staring down at me, for he did not touch me for a minute. Then he worked one arm underneath me, and I heard him grunting, breathing shallowly. Oh yes. I'd hurt him badly a couple of days before. I don't weigh that much, but it must have nearly killed him to hoist me inside the trunk to begin with. Even Harry had complained about it. Heavier than I look. Ha.

Malachi hesitated, and withdrew. He was thinking hard, watching me. I kept my breath faint and resisted the temptation to groan. He made another try with the other arm, and he achieved similarly lackluster results. He grunted again, whimpered slightly, and pulled away.

Ah, I understood.

He was holding something in one hand. Something he didn't want to put down in order to pick me up. I fought the urge to peer out through my hair. There was really no need. I knew it must be a gun. All the more reason for me to be as cumbersome as I could. If I could make him put it down, I could overpower him without too much trouble.

Clunk.

He did it. He set it down—on the bumper, I'd bet. Keep it close at hand.

Just to make sure, I waited until I felt both of his arms worming their way beneath me. He was pulling me up, lifting me slowly, laboriously, from the trunk; he was holding me pressed awkwardly against his chest. His face was close enough to kiss.

Where was it I'd stabbed him? Which side of his chest? Or was it more his shoulder? I must not have gotten him as good as I'd thought. Still, he was bound to be sore. My left arm is weaker than my right, but it was the one that was dangling free. My right one was pinned between our chests, and although I could have wiggled it loose it would have taken too much time. I needed to surprise him.

He'd hoisted me out nearly to my hips when I swung.

His groin was not my first pick of targets at such an angle, but anything else would have gone wild. As it was, I didn't come up from underneath—it was more of a flat punch—but I must say, he *was* surprised when my fist nailed his crotch. He was so surprised, in fact, that he dropped me and jerked his head up, smacking himself on the raised lid of the trunk. I couldn't have planned it any better even if I'd had time and the foresight to try.

I fell halfway out and down, catching myself on my hands before I could do a face-plant in the dirt. I flipped forward, landing in a crouch behind the car. Meanwhile, Malachi instinctively brought a hand to the back of his head and one to his balls.

We recovered at about the same time, and we both went for the gun.

Neither of us found it; he must have knocked it off the bumper when he slid me out of the trunk. Yes, there it was—under the car beside the back tire. Since I was closest to the ground, I saw it first. I ducked beneath the car in its pursuit.

Malachi grabbed my foot and began to tug. I started to kick out with the other leg, but he caught that one in his free hand. I let him have it. I even let him drag me out from under the wheels, feeling the dirt and rocks crawl up my shirt and scrape my stomach. No, no more struggling from me.

I let him extract me because *I* had the gun.

I pivoted in his grasp. He held on to my feet, but his arms were now crossed, elbows bent at uncomfortable angles. Malachi had pulled me into the sunlight only to stare down the barrel of his own pistol.

"Hey there, Sunshine." I smiled.

He let go of my legs and his body sagged forward a little. A dark spot was spreading below his right collarbone; he must have split a few stitches. He backed a step or two away, out of my personal space. I kept the gun trained on him with one hand and used the other to pull myself up against the vehicle.

Above us, the sky was blue, going on gray. I could swear it was about to rain, or perhaps it was getting dark. The day could not be as late as it looked unless I'd been out of it longer than I thought. I heard a rumble somewhere distant—an oncoming car, I hoped, but it was more likely thunder.

I wiped a stray tangle of hair out of my face.

"I'm not who you think I am," I said, just for the record. My voice was only barely quaking, so it came off well. "You've never understood—not even for a second."

He didn't reply. He stood there patiently, waiting for me to shoot him. Making peace with his God, or something like that. Bleeding profusely, at any rate. If there was one thing Malachi knew how to do besides pray, it was bleed.

"What do I have to do, Malachi?" I think it was the first time I'd ever called him by his name. "Do I honestly have to kill you?"

"Yes, Avery—"

"I'm not Avery!" I yelled, and the coming thunder gave me an echo. "I'm not Avery, you insane son of a bitch! I'm your sister!"

"That can't matter. You're *here,*" he retorted. I couldn't tell if I'd told him anything new or not. Had he known all along that we shared a father? Had he cared?

"What? What's that got to do with anything?"

"You're here to start the summoning. You're here to bring Gray back." His lower lip was set in a stubborn line. I found the expression distractingly familiar, but then I remembered it was one I'd seen in the mirror. That realization enraged me all the more.

"I'm here to *stop* the . . . the summoning! Don't you get it? If I don't stop it, my aunt Lu is going to die—and then I'm going to die—and I don't particularly *want* to die, dammit, so I'm here to put an end to this whole thing!"

"I don't believe you."

"I don't care!" My voice had climbed to a higher, frustrated pitch. "It's God's own truth! And if I have to shoot you in order to see this out, you can bet your sweet ass I *will.*"

"Don't *you* swear before God."

"Why not? *He* knows I'm not lying, and if you two were really on such magnificent speaking terms, He'd tell you that!" More thunder, closer now. Or was it thunder at all? It wasn't rolling in crashing peals, rather it seemed to come in one rushing wave.

Closer. Definitely closer.

But what to do with Malachi? The weight of the gun was deeply tempting, but I knew myself better than he did, and I knew that I wasn't going to fire it. I did want to put it down, though, because the thought of standing in a thunderstorm while holding a raised hunk of metal didn't much appeal to me.

"Forget it." I waved the gun at the car. "Just forget it, and get in the trunk."

"What?"

"I'm not going to kill you—even though I bloody well should. But since I can't have you following me, either, get in the trunk before I start using your less vital body parts for target practice. *Do it!*"

His internal debate was written all over his face, but I never had time to learn whether or not he would have eventually obeyed, for it was then that the thunder hit us. The wave struck us both, shaking the swamp and leaving the air smelling of sizzled ozone, so there might have been some lightning too. Then, after it had run us over, it was gone, except for a residual rumble and the ringing in our ears.

At least *my* ears were ringing again when I picked myself back up.

No part of Malachi was doing much of anything, except lying in a loose pile, the whites of his eyes peeking out as pale as boiled eggs. His tongue lolled past his teeth at the corner of his mouth. A trickle of blood dampened the base of his nose.

If he wasn't really unconscious, he was *way* better at faking it than I was.

Funny, I almost wished he was awake. I needed to ask someone— even just to hear the question aloud—*what was that?* I needed to hear that it wasn't just me, and that someone else was confused and frightened too.

But no, it was definitely better this way, better to have him lying there beside the road where someone might find him. I thought about tossing him in the trunk anyway, just to be on the safe side, but it seemed like overkill. He needed medical attention too badly to pose any real threat, and furthermore, I had his gun. Let someone find him and take him to the hospital, or better yet, call the cops.

I checked the safety, then stuffed the gun down the back of my jeans, wincing when the cool metal touched my warm back. I didn't really think that a gun would be any use against whatever energy had bowled us over, but I may as well hang on to it all the same.

You never know. Someone human was doing this, and someone human might need to get shot at.

And then I heard the voice, calling from the trees.

He's coming. He's coming, baby. You get yourself gone.

II

The Death of the Sisters

I

"No," I said, to myself or to whoever could hear me. "No, of course I won't. Mae, is that you? Mae?" I scanned the tree line for some grand sign, or for a glimpse of a ghost who must be there. I saw nothing but endless rows of knobby trees and wet green leaves. For another moment, all was still except for the distant, incessant trickling of water and a choir of insects.

Just when I thought I might have imagined it, the voice came again.

He's coming, baby. You get yourself gone. Get yourself gone.

It was coming from the woods, just beyond where I could see through the foliage. The voice was almost normal, almost a fearful warning. But not quite. No living throat made that sad cry. These were ghosts I knew and loved.

I took a last look at Malachi, dribbling blood and saliva into the grass. He wouldn't be coming after me, not anytime soon. And I had his gun. The weight of the weapon pressed between my belt and my skin made me feel more secure, as though I could defend myself against the dead, or against those who had the power to raise them. I crouched down, tied my shoes tight, and stomped through the grass and mud, and between the tall old trunks. In a matter of seconds, I'd lost sight of the car behind me.

Get yourself gone, girl.

"Mae, where are you?"

Underneath the high, leafy canopy, the world was even darker than out by the road. Although most of the ground was solid enough, I had a hard time seeing where the forest floor was dirt and where it was mulch. My shoes squished as my feet sucked at the mud.

One sneaker sank at least two inches into the muck.

I lurched forward, grabbing a tree for support. A slick salamander, red and black and brown and a little bit gold, scurried up the trunk, away from my falling hand. I watched with relief as it shimmied higher, hiding itself on a low branch. For a dozen reasons, I was glad I hadn't crushed it.

I looked back towards the road. With a twinge of alarm, I realized I wasn't sure which direction I should be checking. The disorientation was dizzying, and my inner panic button was dangerously near to being pushed; but they wouldn't leave me here. The women had never proved anything but helpful before. They wouldn't let me die out there in the woods.

I hoped. I prayed. I even asked it aloud. "Mae? Willa? Luanna? I know you're here. You have to be. Oh my God, don't leave me out here. I don't know where I'm going." *And I'm sore, and I'm tired, and I have no idea what I'm doing,* I thought, but I didn't add that part. They probably knew it already. I clung to the trunk with one hand while the salamander's oil-black eyes stared down.

Yes—there, through the trees. A flash of color. A smudge of light or motion.

Then again, very distinctly, I saw yellow, a tall streak.

I staggered towards it. "Mae?"

But this was no ghost. And it was not Mae. A woman in a corn-colored dress knelt at the foot of a tree, the trunk of which was as big around as a toolshed. She was using a dull knife to scrape greenish-brown moss from the trunk, collecting it in a cloth bag in her lap. Patches of sweat dampened her dress from her shoulders to the small of her back, and her feet were bare, sticking out from underneath her thighs and twitching as her arm worked the blade.

"Hello?"

She didn't answer.

"Hello?"

The woman's head lifted, and cocked to the right. She'd heard something, but it wasn't me. I was staring down at Willa. Not the ghost Willa, who had come to my dreams, but the living, breathing woman Willa. Her flesh did not hang loose off her cheekbones, and her lips were full and firm. Her eyes and skin were not the pasty, postmortem gray I'd always seen. She was the color of black tea with a small spoonful of cream, and her eyes were olive-brown. A sudden swelling in my throat reminded me of the obvious—she looked a great deal like Lulu.

But her eyes were not looking for me. They were searching for something else, a different presence. One I'd not detected.

Who's there? she asked, and only then was she betrayed as a figment. Although this apparition looked as solid as the woods around us, her voice remained the hollow echo that marked the speech of all the ghosts I've ever heard. *Avery, is that you?*

Yes, ma'am.

He stepped from behind another large tree. He was wickedly handsome, as dark as European chocolate, with ivory white teeth. A cream undershirt showed from beneath the cotton plaid button-up he'd half tucked into a pair of dirty black pants. It would have been easy for me to say he resembled Dave, but he was so much bigger, and he walked with a sense of masculine aggression that my uncle generally lacked. This was a man accustomed to being obeyed.

It's just me. His words had no more volume than Willa's, but I heard each precise letter when he spoke them. He walked up close to her then, and picked at the moss on the tree. *What are you doing getting this? We don't need any. It ain't the right kind.*

Willa lowered her eyes to the bag sitting across her knees. I thought I saw fear beneath her lids before she averted her eyes. Fear and something else . . . guilt. *Sure it is,* she nodded, but Avery didn't believe her and neither did I.

No, it ain't. This is good for some things, but not for what we need tonight. You know this isn't what I asked for.

She looked up at him. *Honest I don't. I thought this was what you said.*

Well, it ain't.

What kind do we need, then?

Never mind, he said. *I got it already. I got almost everything I need to make it work.*

He turned his back to me and offered her his hand, as if to help her rise. But in the other hand, behind the small of his back, he held a long, serrated knife with a wooden handle. *I only need one more thing, and you can help me with it.*

Oka—

The knife cut her word short.

She tried to move backwards but he held her by the shoulder, at the crook of her neck, and he would not let her fall. Blood gushed over his hands, and down the front of her dress in dark orange streaks where it wet the yellow fabric. She clawed at his arms, and pushed at his chest, and kicked weakly at his legs . . . and then went slack.

Her knees unlocked and she folded to the ground, still sucking at air through her slashed throat.

While she lay there soaking the grass around her, not completely unconscious, Avery took the big knife to her wrist and began sawing. I clapped my hand over my mouth and turned away, but I could not escape the sound of splintering bone and snapping veins, accompanied by the woman's gasps of astonished agony.

Avery was strong, and he worked quickly. When I dared to look again, he was dumping out the contents of Willa's little bag, and replacing them with the gory trophy of her right hand. He stood and tied the bag onto his belt. Then he hoisted her up, slinging her over his shoulders and carrying her away. One of those naked, calloused feet still jerked faintly against his back.

Go on, girl, Get yourself gone.

I heard it again, more urgently. I followed Avery's gruesomely laden form anyway, staring fixedly at the knife he'd shoved down the back of his pants, just like I was toting my gun.

Someone had to know. Someone had to see. I owed them this much.

I must have said that last part aloud, for a response came unbidden from the trees.

No, you owe us much more.

II

Avery carried Willa to the edge of a fetid pool that reeked of rot and disease. He dropped her in, splashing his ankles with the smelly black liquid. She didn't sink fast enough for his liking so he put his foot on her back and pushed. Bubbles gurgled up from her dress, from her lungs, and from her hair. And then she was gone. She did not rise.

Avery shook his leg, driving the worst of the water away. Somewhere, not far off, I heard the low plop and ripple of something quite large entering the pool. Soon after, a second plop, and more ripples. Then came the yellow periscope eyes and the long, scaly heads. I marveled to see how quickly the forest had given way to wetlands.

He left the pond purposefully, striding almost happily between the trees, bouncing on the balls of his feet. Sometimes when he turned or shifted I could see the bag at his side, and I could see how the bottom grew damp and deeply red.

He nearly ran into Luanna, who threw her hand to her chest and gasped when he came charging at her between the trees. She too was perfect and alive as far as I could tell, but when she spoke it was the same tinny, faraway sound I knew and recognized from my child-hood.

There you are. I was just coming for you.

He smiled. *Were you, now?*

Oh yes. I got the last of the roots to grind down for tonight.

Let me see.

She hesitated. *I told you I got them. Let's go back home and get this started.*

Let me see them, Lu.

All right, then. No need to be that way. She handed him a bag much like Willa's, lumpy with its contents.

He opened it up. *This ain't what I said for you to get.*

It is so.

I said it ain't.

She shrugged, but her shoulders trembled with it. *Maybe I'm wrong. I thought that's what you told me.*

Avery threw the bag down and cuffed her with the back of his hand. She clutched her face and wavered, but didn't fall. *A pinch of this would throw off the whole batch! You were gonna go on back home and mix it up before I could see it, weren't you? That's what you were gonna do. You women are out to get me, that's what it is. Either that or you're all stump stupid, and I know that ain't right. What's this turned into now, Lu? Why are you three trying to interfere with what you know I mean to do?*

Ain't no one interfering, Ave. I just made a mistake, that's all. She was just beginning to notice that the filth on his clothes wasn't entirely made of swamp scum and mud, and she was getting nervous, though she did her best not to show it. Only the quick twitch of her eyes betrayed her fear. Left to right they went, and right to left, intuitively seeking some exit even before the danger.

He took her quickly, though not so quickly as Willa, for Luanna was not taken off guard. She screamed and tried to run when she saw the knife, but he caught her hair in one huge fist and yanked her head back to be beaten and sliced. She didn't go down without a fight. Once, twice, even a third time she nearly got loose, only to be drawn back into his sharp embrace. I wanted to applaud her for it, but my stomach was turning, wanting it to end.

Luanna fought back like a jungle animal, and although Avery eventually took her down it was not without losing a handful of hair and flesh of his own. Towards the end I turned away, unable to watch another moment of ripping fabric and shearing skin. God, I hated myself for my revulsion. I hated myself for wishing she'd quit struggling and just give up already, so he wouldn't have to mangle her any more.

Finally she died, but even then he did not quit hitting her. When he was done, there was little left of Luanna to be recognized. Everything was covered with mud and blood from the random chunks of flesh torn in the fray. Her face was nearly gone, and what remained was blue or black. It was only afterwards that it dawned on me that she went by "Lu," and I wondered if it was more than coincidence that women with this name could fight so hard.

Eventually Avery's rage was satiated and Luanna's hand was tied up in her own small cloth purse. Avery carried her to the same dark pool where he'd sunk her sister. I did not see Willa's body, and I did not see any horrific, bloody-mouthed alligators, but I could not help but notice the ominous floating eyes lurking quite close.

III

Still, I followed.

Avery hiked with half-hopping steps between the trees, along a path he must have known well to walk so quickly. He was going deeper, farther back into the wettest lands that could still be called land and not a sinking stretch of mud. All the way I watched his back, swaying and dipping to dodge the low limbs and the softer patches of earth. A second bag hung at his side, jostled by his shifting hipbone, containing a second hand that leaked blood through the soft fabric, staining his pants in short pendulum swipes of russet brown.

One to go.

"No, no, no, no, no," I murmured to myself, keeping time with Avery's expertly stomping feet. He was getting ahead of me, but not by much. I knew what must happen next and I chanted against it, *no, no, no, no, no,* but all the prayerful begging in the world can't change what has already passed. I'd like to say that nothing can, but a brief while ago I would have said that nothing could bring back the dead, and now my opinion on the matter was not nearly so certain as before.

I tailed Avery maybe half a mile to a wood-slat cabin, set on short stilts to keep it from sinking or flooding. Three crooked steps led up to a narrow porch and an open door that swung without a screen. Clattering, boiling sounds of cooking came from within, and a pungent, earthy odor steamed from the stovepipe chimney that leaned out from the wall. Avery kicked the excess mud and gore from his shoes against the bottom stair.

Avery? Mae called from within.

You got it all ready? He went up the steps and stood in the doorway for a minute before going in. He used the back of his foot to close the door.

I climbed the stairs behind him. They creaked and groaned

beneath my weight. Surely this was no phantom place. A stray nail was solid enough to snag my shoe. But why didn't they see or hear me? I didn't understand, but I was too fascinated not to watch. I didn't let myself in; I stayed at the window like a cowardly peeping Tom.

Mae nodded. *I got it all ready. Don't you smell it? Lord, but it's enough to clear out the swamp, it stinks so bad. Where's the girls?*

Out there. He waved towards the door.

They not done getting their share yet?

No, they ain't. Where's my little one? You didn't let her go out alone, did you?

Mae's eyebrows came together just a tiny bit. *She's right out back, playing with the frogs in the puddles. Once they started their croaking, there was no keeping her in here. She about drove me crazy, bouncing around calling out 'ribbit, ribbit,' until I sent her on out—*

Avery put his hand on her cheek, and traced the curve of her face. Mae stopped talking. She touched his arm. I thought for a moment—that is, I tried to make myself believe—I thought they might kiss, and everything might be all right. Avery reached back behind her neck and firmly, but almost gently, he held her and kept her from falling backwards. She laughed and turned her back to him, thinking he meant to play.

I turned my back to the window, not wanting to see. Her frightened squeal, and her gurgling cry—I heard them, and this was enough. I heard her fall against the bed in the corner, and I heard the straw stuffing that made up the mattress crackle beneath her body as she thrashed against the fast falling knife.

And then everything was still. I waited for more, but no more came. Maybe as long as a full minute I stood there, back to the rough slat wall, panting as though it was my throat that had been slit with a rusty-edged knife. Something had changed in the swamp around me—something signaled a shift and a warning, and I braved the window's view once more. I couldn't see much of what

I feared; Avery was facing the wall away from me, his back hunched over the bloody form on the bed. His elbow jerked furiously back and forth as he sawed off his third trophy.

I couldn't stand it.

I stepped aside and put my hands on the split-log rail of the porch to hang my head, fighting the dizziness and nausea that was creeping up my throat. My hair hung around my face in a wavy black curtain, one I did not care to part. I could not look through that window again or I would go more mad than my cousin, and with madness I could not save Lu or even myself. I'd seen enough.

Yes, now you've seen enough.

I raised my head just enough to see out from between layers of hair with one wet eye. They were all three there, Willa, Luanna, and Mae, standing before me in the damp overgrowth that passed for a front yard. They appeared the way I had always seen them before, dead and unhappy. Three furies, or three fates . . . the Gorgon sisters once beautiful, made into sad monsters.

"What do you want from me?" I asked, having half an idea but needing instructions.

Your mother-aunt will be dead at sunset, Mae said, nodding towards the sun. It had already fallen behind the trees and would soon be level with the horizon. I had light enough to see by, but not much more than that.

The energy that hit you, that was his call for her life.

It's gone to claim her.

If you kill him, the wave will wither before it reaches her.

I glanced sideways into the window at the hulking form, still looming and carving at Mae's corpse. "I can't kill him. I don't think I can even look at him."

But you will kill him. Or all is lost.

"What do I do?" I asked desperately, clutching the rail with my hands and forcing back a wad of rising vomit. The women remained immobile, stiff as statues except for the swaying of their garments, pulled at by a wind I couldn't feel, touched by a peculiar breeze that didn't brush anything around them.

Why ask us? Luanna finally shrugged. *Go and make your own try if you want to save her.*

Willa agreed. *Go on, now. You've come this far. Would you kill her now by waiting? She who hesitates . . .*

Yes, she who hesitates . . .

She who hesitates . . .

Once again I begged their aid, "What do I do?"

Mae shrugged as casually as if I'd asked her for the time and she had no watch. *How should we know? As you've now seen, we failed. We would have stopped him if we could, but our try came too late. We were weak against him, because we loved him.*

"I'm not strong enough."

You are. He's seen to that. He's given you everything you need. What did you think those draughts were for? Why do you think his old sister still lives? Oh yes, darling. You're plenty strong now.

I stood on the rickety porch, clawing at the rail that would give me splinters if I held it any harder. I still smelled the tangy, earthy cooking that spewed out steam and smoke from the stovepipe, and the sun was sinking even as I stood there.

I steeled myself, prepared for the worst, and looked in the window again. There was a familiar shape—no, not the same one, but with a smaller, thinner back—hunched over a form lying prostrate on the bed; and instead of bare black feet thrashing against the mattress, the prone legs now occupying that space were clad in muddy tennis shoes not so different from my own.

So this was the shift the woods had signaled. I was back in the real world, if in fact I'd ever left it.

I reached for the door and pushed it with my fingertips. It bounced inward with a squeaky jolt. The man at the bed stopped what he was doing. In one of his hands I saw a thick twine rope dangling. He was not cutting the body on the bed, he was restraining it. I was so relieved I took a deep breath.

From the kneeling, skinny body came a familiar voice. "You came in time. I knew you would." That voice was strong, and deep—it did not seem to match the wrinkled hands that held the rope. And I had heard it before, in my stranger dreams and lucid fears.

I started to reach backwards for my gun, but something made me reconsider. "Who are you? And what are you doing to . . . him?" Yeah, I *did* know those shoes. I knew those dirty jeans.

He laughed, low and mellow. "I'm not hurting him near so much as you did. Boy, but I knew I did right giving you the medicine. Of course, you're mine anyhow. I knew you'd be tough. But this one, he's the vessel. I won't be harming him. I need him." He spoke so smoothly, it was like being on drugs and listening to Barry White. Impossible for that voice to belong to those skinny arms, that bony back.

"Who are you?"

"You know who I am."

I argued, but my protest was a lie and we both knew it. "No. I don't."

"You do. But you're afraid. There's no need for it. I'd not harm you any sooner than I'd harm *him*." He twisted his neck just enough to see me with one brown eye, the whites gone yellow with age. "Naw, I'd not harm you none at all. You're here to help me."

"I'm . . . not. You're crazy. I'm not going to help *you*."

He nodded and his jowls flopped. "Oh yes, you are. You've come back to me. You know you're mine. You've always known. That's why you're here." He returned his attention to my poor cousin, wiggling and whimpering. He tightened one last knot.

"I'm here because you're trying to kill Lulu. And I mean to stop you." A slim, pale ray of light squeezed in past the gauzy burlap curtains. I had just a little time. A few minutes, maybe. I reached

258

for the gun; I pulled it out from my pants but let it hang down at my side.

"There ain't no stopping what's already done."

"I've got until sundown."

"Maybe." He rose to his feet and faced me for the first time. He still stood with that aggressive confidence I'd seen in the visions. He stood like a man who knows something that you don't, and it's something that can make the difference between living and dying. "Maybe you do, and maybe you don't. But I do know you'll not kill me. I've lived too long to be taken by my own child."

My fingers went numb, and then weak. The gun slid loose and clattered to the wood floor. I did not hear or feel it fall. "I'm not— I'm not yours. I'm not."

He cocked his head and smiled without showing any teeth. "Come now. You know better than that. Say my name, girl." A pair of drawstring pants were pulled tight around his narrow waist, and the shirt that was tucked into them was gray and threadbare with age. His feet were naked except for grime, and his once smooth skin had gone ashy and dull. I remembered, someplace in the back of my mind, the letters from this place—one to Pine Breeze. Eliza must have been here to visit, at least once or twice, though it was hard to imagine her in such a place.

"It's not possible," I breathed.

"Say my name. He's awake now." He pointed down at the body, now quivering with fright and straining halfheartedly against the ropes. "Say it, and let him see that you were right all along. Won't that feel good, now? Won't it be right to show him he was wrong? After all he's put you through, I wonder why you aren't throwing it in his face."

He stepped aside and I saw Malachi's face, gagged by a dirty rag, eyes bugging out of his skull as he stared up at the man who'd bound him. I looked back and forth between them, unable to move or act or think straight.

"Avery." It barely came out. Surely I hadn't said that aloud. It could not be true. It could *not*. But Malachi knew, more certainly than I did. I could see it in the bulging veins at his temples and the paralyzed jerking of his hands.

"Say it so he can hear it. You say my name, and you tell him you were right."

"Avery." There. It was out, and loud enough to be heard. Malachi closed his buggy eyes and tears of frustration welled out from the cracks. "You can't be. That's not possible." Even as I contradicted him, I knew it was pointless.

"And you can't be my long-lost baby, but that's so too."

I faltered, realizing I wasn't holding the gun. I felt around for it, but didn't find it. I didn't even look down at the floor. I couldn't look anywhere at all except at him, and it didn't seem important, some-how. I'd walked in with a gun, and now it was gone. Not in my hands. Didn't matter. Nothing mattered except to see him some more, and to hear him talk. "You're wrong," I argued again, maybe just to hear him speak.

"Now, why would you fuss, when you know it's a fact? You're my child—I know it, you know it, the women know it—" and here he gestured at the door, as if he'd known all along they were there. "Even the spirit at the hospital, this boy's momma, she knew it. She smelled it on you right away."

"Wha—what?"

"You know that place—that place where you were born. That angry old bitch knew by your smell that you must be mine, but that's not why she tried to scare you so bad. Malachi, when's your momma gonna give up and go to rest? All the folks she hates are dead. I'd send her on myself if she'd listen."

Malachi mumbled a furiously garbled answer, but I didn't under-stand or care. The air inside the shack was so heavy I could feel it pressing down against my skin; I could have taken a handful of it and squeezed it into some shape. Or perhaps it was just the smell of the evil herbs churning and boiling as the night approached. The night—yes, the night was approaching. I only had until sundown.

Maybe until sundown.

Hang on, Lulu, I prayed, trying to pull my thoughts together into something coherent enough to be useful.

"What are you talking about? That thing—that thing that talked to me at Pine Breeze? You sent it there?" Just stringing the words together was almost more than I could do. What was he doing to me? Was it magic, or hypnotism, or simply a very difficult truth that pressed so heavy on my sanity? "Did you send that monster after me, to chase me off?"

"Aw, don't talk about this boy's momma that way. It ain't right, or polite." He reached down and actually scratched Malachi's head, almost with affection. "And I didn't send her there after you, no way, no how. I raised her, that's a fact; but I only meant to ask her some questions. I only wanted to know about you—the rest of your kin—and she knew better than anyone. She seemed the one to ask, and I wasn't about to let her being dead stop me.

"I didn't know she'd take off like that, though. I didn't know she'd be so wild and strong! She just took straight off, she did, and I couldn't snatch her back no matter what I tried. So I just let her go on and get lost. I didn't know she'd go back to that hospital, and I *sure* didn't know that nutty old woman would still be hunting after your momma."

"You must be . . . you must be twenty . . . or thirty years . . . older than Eliza." My next question was so huge I could only ask it in one word. "How?" Even at his advanced age, Avery was half a head taller than me and I sensed no weakness about him. Except for his appearance, there was nothing in his demeanor, posture, or attitude to suggest he was any older than I was.

"Twenty-seven years older, at my best count. I was around your age or thereabouts when she came along. So I'm old. What does that mean against forever? Against what's going to happen tonight?

Eliza's old too, but she's old 'cause I let her be. An' if she wants to cooperate some more, she can live to be older still."

I looked quickly at the woodburning stove. Several pots bubbled with different colored brews. "Her medicine," I said, and, glancing a bit to the left, I added, "And that damned book," almost wanting to laugh at all the effort we'd wasted searching three states off the mark.

"She wouldn't have lasted this long without me—without my formula. It ain't perfect, as you can see by my old bones and her bent little body, but it's been working well enough. Tonight, when John comes back, he'll show me how to fix it. And once it's fixed . . ." He waved one long hand and let my imagination fill in the rest.

"How many people need to die for you to live forever?" Malachi was looking pointedly back and forth between me and something on the floor. Trying to tell me something. What? Oh yes. Beside me. The gun. He was trying to remind me that I had a gun, but I couldn't hang on to the thought without concentrating, and it was hard to concentrate when Avery was talking.

"You won't stop me," he said, and with each word my confused focus wavered, then came together enough to remember the firearm again.

From the corner of my eye I saw it there, about two feet south of my right hand. Squat, grab, fire. How fast could I do it? Better be quick. The little ray of light that had fallen in through the curtains was fading and my aunt was dying.

"Like hell I won't."

"You won't," he said with enough of that intimidating confidence to frighten me. He stepped forward in two long strides. Where had he gotten *that*? Where had he been hiding that knife, that huge knife big enough to be a machete?

He smiled, and this time I saw his teeth, as jaundiced as his eyes. "You won't even *try* to stop me, my baby. In fact, you're going to give me . . . a hand."

A sudden understanding of the threat jolted me free of my stupor; I dropped to a crouch and grabbed the gun. Too late—he was too close. He stomped one huge foot down on my wrist before I could pull the trigger, and I no longer had any doubt that he was as strong as he sounded, and a hundred times stronger than he looked.

I shrieked and tried to yank myself out from under him. With a mighty heave I pulled away, and his balance faltered, but that move cost me the gun; I had to leave it beside his foot to extricate myself.

Avery ignored the gun and brought the knife down right where my arm had been. The blade stuck into the wood, but not so hard that he couldn't retrieve it. He held it aloft again, and we circled each other like fighting dogs. I was still on the floor, in a crablike backwards crawl trying to get away from him, but I had nowhere to go. He was now between me and the door, and the only window was beside it.

"I don't want to kill you," he insisted, knife securely poised in his grip, loudly contradicting his words.

"I don't believe you."

"All I need is your right hand—no, not even that if you'll hold still. I need your fourth finger—and that's all. That's all I need to use your power. And it's mine to take. I gave it to you."

"No part of my body is yours to take. You stay the hell away from me."

He lunged forward and I scrambled backwards, knocking into the wall and sliding along it until we opposed each other once more. "But I need your power, child. I can either take it from your hand, or I can kill you—it's up to you. To kill you would return it to me just as surely, but you've got to believe I'd rather see you alive."

"But I don't believe it. And I swear to God that if you touch me, I'll feed you your heart."

Avery laughed, and the knife turned in his fist. "No, my pretty one. You don't want my power. And if you kill me, you'll take it whether you want it or not. That's another reason you've got to let me have my way."

"Forget it. And I don't need your power. I just need you to leave us alone."

"Have it your way, then. I'll still have it my way too." He dove for me again.

I scrambled back to the left, towards the stove, and as he bore down on me I reached up, feeling madly about for anything I could use as a weapon. I seized on a handle, and without looking up to see what it was I flipped it forward. A small pot, filled with a smelly, boiling liquid, sailed over my head and caught Avery in the side of the face. He reeled away, catching himself against the far wall and wiping at the dark, hot liquid.

Something about the way he recovered himself, eyes narrowing and shoulders stiffening, made me cringe. Now I'd made him angry. I expected him to make some battle cry or villainous threat, but he did neither. Instead he charged forward again, and this time he caught me by the shoulder before I could dart a hasty evasion.

He raised the knife and drove it down hard—I caught his forearm but not soon enough. The knife went in just above my left breast, but not too deep. It tore skin and scraped against bone, but did little other damage. The sound of the metal inside me made my teeth ache as much as the split flesh stung, but that was all. *It could be worse,* or so I frantically assured myself. *I'm not bleeding bad. It could be a lot worse.*

I pulled my legs up between us and pried him back enough to force him to retract the knife. I held him at bay like that, with my feet against his stomach, one of his bony arms in my fist, keeping that enormous blade clear. With the other arm we wrestled each other, his fingers reaching for my throat and mine clawing at his face, digging for eyes or other tender spots.

Everything I touched felt like thick, wadded parchment. He was made up of false parts, all stringy skin and wrinkled leather. I scraped at his cheek and neck, and where blood should have oozed there was nothing. It wasn't working.

Time to change my approach.

I closed my hand into a fist and started swinging. I didn't have enough room to get a lot of force behind it, so I aimed at what was close and possibly vulnerable. First I popped his nose, up from underneath. I heard something crack, maybe even break, but he was unimpressed. I hit it again, with no more effect, so I switched to his throat—his Adam's apple was bobbing right above my face so I punched it for all I was worth and he gagged. He sucked in a jagged breath and gave a tiny convulsion. The victory was a small one; I'd barely distracted him, but if nothing else, I knew now that he *could* be hurt. It would take a lot of doing, but all this effort might not be futile.

Mentally crossing my fingers, I let go of the hand that was going for my throat. In the split second before his fingers closed around my windpipe, I grabbed at the hand with the knife and bent it, aiming the tip of the blade at Avery's own throat and shoving with all my strength.

It went in.

Not much, not deep—no deeper than he'd cut me—but he let go of my neck and pulled himself off me. He pressed his fingers to the wound, and when he removed them I saw the gash I'd made oozing with dark, thick blood. It swelled thickly to the surface, not splashing or running but only making a small spot of heavy slime beneath his jawbone. It looked appallingly like the sort of fluid that might leak from a corpse.

While he stared at me, and then down at his dirty fingers, I climbed slowly to my feet, bracing myself against the stove and trying not to touch anything hot. There were two more pots bubbling away, and I'd use them both if I had to.

"All right," he finally said. "No more games. We'll do this *your* way, and see how you like it."

With that, his eyes rolled back in his head and he pulled in a great breath of air. I could hear his lungs expanding, and expanding, and expanding. I knew there was no way they could hold so much. Even the pressure in the room dropped, and my ears ached until I flexed a yawn and they popped. My sinuses swelled in my head, and my chest felt weak. Still Avery's mouth was gaping, pulling every molecule of oxygen into himself.

His hands clasped one another, and gradually he raised them up higher, past his elbows, past his shoulders, above his head. And when they could lift no farther, his eyeballs swung down into their proper position. He opened his palms. And a great shock wave, much like the one I'd felt by the side of the road, burst through the cabin.

Malachi, from his somewhat limited position hog-tied on the bed, merely curled into the corner. But I was standing there like a fool when it hit, and I was thrown against a wall—no, through a wall—no, *half* through the wall, and half out the window. My head blasted through the glass, and my neck and collarbones followed. When the last of the vibrations died away, I was hanging over the windowsill, glass shards peppering my hair and clothes.

I lifted my head, dazedly wiping my hair out of my eyes. Willa, Luanna, and Mae were still standing there, right where I'd left them in the yard. Willa and Luanna gazed dispassionately upon me, knowing the worst they had to fear was another member in their ghostly troop; but Mae's hands twisted in a mortal gesture of anguish, and her sunken eyes were strained.

You should have listened to me. I told you to get yourself gone. I was afraid of this.

"O ye . . . of little faith," I breathed.

I put my hand down on the ledge to push myself up, but jerked it back when I settled on fractured glass. Instantly my palm spurted blood, but it didn't much matter. My shirt was sloppy with it too. Warm blood also trickled down through my hair, dripping one trail south behind my ear and one down my forehead.

Afraid of touching more glass, I heaved myself backwards and up, returning to a standing position. I turned around and Avery was there.

Right there.

Nose to nose with me.

Before I had time to think myself a new plan, I did what every woman instinctively does when standing that close to a man who means her harm. I brought my knee up sharp and fast—and hit nothing.

He was gone.

To my side.

One of his huge, thin hands caught my head and slammed it down on the stove. By pure luck my face missed the flames, but a searing pain across my forehead announced that I'd not gotten away from the fire scot-free. I fell to the floor, and it was mercifully cool.

Then he was on top of me again, pinning my arms to the boards with his hands, which meant his knife was all but useless, except for the fact that its handle was bruising my wrist. I wriggled and struggled, refusing to give him enough slack to make use of that terrible knife. But I was pinned.

The teeny wound I'd made on Avery's neck was closing, sealing itself as I looked up from underneath him. He saw me staring at it and cackled, though he was a bit winded. I found hope in the breaks of his voice. "You could have had . . . this power too—and much more. I would have given it . . . to you."

"I'll take it yet, you son of a bitch."

"Oh, so you want it now?" He grinned. "Only if you kill me."

"Gimme a minute," I growled with more assurance than I felt. But, summoning my last drops of adrenaline, I put all my weight into my right side and heaved. Avery lost his balance and our fight began to roll. I found that if I fought my natural inclinations and pulled my body closer to his, he couldn't get enough leverage to stay on top.

It worked until we hit the bed. Avery's back collided with it, and he let go just enough—and my skin was just slick enough with my own blood—for me to jerk one arm free from his grasp.

In my flailing to get away, it was by simple accident that I elbowed him in the eye; but it worked so well I didn't complain. He let go of my other arm, and of his knife as well. It clattered to the floor and I reached for it, but he swiped it away first. It slid under the bed beyond either of our immediate reaches, so we both turned our attention to my gun.

Malachi's gun. The one I'd brought inside with me.

On the floor near the door. We saw it at the same moment. I shoved off from against the bed—the shack wasn't any bigger than a large bedroom and I could have cleared it in a single leap, if Avery hadn't grabbed my foot and yanked me out of the air.

I fell on my face and palms, kicking at him with everything I had left. But my hands were sticky-slippery, and I couldn't pull myself up or get any traction to escape. My fingers ached and my head ached and I was bleeding from places I couldn't even see without a mirror, and Avery had me like a fish on a hook.

Next to the gun, the door was open. As I flailed against my grandfather, who was reeling me in, one chunk of pants leg at a time, I saw the three ghosts outside. As one, they raised their heads as if they heard something approach.

Mae shook her head, her eyes wide. *She's coming, child. You must kill him now, before she reaches us, or it is too late.*

Oh God. Mae was right. The shadows were so long they were steadily blending into darkness, and Lu would be dead in a moment if I didn't act. It couldn't end this way. I couldn't come so close only to blow it at the last second.

Lu was counting on me.

Dave was counting on me.

All those monks, or priests, or whatever they were, at that

church in St. Augustine, they were counting on me too, whether they knew it or not.

Avery got his hands inside the waistband of my jeans and yanked me back, me still without the gun and him exerting one hundred and thirty years of accumulated strength against my fear. He thrust his hand down onto my neck and tacked me to the floor with his thumb and middle finger, pressing against my throat and completely cutting off my air. With his other hand he collected both of mine, holding them against the ground.

When you're not breathing, you don't struggle long and you don't struggle hard. My fingers flapped uselessly against his wrist. I felt my blood rise to my skin's surface, and my face went hot. I didn't close my eyes, but after a minute I couldn't see.

That's why I was confused when he let go. I was so confused that for a few seconds I just lay there, wondering why he wasn't hurting me anymore. Then, as my vision cleared, I was almost tempted to laugh.

Of all the unlikely heroes, Malachi had flung himself off the bed and onto Avery's back. His hands and feet were tied, but that only meant he couldn't let go of Avery's neck even if he wanted to.

Together they twirled and spun as Avery tried to shake him, and Malachi's bound wrists hung heavily at my grandfather's throat. His full weight (though it couldn't have been much) was dangling down Avery's back, pinned at his neck; Avery was wearing my cousin like an unwieldy cape.

While he was thus distracted I turned over, dragging myself to my hands and knees.

My head drooped down and my eyes were watery, but I could see the gun just a few feet away. One raw palm after another, I crawled towards it. Slowly. Painfully. One scraped knee after another I propelled my broken, bloody body to the one thing I prayed would save me. I clawed towards that damned gun like it was the Holy Grail.

It had to be.

If it wasn't, we were all dead.

I dropped one hand down onto it and it slipped around in my fingers. With both hands I picked the thing up and held it firm, then rose to my knees, aiming at the struggling duo. They were still waltzing about, Avery trying to shake Malachi, and Malachi determined to hang on.

I flipped the safety, pointed the barrel, pulled the trigger tight.

The first shot threw me backwards, almost out the door, but my shoulder landed up against the frame. I put one leg up on the wall to brace myself and fired again.

And again.

The rotating tussle of wrestling limbs jerked and jolted with each bullet.

I wasn't sure who I'd shot and I didn't care, not even a little bit. I just kept on shooting until the gun was empty—six shots, I guess, it was some kind of a big pistol and I think it was fully loaded when I began. All I really know about guns is where the safety usually is and which end's the dangerous one, but at the time that was all I needed.

When the chambers were empty, my ears were humming and both of my adversaries were down, splashed with gaping red holes. Twitching. Both alive, but both hurt.

I hauled myself to my feet, propping myself against the door and letting the gun hang at my side like an anchor at the end of my arm.

Malachi was struggling to pull himself off Avery, who had fallen beneath him. One bent arm at a time he pried himself loose, crawling off to the side and leaning with his back at the bed. He was bleeding from nearly as many places as I was, but none of them appeared critical except the freshly reopened wound on his chest, which had dampened the front of his shirt down to his navel.

Avery was pushing himself up, lifting his chest off the floor and steadying himself on his elbows. A black, sticky puddle mucked up the boards beneath him, but I didn't trust it. His head was wobbling, but he was alive, and in a moment he would be on his feet. And I was out of bullets.

But the knife was beside the stove.

I stumbled towards it, almost falling when I picked it up.

"Eden, let me. . . ." Malachi insisted.

I ignored him and stood over Avery's trembling back. I lifted the knife high, trying not to wonder if I had enough strength to send it all the way through his neck. It was heavy, and it was sharp, but after all the trauma, were my arms enough to wield it?

He raised his head and one of his eyes met mine. The other was a vacant, gaping crater. Yellow fluid and black blood congealed around the sides of the wound, already healing from my lucky shot. But he was down, and he was beaten. He simply wasn't dead yet, and it was up to me to fix that oversight. My arms wilted a little, dropping the knife to my waist level.

"So you'd take me, then . . . just like that?" he said, voice halting and wet. "But you were here to help. I made you strong. I brought you here."

"You killed me once, and I came back—but it was never to help you."

I don't think he heard, or at least he was not listening to me but to something or someone far, far in the distance. "Then I misunderstood. For what it's worth, I never killed you. But now I know the way he wants it . . . and I agree to his terms. So take it—do it if you're going to." He stared back down at the floor, his head sinking between his shoulders.

He didn't have to tell me twice. I pulled the long knife up over my head and swung it down like an ax. It clicked between two of the vertebrae in his neck, splitting them neatly, and continued on through the muscles that held up his head, and the tubes that went to his stomach, and the pipes that serviced his lungs.

His body collapsed, sinking spread-eagled to the ground.

A great gust of hot air gasped out of the hole where his neck had been, but his head was still attached by some cartilage, meat, and skin. With renewed vigor I hacked viciously away at the last bits until his head rolled clear, jaw slack and yellowed teeth leering from pale gums, one brown eye glaring up and out of the skull.

The eye blinked twice before its light went out. His last words came slowly, his tongue stiffening with death. "Take my curse, child . . . and *live with it.*"

Then all of him—now both parts of him—withered and went still.

I opened my fingers to drop the knife. It stuck to my palm, lightly glued there by all the blood. I shook my wrist and it fell clattering down between his body and Malachi, whose head had rolled backwards against the bed. He'd either died or passed out again.

For a moment, I thought I might join him. My head was swimming with bubbles and stars, and my skin was tingling all over. Perhaps the shock of my injuries was wearing off and I was on the verge of feeling every cut, every sore. Perhaps I was dying. Perhaps . . . but then I put my hand to the knife wound at my breast and felt that it was dry. I peeked inside my shirt and saw that it had shrunk to a red, swollen line.

Already. How could that be?

Take my curse, and live with it.

Every passing moment I felt stronger, and drier, and less damaged. Oh, the room was still weaving back and forth, and I ached from every joint, but my bleeding had stopped, and the sharp immediacy of pain was fading. "Some curse," I said. "If this is the worst of it, I'm going to save a fortune in doctor's bills."

I surveyed the room. Malachi's eyes flitted but didn't open. So he was alive after all. Maybe. I waited for another flicker, but none followed. Then again, maybe not. I didn't much care. A pair of long, light curtains swayed around the window I'd broken with my head.

I ripped them down and wadded them up, then dropped them on top of the stove. They ignited immediately. I watched with satisfaction as orangey flames sprouted and spread, eating the curtains and starting on the walls.

I picked up the knife again, and used it to fish some burning chunks of wood out of the stove. I scattered them around, watching them char the floor and ignite the rug by the bed. Then the bedspread caught, and the fire worked its way up to the pillows. Bed, walls, bits of floor all sparked into spreading heat. The shack was a hundred years old and not in the best state of repair. It would burn fast.

I stood in the middle of the increasingly warm room and surveyed my handiwork. Satisfied that the place would go completely up in smoke, I turned to leave.

But Malachi was awake again. His wheedling voice whispered over the hungry crackling of the fire. "You . . . you can't leave me . . . here," he said, smoke choking his words and raising tears in his eyes—or maybe he was only afraid.

I hesitated in the doorway. "Why not?"

"I'm . . . sorry. About . . . all of it. I . . ." My cousin-brother coughed and tried to raise his head to an upright position. "I was wrong. Please . . . don't leave me. Help me. I'm sorry. Never . . . never again."

A small thread of fire was working its way along the blanket towards Malachi's wobbly head. I watched as it approached him, devouring the cotton sheets and spitting them out as coal and ash. I could let it take him. I could leave him in the shack, and even if someone found out what I'd done, no one would care.

Self-defense. Ample precedent. I wouldn't even have to lie.

The flame sneaked up to his collar and singed it dark, then attacked his hair. He didn't feel it, or if he did, he lacked the strength to do anything about it.

Decisions, decisions. I sighed. It wasn't so difficult after all.

I stepped forward and patted at the flame with the back of my hand. Malachi dodged away, thinking that I was trying to hit him. "Stop it," I commanded. "You're on fire. Let me put it out."

He looked at me with those huge, watery blue eyes, rimmed with red from the pain and smoke. For the first time I saw written on his face not maniacal certainty, but fear. Everything he'd spent his life believing had been wrong, and now he had nothing but . . . well, nothing but *me,* and the relationship we'd established thus far did not amount to much. But he was my brother. And he was going to die if I didn't do something.

I reached down and wrapped one of my arms behind him, under his armpits, and pulled him to his feet. "Come on. This place is going to go." I guess I'm just not one to say "I don't care" and really mean it, even if I think I do.

He nodded and did his best to follow orders, flopping one foot down in front of the other in a pitiful attempt to walk. It was enough. We limped together onto the porch and down the stairs, and then into the yard.

Avery's house fell down behind us, spewing a burst of heat against our backs and collapsing into a pile of flaming rubble. We stumbled across the wet, thick yard where the women no longer stood, and we weakly began our way back towards the road. Except for the light of Avery's pyre, the swamp was dark.

I was just beginning to wonder how we'd find our way out when a bobbing white light charged forward at us from between the trees. "Eden? Eden, is that you? Are you all right? Dear God, it's taken me forever to find this place! I saw the fire through the trees, and *dear sweet Baby Jesus—is that . . . ?*"

"I'm fine, Harry," I cried back, though it was possibly something of an overstatement to use "fine" in such a context. "Yeah, it's Malachi. It's okay, though."

My brother put his head down on my shoulder and lurched along beside me. "Thank you. I know . . . you didn't have to do . . . this for me. I mean . . . after all I did to you . . . and everything."

"Aw, Malachi," I said, awkwardly patting his ribs with the arm that held him up. "It's okay. I was never very afraid of you anyway."

12

Finis

I still see ghosts, but then again, I always saw ghosts. Now I see them more, that's all. And my dreams have settled down. Most of them are like Dali paintings, just like before this whole mess started. Well, except for that one dream. I had it just last night.

In it, I was very small, maybe five or six years old. I was back there, in the swamp at Highlands Hammock, and the day spilled bright through the leaves overhead. Not long before, it must have rained, for the yard behind the shack was made of mud. Teeny frogs hopped and croaked, bouncing on thin, springy legs between the puddles. I was enchanted by their shiny, bulgy eyes and bright skin.

The frogs liked me too.

I picked them up gently and kissed them, seeking not princes but friends. I helped them climb out of mud-slick holes and put them back in the water if they roamed too far from the soft places. Sometimes, when the pools were filled with tadpoles, big black birds would lurk about like vultures, picking off the squirmy black babies for a quick snack.

I always chased the birds away from the ponds and puddles, determined to save my frog buddies; but then I climbed a tree and saw a nest filled with downy baby birds, chirruping with hunger, waiting for their parents to bring them food.

My mother smiled when I asked her—should I chase the birds or let the frogs get eaten? "Well," she said, "they all gotta eat. It'll balance out in the end, with or without you chasing 'em."

So when I saw a bird get a frog, I closed my eyes and remembered the baby birds and how they'd all gotta eat. And this was how it was bound to be, whether or not I was there to interfere. But in the meantime, I played with the frogs in the backyard, and I loved them while I had them. And I was always careful not to step on them, even though they were sometimes hard to see out there in the grass.

I crouched down and poked at one, pushing it onto my open fingers. Its little throat inflated and it let out a happy gribbit.

"Hello, froggie."

Behind me, up in the cabin, something splintered and broke. It sounded like someone was falling. I scrunched my forehead and listened closer. No, there wasn't anything. All was quiet. Mother was cooking. She must have dropped something.

My froggie's throat swelled again and it started its hoarse song. I held him up to my face and felt his whispering breath. They usually didn't let me hold them so long. It was the neatest thing I'd ever seen. I wanted to share it with my momma. I stood slowly, making sure not to disturb the frog prince and his music. I covered him with my other hand, cupping him carefully so that his singing echoed around in my palm.

With cautious steps, I made my way back to the house.

Gotta show Momma.

I shifted my eyes from my hands to the ground. Gotta walk easy. It took me five full minutes to get to the front of the house.

One step. Took it so soft it didn't even creak.

Two steps. Didn't make a sound on that one either. I stared at my hands, then stared at the ground. I stared at my feet. Lifted them again . . . so slow. Stared at the top stair of the porch. Stepped up onto it without a sound.

I held out the frog and lifted my head, prepared to announce my wonderful new pal—and stopped myself. My father was there. His back was to the door. My mother was on the bed. She wasn't moving. Her arm was hanging down, almost touching the floor. A long trail of red spilled down it, dripping from her middle finger to form a small puddle on the floor.

Another drop fell with a little splash.

And another. And another.

My father was doing something to her—something I couldn't see. His arm was cranking back and forth, and the one-roomed home was filled with the sounds of uneven sawing, the rubbing of sharp metal teeth across something solid but wet.

The little fellow in my hand chose exactly this moment to speak.

Gribbit.

Gribbit.

Gribbit.

My father stopped what he was doing. He turned. And I saw . . . and I saw . . . I saw what he was doing. I saw Momma's right hand hanging by a sliver of skin. I saw the white bones poking through the red, shredded flesh. I saw her eyes gone up in her head, and her mouth open and her skin going pale and gray. And my father had done this to her.

And he had seen me.

I took one step back.

"Now, pretty one . . . now . . ."

I took another step back.

"Miabella."

Without taking my eyes away from my father's, I squatted down and put the frog on the edge of the porch. It hopped down and disappeared into the weeds.

"Miabella," he said again.

But by then I was already running.

My little legs pumped hard, and fast, and my bare feet did not even notice the twigs and roots they stomped across. I was always barefoot, and the naked ground did not intimidate me. It did not slow me.

Footsteps pounded hard behind me, drawing closer until I took a turn through a more narrow place, a place where the trees grew closer together. A place where the ground was soggier, and then downright wet. I was splashing and ducking, and he was not keeping up. I didn't know where I was going, but my father couldn't catch me, and that was all that mattered.

"Miabella? Miabella! *Miabella!*" He was crying louder, but his voice was growing more distant. I was losing him. I was getting away.

And then I was falling.

Falling through water, so black and thick that when I opened my eyes I saw nothing. My feet could not feel the bottom below, and my hands could not find the air above. At first I went wild and thrashed, fighting to find which way might be up, even if it meant my father was there. But the water was all mud, and creeping things were swimming about. I felt small, webbed toes shove off against my arm and was less afraid. No, not afraid at all.

My father was above, covered with my mother's blood.

I had gone below, with the creeping things, and the hopping things. It was better there. The frogs would care for me, as I had cared for them. They would keep me safe here in the mud, where I played with them when the sun was warm and the grass was tall.

They would . . . sing me to sleep in this new . . . in this new, thick darkness. They . . . would watch over me. They would . . . protect me. The frogs were my keepers, and they would keep me . . . from

279

harm. Yes. Everything . . . was going to be . . . fine. The frogs would help me.

Or perhaps the
. . . birds.

Epilogue

"You haven't got a mark on you," Lulu said, shifting to position herself more lazily in the big bed she and Dave share at home. "Rather miraculous, I'd say."

"No more so than your recovery." I squeezed her hand and she let me, then pried it away in pursuit of orange juice.

"Nothing to recover from."

"And there was nothing to mark me," I retorted, watching her down the juice and reclaiming her hand when she set it down again. I played with the wedding ring there, twisting the band in a groove around her finger. "I don't know why you were so worried, anyway."

She sighed and leaned her head back into the pillows, which aimed her eyes safely away from me and at the ceiling. "That old woman, you know. That's all. And that damned boy. They never did catch him, did they?"

"I don't think they did, no. Not last I heard."

Harry had argued about that one, at first. But in the end, I couldn't let them take Malachi. I'm not sure why—maybe because he'd tried to help me, or maybe because I was still so sorry for him, even after all this time. Maybe it was just as simple as that Malachi was the only link I had to my father, and though he hadn't wanted anything to do with me, I wanted some connection to him regardless.

Malachi made me feel less marooned. He made me feel like there was someone out there I didn't have to explain anything to. That's why I bullied Harry the way I did, and got him to take my brother back to the monastery. There he'll be cared for by the priests and the other penitents in their quiet, reflective world. I can't think of a better place for him. Lulu and Dave would probably freak out if they knew, and insist that I take him to the police, and let them handle him.

Maybe one day I will, and maybe I won't. He's family, after all.

And whether Lulu meant to or not, she's managed to teach me that there are times you should forgive family, even though you don't want to, and even though you wouldn't forgive anyone else on earth if they treated you that way. I felt a strange little ache when I thought about Lulu and her mother, and how they'd gone for fifteen years with a wall between them because of a misunderstanding. Sure, Grandma could have and likely *should* have handled things differently; she should have let Lulu and Michelle go and visit my mother. She should have told them what was really going on.

Then again, my mother could have told them too, and she didn't. It was hard to sort out, though it might have been easier if I'd known either of them at all.

"It's kind of your fault, you know," I complained gently at my aunt, who was posing there on the duvet. She was so beautiful that it made my chest hurt; and I was so happy that she was alive, and she was well enough to be pretty while weak. I was delighted that she was healthy enough to milk the hospital visit for every ounce, and I was overjoyed to see Dave bouncing from room to room, playing nursemaid.

"What do you mean, my fault?"

"I mean, if you'd been willing to talk about my mother once in a while, I wouldn't have wondered so hard that I went talking to other people."

"But I didn't know the answers to half of what you wanted."

"That seems to be true," I admitted, "but the answers wouldn't have been half so important if you'd been . . ." I dropped it. There wasn't a good way to finish the thought, so I didn't. "All I want to say is, I wish you'd been more willing to talk about her. If I'd known *something*, I wouldn't have been so desperate to know anything at all."

"You never asked much."

"Touché."

She was right, I hadn't. I didn't want her to think I didn't value the people who'd brought me up, and I didn't want her to think I loved her any less because I was curious. An image flashed through my head, of Dave, there in the hotel lobby in Macon. I hadn't wanted to talk to him about finding my father for the same stupid reason. Poor Dave. He has his questions, but he's so happy to have us both back that he doesn't ask them. I love that about him. I love him more than I think I could love him even if he *were* my biological father. Family is family, and I say he's part of mine.

I could have gone on—I could have said more, and said it pointedly. I could have told her that I finally understood. But what would be the point? She didn't talk about Leslie because it was hard and it hurt her. I love Lulu, and I'm glad I could save her, but things are different now. She's lost her secrets and I've lost my ignorance. And now there's a wall between me and her. It's not like the one she set up to keep her own mother at bay, but it's there all the same. I'm not sure what it's made of, and I don't know how to knock it down, but every day I seek some way to climb it.

I made my first move a few weeks later, when I invited her to join me at a coffee shop downtown. I showed up early.

Ms. Finley was waiting at one of the small round tables by the door. She smiled when I came in, and her smile turned puzzled when I handed her the bag. The grin went bright again when she looked inside.

"Where'd you pick this up?"

"Atlanta. Went there for a concert last week. I hope it's the right color."

"Can't go wrong with bone. Good shade for an old broad. Matches just about everything and dresses up nice. I think my old one had brass buttons, but I don't remember. This is nice, thank you. What's the occasion?"

"I just wanted you to talk."

"Why me? I gave you just about everything I could, though I'm happy to come out and be social. And of course, I thank you for the sweater."

"You're welcome, Rhonda. Thing is, this time, the talking isn't exactly for me."

Lulu's tall shape cast a shadow past our table as she breezed by the big window and reached for the coffee shop door. She nodded at me, then at my table-mate, though her forehead was wrinkled with curiosity.

"Have a seat," I told Lulu, offering up mine. "This is Rhonda Finley, but she used to go by Marion. Rhonda, this is—"

"I would have known her as surely as I knew you, even if I saw her on the street. I'll try not to dislike you on sight for looking that much like you did as a girl." The older woman rose and extended a hand. From polite habit, my aunt took the hand—though she was too surprised to speak. She recognized the name and it shocked her. When she looked my way for an explanation, I shrugged it off.

"What do you want? The regular? I'll get it at the bar." I ushered Lulu into the chair and dug a ten-dollar bill out of my front pocket. She always gets chai. She orders it cold in a glass all summer, and hot in a latte mug all winter.

By the time I returned with the beverage, the two were talking without me. That was fine. At least they were talking.

While we were out, I got my first phone call on the cell phone I'd broken down and gotten when I returned from Florida. It was

Malachi. He didn't leave his name, but I knew the voice, and even though I left him with a solemn vow of no more attempted homicide, I cringed to hear him speak.

He left a number. I deleted the message without writing it down.

My feelings about him are too mixed to sort out properly quite yet.

But bless his heart, he learns fast. He didn't call again, but just the other day I received a letter that said what a phone call might, and I didn't have to pretend to any small talk.

He says that God still speaks to him, but then again God always did—now He just talks more, that's all. Now Malachi understands, and there is less confusion. He knows where he went wrong, and God has forgiven him for his mistakes. Each day he sends up a prayer for me, that I might find clarity and resolution.

I sure hope God listens better than Malachi does.